ROBERTS

A **TOM WAGNER** ADVENTURE

Thriller

Translator: Edwin Miles / Copyeditor: Philip Yaeger

Imprint: Independently published / Paperback ISBN 9798437981634, Hardcover ISBN 9798449090218

Cover Art by reinhardfenzl.com

Cover Art was created with photos from: neo-stock.com & depositphotos.com: I_gorZh, nejron, paulvinten, genious2000de, Patryk_Kosmider, Foto-VDW, YAYImages, jag_cz, emrahselamet, a.horoshun.gmail.com, nikkytok, udon10671

www.robertsmaclay.com

office@robertsmaclay.com

CONTENTS

"The truth has only one color. Lies have many."

Melchior Kirchhofer

1

JERUSALEM

It was a cruel silence and it seemed to drag on for an eternity. But in reality, it was no more than a few seconds.

The dull pressure in his ears gave way to a steady, high-pitched whistling. There were other sounds, too, but they seemed to come from far away. He opened his eyes slowly. A brilliant void slammed painfully into his head, and he squeezed his eyes shut again. Above him, scraps of paper rained down like confetti at a parade. *Was that snow mixed with the confetti?* he wondered. Where was he? What had happened? Why was he lying on his back?

Then came the pain, crashing through his body like shock waves. He sighed and tried to sit up.

The shrill whistling sound gradually faded, and the other sounds grew louder, forcing their way relentlessly from the background into the foreground. Screams. Human screams. Crying and wailing. What he saw before him was so surreal that at first, he could not process it at all. Ghostly figures wandered helplessly through a brown fog. But it was no fog. It was a cloud of dust, endless, like a sandstorm frozen in a moment.

Then his memory returned. The quaking, the heat, the shock of the blast. The explosions had blown him and everyone around him off their feet. The microphone, decorated with a red cube upon which were emblazoned three white letters, was still in his hand. He looked down at his clothes and saw that he was completely covered in dust, as if someone had rolled him in flour.

"What happened?" croaked a voice behind him. He turned around.

"I don't know for certain. Explosions," Jack said, on his feet now and standing over the other man, who still lay on the ground. He knew him: his colleague, his cameraman, his friend. Mason. Like him, covered from head to toe in dust. Mason sat up and Jack stretched out a hand, but the cameraman ignored it. Instinctively, like the veteran he was, he felt around immediately for his camera. He found it and stood up, hoisting it to his shoulder.

"We're good. It survived," he announced after a quick inspection.

"Hello? Are you still there?" Jack said, speaking into the microphone. He replaced the earbud in his ear—it had been knocked out when he fell.

"Thank God you're all right," said a woman's voice on the other end. "You're still live. What happened there?" she asked.

Still a little stunned, Jack stood motionless and stared into the black lens of the camera.

Deep breath, Mason signaled to him.

Jack looked around. The dust was beginning to settle, but what it was revealing was becoming more and more horrific. He could say nothing. Still holding the microphone, he simply stood with both hands held to his head and turned in a circle. Bodies lay on the streets, cut down by flying debris. Car alarms howled through the chaos. People covered in blood staggered past, dazed, while others administered first aid. A woman knelt in the middle of the street and cradled a tiny, lifeless form in her arms, her agonized wail filling the air around her. Countless people ran past, ignoring her. In minutes, the crowd that had gathered for the unprecedented event had evaporated. They had come to see the Holy Father. Those unhurt or only slightly injured had fled heedlessly in all directions. Many had been trampled to death in the crush to escape.

"We . . ." Jack began, turning back to his cameraman and struggling to put his impressions into words.

"We don't know . . ." He took a deep breath, grasped the mic tightly, and forced his eyes to focus on the camera lens, blocking out everything else around him.

"We don't know yet exactly what just happened. It's horrible," he began again. "All we know for certain is that there have been several explosions at the Church of the Holy Sepulcher here in Jerusalem. The devastation is immense. We have no information at the moment about the Pope and the other church leaders."

2

A LUXURY YACHT IN THE MEDITERRANEAN

Isaac Hagen marched along a wood-paneled corridor to the elevator and rode it down to one of the lower levels of the yacht. He took a keycard from his pocket and held it to a card reader beside the only door on that level, then placed one hand flat on the scanner. He heard a faint buzz, pulled open the door, and entered the room.

On the other side of the plain-looking door was a vast control room, like the bridge of a television spaceship. Along the walls, computer terminals were mounted side by side, an operator at each one. Each screen showed an array of live streams from security cameras across Europe, with maps and countless lines of computer code. The operators murmured into their headsets as their fingers flew across their keyboards.

At the end of the control room were two more workstations, different from the others. Each of them resembled the cockpit of a fighter jet. And in fact that is precisely what they were: state-of-the-art drone cockpits. And both were manned.

Hagen stopped beside the man already standing behind the pilots.

"Nice of you to join us. You're just in time," said Noah Pollock icily, glancing up momentarily from his tablet.

"Sorry, call of nature," Hagen replied, still suspicious of their newly formed alliance. "Why am I here?"

"Project Sanctum Sepulcrum has succeeded," Noah said, pointing up at one of the large monitors on the wall, which was showing a live report from CNN.

"Sanctum Sepulcrum?" Hagen asked, staring at the screen.

"Ah yes, you don't know the details of this one. Sanctum Sepulcrum was another step in bringing about real change. I've accomplished something that my predecessor was unable to," Noah said.

Hagen saw the diabolical expression that appeared for a fraction of a second on Noah's face. "Which is what?"

"I assume you've heard about the Project Cornet disaster? The failed attempt to kill the Pope in the Sagrada Familia?"

Hagen's eyes widened. He hadn't been personally involved in Cornet, but he knew about it. He nodded, unsettled.

"Yeah, I know what you're thinking. It *was* over the top, wasn't it?" Noah continued, seeing the disapproval on Hagen's face.

"But weren't you part of preventing that? You and Tom Wagner?"

Noah narrowed his eyes and looked steadily at Hagen. "That was another life, another time."

Hagen swallowed.

"So, you're back on the Pope?" Hagen finally said, breaking the tension after they'd stared at one another for a long moment.

"Not just the Pope," Noah said, his diabolical grin returning. "Pálffy, Guerra and Ossana had the right idea, but their approach was too complex. They were trying to kill a fly with a hand grenade. They wanted a spectacle for the press, something unforgettable."

Hagen recalled how the world, and Europe in particular, had only just managed to avoid a nuclear cataclysm.

"But you don't need to kill hundreds of thousands of people to get the world's attention. You just have to kill the right ones," Noah went on. "You don't need an atomic bomb to get the job done. I prefer a scalpel to a blunt instrument."

"And a drone attack is more subtle?" asked Hagen, rather testily.

"Don't be an idiot. I'm not looking to start World War III. The drones are just there to observe. A front-row seat, if you will."

"Then how ...?"

"Good planning and good contacts," replied Noah with a smile.

"What if the drones are spotted?"

Noah laughed out loud. "Modern stealth tech and a little grease on the right palms will always guarantee a smooth flight."

"It looks like you succeeded."

"We changed the world today. But the death of the most powerful man in the Church is just the beginning."

A shudder ran down Hagen's back. With one blow, Noah Pollock had wiped out the leaders of the three most influential world religions. And on holy ground, no less. The consequences of such an attack were beyond reckoning. Noah was literally sitting on a powder keg and playing with matches.

Hagen stared at the monitor as the pilot zoomed in even closer on the old part of Jerusalem. At the center of the screen, the Church of the Holy Sepulcher—"Sanctum Sepulcrum" in Latin—was now visible, in high definition. Or what was left of it, anyway. Now, columns of smoke rose from several points around the spiritual center of world Christianity.

"Do we have confirmation?" Noah asked.

Hagen tore his eyes away from the screen and looked at Noah.

"Yes, sir. Sanctum Sepulcrum is a complete success," said a staticky voice from a speaker.

"Okay. Back to base. Over." Noah smiled, removed his headset, and turned to Hagen. "See? We're one step closer to our objective. The leader will be very happy when he gets here."

"The leader's coming here in person?"

"Yes. And everything must be ready when he arrives. I'm leaving that up to you."

Hagen nodded.

Noah turned to one of the pilots. "You know what to do when the team returns to base?"

"Yes, sir."

Noah turned away, and he and Hagen made their way past the terminals, heading toward the exit.

"Sir!" one of the operators called, waving Noah over. Followed closely by Hagen, he joined the man at his terminal.

"What is it?" Noah asked indifferently, tapping at his tablet.

"Sir, we have movement in the old headquarters at the Wewelsburg."

Noah froze. He looked up slowly.

"Say that again."

"We have—"

"That was rhetorical! Get out of the way!" he cut the man off. He shoved him aside and took a seat at the terminal. With a few taps, he called up the surveillance cameras. When he saw what was going on, he drew a sharp breath.

"Tom Wagner," he said through gritted teeth as his fingers flew over the keyboard.

3

AF HEADQUARTERS, WEWELSBURG, BÜREN, GERMANY

Tom stared at the screen.

Four minutes, forty-eight seconds. Forty-seven, forty-six, forty-five . . .

Tick, tock.

Valuable seconds ticked away. Tom, Cloutard and Fábio stared at the timer as if rooted to the spot.

"Boys? Hello? We've got to get out of here." In disbelief, Adalgisa snapped her fingers in the faces of the three men.

"Not without proof," Tom said, and turned back toward the conference room. At least he could grab a few files.

But Cloutard grabbed him by the arm and held him back. "Do not be a madman. I know you want to bring your parents' killers to justice, but you can only do that if we get out of here alive."

"Forget the files," Fábio said, standing up and pointing to a small hard drive, "I've already copied some of them. We won't be leaving empty-handed."

"Okay, okay, I'm convinced. Let's go," Tom said, and he turned in the other direction and headed for the steel door through which they'd entered. But a shrill alarm signal made him freeze. "What the hell is that?" he shouted.

"Shit, shit, shit!" Fábio's voice grew louder with each word. He was instantly back at the terminal, tapping away furiously.

A hiss and a scraping noise. Tom swung back toward the entrance but could only watch helplessly as the steel door closed with a devastating "clang" and the bolts slid into place. They were trapped inside a ticking time bomb.

"Remember how I said we didn't trip any alarms?" Fábio smiled apologetically but didn't look up. He continued to type as he talked. "Well, someone spotted us, and they've taken control of the system. And whoever it is, they're *very* good."

"They? It can only be Noah. Can you get the door open again?" asked Tom.

"Three fifty-nine, fifty-eight, fifty-seven," Adalgisa cried.

"Adalgisa, please, that is not helping," Cloutard hissed.

"I can try," said Fabio, "but not in three minutes ..."

"Forty-three," Adalgisa said. "See? I'm helping!"

Tom moved behind Fábio and squeezed his shoulders

encouragingly. "You've got this," he said, before hurrying back to the steel door.

"Any other brilliant ideas?" Cloutard leaned resignedly against the railing that circled the terminal level, his flask of cognac in his hand.

"If I were Superman, I could rip the door off its hinges and fly us out of here. Bummer . . ." Tom wore a pained smile as he scrutinized the wall, the lock, and the massive steel door.

"Hey," Fábio called. "The timer just stopped. At three twenty-nine."

"What?" Tom leaped down the three steps to the lower-lying terminal level and ran to Fábio. "You stopped the countdown?"

"It wasn't me."

All four jumped when a diabolical laugh rang through the speakers in the control room. Moments later, the enormous video wall on the right side of the hall came to life, and Noah Pollock's ruthless face glared down at them, more than ten feet high.

4

HANGKLIP SUMMIT, NEAR CAPE TOWN, SOUTH AFRICA

At the eastern tip of False Bay, to the south of Cape Town, Eon van Rensburg stepped out onto the terrace. Ten years earlier, he'd bought the entire mountain known as Hangklip and built his personal, twenty-thousand-square-foot retreat on the summit.

Oh, there had been a few problems with the local authorities, environmentalists, and the head tourism office in Cape Town. The peak was a popular hiking destination, after all. But a substantial contribution to the city had smoothed the way—though not so substantial that Kiara, Eon's wife and bookkeeper, had taken much notice.

The van Rensburgs' marriage was a serendipitous affair. Eon, heir to his father's diamond mine, had been a guest at the Vienna Opera Ball in 2001—where more business was done to the strains of waltz music than in the C-level suites on Wall Street. Eon was planning to sell the entire conglomerate that his grandfather had founded, and his father had built up to dizzying heights of wealth and prestige. He envisaged a tidy profit and intended to devote himself more to philanthropy when the deal was done. He wanted to indulge his passion for collecting old artworks and antique artifacts, and he would invest the rest of his fortune in charitable organizations. Not without ulterior motives, of course—all due respect to charity, but one had to live on something, after all.

Industrialists, politicians, mafiosi, arms dealers, and lobbyists of every type and nationality gathered at the Opera Ball, sharing their private boxes as a matter of course. Eon spotted the woman while still involved in preliminary discussions. His father had taught him that if you wanted something you had to take it, and not waste time asking permission. Eon approached Kiara. They talked. They waltzed, drank champagne, danced some more, and at the end of the night they belonged to one another. Eon shook off his business partners and Kiara slipped away from her escort, a Russian oligarch. At four in the morning, after the last waltz had died away, they left the opera house, crossed the street, and went to Eon's suite at the renowned Hotel Sacher. In the four days that followed, they put the huge bed in the suite to the test. Eon left it only once, for about half an hour—long enough to visit a jeweler on Kärntnerstrasse and buy an engagement ring. They had been inseparable ever since.

They shared not only a bed and the appetites they sated in it; they were true soulmates. Their love of luxury and the finer things in life bound them together as much as their fascination for the art and culture of past civilizations. Kiara had a flair for finance and Eon had an eye for art and the necessary contacts, all of which they steadily developed.

The couple owned a real estate portfolio that extended around the globe, but Eon's Cape Town home was always their true haven. Eon loathed modern architecture, and instead had built a true palace on the summit of the Hangklip, constructing it in the style of the Victorian manors so typical of Cape Town. Of course, there were some modern touches, among them an infinity pool and a helipad. And the entire mountain was protected by ultramodern surveillance equipment and an army of security personnel—due less to the usual priceless items, like cars, watches, and jewelry, than to the private museum the van Rensburgs had established.

"Honeybee, we should talk about the exhibition again. The reception is in two days."

In twenty years, they hadn't been separated for even a day, and yet Kiara's voice still sent a warm shiver up Eon's spine. Wrapped in a filmy garment for which the word "robe" was far too clumsy, Kiara strolled out to join him on the terrace. The garment was a work of art, stylish but erotically charged—a breath of nothing, covering just enough to not seem cheap while still giving the imagination plenty to feed on: everything that Eon could not get enough of.

She held a cup of coffee in her hand but kissed her husband on the mouth before giving him the cup. Eon drank a mouthful of coffee then slapped Kiara hard on her ass.

"Ouch, goddamnit," she protested playfully, her sidelong glance making it abundantly clear that her complaint was not to be taken seriously.

"Forgive me, my queen," Eon said, pushing the robe aside to inspect Kiara's fire-red rump. "I completely forgot that our little session last night had left its traces. But you are not alone," he said, and he lifted his T-shirt to reveal a collection of colorful welts and bruises. They smiled mischievously at each other, both happy they shared the same interests—in every area.

"Master van Rensburg. You are awaited in the museum."

Eon hastily adjusted his T-shirt and Kiara chastely covered her rear. The servants didn't need to know that they spent their nights chasing each other around the bedroom with riding crops. They grinned.

"We'll be right there, Harold." Eon flicked his hand toward the servant as if shooing away a bothersome fly.

"Don't be so condescending to poor Harold, honeybee," said Kiara. "It's not his fault you and I are freaks."

5

AF HEADQUARTERS, WEWELSBURG

"Tom, Tom, Tom. What are you up to now?" said Noah. "Sticking your nose into things that don't concern you, I see. Again."

"Maybe, although I don't see that you're in any position to judge. Someone whose spent their whole life as second-in-command, always taking orders and playing the yes-man . . . you probably can't even think for yourself anymore, right? But I can't blame you, of course. First it was Mossad telling you what to do, then the Cobras, and now it's AF. You probably can't tell good from evil at all."

Noah was about to reply, but he never got to it. Taking precise aim, Tom first took out the surveillance cameras and then the video wall itself, squeezing the trigger with a stony expression on his face.

"*Pour l'amour de Dieu,*" said Cloutard, flinching at the noise and spilling some of his precious Louis XIII.

"We've wasted enough time with those guys. No more.

Bickering like kids is the last thing I want. I'm done with Noah, for good."

Cloutard nodded. Noah had once been Tom's best friend and Tom had struggled with his betrayal for a long time. But it looked like that was finally behind him, Cloutard thought.

"Fábio, the door. How far are you?" Tom asked.

"Give me ninety seconds," Fábio said. "The guy's good, but I'm better."

"Honey, we only have sixty," Adalgisa said, drawing a sharp breath. The timer had reappeared on his monitor —and as a parting gift, Noah had reset it.

Sixty seconds. Fifty-nine, fifty-eight, fifty-seven . . .

"We've got another problem," Fábio said. "I can open the door, but it will close again immediately. You've got to jam it with something."

Tom looked around. "Okay, Mr. Criminal Mastermind, give me a hand." He grabbed Cloutard by the sleeve and dragged him toward the conference room. "The table."

They heaved the enormous table over and Tom began to unscrew one of the steel legs. Cloutard did the same.

"Got it!" Fábio cheered.

With a rumble and a hiss, the steel slab swung open.

"Get a move on! It's going to close again!" Fábio shouted, his fingers flying expertly over the keyboard. Tom and Cloutard ran back.

"Are you sure these will hold?" Cloutard puffed.

"Nope," said Tom.

"Twenty-seven, twenty-six," Adalgisa threw in.

"Quick! The door's already closing."

"Twenty-three, twenty-two . . ."

"Now!" Tom yelled, and he and Cloutard wedged the steel tubes between the door frame and the door itself. The hydraulics immediately began howling.

"Come on, move it!" Tom pushed Cloutard through the gap and beckoned frantically to the other two. Adalgisa ran through, disappearing into the corridor behind Cloutard. Fábio stuffed his gear into his backpack, ran to the door and likewise slipped through.

A loud crack sounded and Tom jumped back. One of the table legs was beginning to buckle under the enormous pressure of the hydraulic motor.

"Come on! There's only ten seconds left!"

Tom looked back one last time and was about to slip through the gap when he saw it. The portable hard drive with all the proof had slipped out of Fábio's backpack and was still lying on the terminal desk.

"The drive!"

Without thinking, he turned and dived for it.

"Are you crazy? The door!" Cloutard shouted through the gap.

"The evidence!" Tom shouted back. He reached the terminal in three big steps, grabbed the drive, and turned back. The floor lurched underfoot as the first charge exploded, and Tom almost stumbled. Out of the corner of his eye, he saw an immense fireball racing at him. *Crack!* One of the table legs folded. Tom dropped to the floor. Like a baseball player diving for home base, he slid across the floor and through the narrowing gap in the door. For a moment, a gout of flame lit up the passageway and the shocked faces of Cloutard, Fábio and Adalgisa. The second table leg snapped like a toothpick and the door slammed shut, just as Tom's slide brought him to a stop at his friends' feet.

They ran. Stones and dust rained down from the tunnel ceiling with every successive explosion. The earth rocked, but they struggled toward the exit. It was like running along the corridor of a ship caught in a gale. Just as the dust cloud from the collapsing passage caught up with them, they burst from the tunnel mouth into safety.

6

VIENNA GENERAL HOSPITAL, AUSTRIA

HELLEN OPENED HER EYES—THE SMELL OF FRESH COFFEE had awakened her. She groaned and sat up straight, rubbing the sleep from her eyes. Since her mother's emergency operation, Hellen had not moved from her side. The doctors said that her mother had come through the operation well but there was swelling on her brain, and they had put Theresia de Mey into an artificial coma. Hellen had fallen asleep in an armchair beside her mother's bed. She stretched. Her back hurt.

"Here. I thought you could use this," said Edward, handing his daughter a cup of hot coffee. He'd sneaked back into the room just moments before.

"Tha-a-a-ank you," Hellen yawned, and took a cautious sip. Slowly, she began to revive. She stood up and moved around a little to get the blood circulating.

"You should go home. Take a hot bath and get some rest. You can't do anything here."

"I'm fine, really. I want to be here where they wake her up."

Hellen stood at the foot of the bed and looked at her mother's seemingly lifeless body. The respirator sighed rhythmically, and Theresia's chest rose and fell almost imperceptibly. The sight of her mother's pale, sunken face once again caused tears to brim in Hellen's eyes.

"I wish Tom were here," she whispered, and quickly dried her eyes. Edward went to his daughter and took her in his arms.

"Where is he, anyway?"

"He and François are off on some harebrained chase again. But he couldn't know that—"

"Hellen, you have to stop constantly looking for excuses for Tom's behavior," Edward said, and he looked intently at his daughter.

"I know. But what can I say? He's like a nine-year-old with a sugar rush, but I love him."

Hellen laid her head on her father's chest, and he stroked her hair softly. There was a soft knock on the door. Hellen separated herself from her father and looked over at the man who'd just knocked.

"I didn't mean to disturb you," said the doctor, standing at the gap in the door. "I just wanted to give you a quick update."

"Please, come in," said Edward. Hellen put the coffee cup on the nightstand and stood beside her father, arms hugging her chest.

"How is she? Will she recover?"

The doctor looked up from his clipboard and smiled. "Yes. She'll be back on her feet before too long. The swelling has gone down, and she has stabilized nicely. She still has a long road ahead of her, but based on my experience, Ms. de Mey should make a full recovery. We should be able to wake her in a day or two."

With every word the doctor spoke, Hellen's arms relaxed a little from their tightly crossed position and slowly sank to her sides. When he was finished, she threw her arms around him, tears of joy filling her eyes.

"Thank you! Thank you!"

The doctor let out a surprised laugh.

"She's going to get better!" Hellen said, now embracing her father.

"Then we'll finally find out what she wanted to—"

"What's going on out there?" the doctor interrupted him, stepping out into the corridor. Several staff had just trotted past the room. Hellen freed herself from her father's embrace and they followed the doctor outside.

"What's happened?" Hellen asked one of the nurses before the woman disappeared into the staff room.

"I don't know. There's been some kind of attack."

With the nurse and the doctor, they entered the staff break room, where several people had already gathered around the television and were watching a special broadcast.

"The details are only reaching us slowly," said the news anchor onscreen. "What we can tell you is that, about half an hour ago, a series of large explosions rocked The Church of the Holy Sepulcher in Jerusalem. We don't yet know the extent of the damage or anything about the victims."

On the screen were the first images of the destruction. Video from a CNN live feed was being broadcast and the anchor translated.

"As part of a trip to the Middle East, the Pope was to preside over an unprecedented meeting of the leaders of the world's major religions. The head of the Catholic Church faced heavy criticism in the lead-up to the trip, as meetings with leaders of declared terrorist organizations were also on the itinerary."

"Oh my God," Hellen exclaimed. She stared at the television in shock. Edward put an arm around her shoulders. Barely breathing, they listened as the report continued.

"We have just received the sad confirmation that Pope Sixtus VI is dead. Members of the Jewish delegation and the Muslim imam were also killed."

Hellen drew a sharp breath. The Pope was dead. She had grown very fond of the old man after she, Tom and Cloutard had saved his life in Barcelona. *Tom will be devastated*, she thought. He and the Pope had shared a special bond ever since.

". . . the Israeli president has declared a state of emergency in the expectation of rioting and possible further attacks. We return now to Austria, where ongoing storms have flooded large areas of the country. The city of Innsbruck has been hit particularly hard. The Inn River has . . ."

Hellen drew her father aside. "This has to be AF's work. I'm sure of it," she whispered in Edward's ear.

"You can't know that," Edward replied.

"Who else could it possibly be?"

7

VAN RENSBURGS' PRIVATE MUSEUM, HANGKLIP SUMMIT, SOUTH AFRICA

FRESHLY SHOWERED AND DRESSED, EON VAN RENSBURG and his wife, Kiara, made their way to the top floor of the house. They stopped at a security checkpoint that was staffed around the clock.

"Good morning, sir, madam," said the guard on duty.

"And good morning to you, too," Kiara replied.

"Mr. de Waal is already inside, Master Rensburg," the guard said.

"Thank you."

The guard flicked a switch, the doors parted with a barely audible hiss, and they stepped into the Holy of Holies—a collection of artifacts, relics, and objets d'art unmatched in any other private collection in the world. Many of the exhibits were officially classified as lost, or it was not widely known that they had been recovered—a chest of bars of Nazi gold from Lake Toplitz, for example. Beside the chest hung two paintings: Picasso's "*Le pigeon aux petit pois*" and Caravaggio's "Nativity with St. Francis and St. Lawrence." Display cases nearby were filled with jewel-studded crowns, ancient weapons, and mystic-looking books and codices.

"If François Cloutard and Berlin Brice knew what we have here, they'd drop dead of a heart attack, honeybee," said Kiara, leaning on her husband's shoulder. Her right hand stroked his chest and began to wander down over his stomach. Torn between desire and propriety, Eon pushed his wife's hand away. She could still drive him crazy . . .

"A lot of these items can't be on display when the guests arrive," said Eon, looking around.

"Quite, Master van Rensburg," said a gaunt man with a no-nonsense expression and an ugly scar extending across his right eye and down to the left corner of his mouth.

"Ah, there you are, Wikus. How are the preparations going?" Kiara asked. Although Wikus de Waal was on her payroll list, she still shuddered every time she saw him. She was not comfortable around him at all. But Eon never tired of pointing out how well he did his job. And his tasks were many and varied.

"The exhibition is almost complete. Tomorrow, we will start removing those exhibits not intended for the public eye and exchanging them for other items. We'll only need a day for that. Unfortunately, we still haven't received the centerpiece of the exhibit from Vienna."

Eon's and Kiara's eyes widened in dismay. "Oh, my God, honeybee," Kiara said, fanning her face with one hand, although the air conditioning in the gallery kept the temperature at precisely seventy-two degrees. Kiara had a talent for theatrics—another thing Eon loved about her.

"Don't worry, my queen," he said. "Wikus will sort everything out on time, just like he always does."

He looked expectantly at the gaunt man, who replied, "I am afraid the Viennese are in breach of contract. We have not heard from them for several days."

Kiara was on the verge of fainting—feigned, of course. *One of these days she'll win an Oscar*, Eon thought with a smile, and he laid a hand reassuringly on his wife's shoulder. She flinched. Her shoulder, too, had felt the sting of the riding crop.

"Take the jet and fly to Vienna immediately," Eon said, his voice abruptly icy. Kiara looked languidly at him. She loved it when he exercised his authority. "Bring back what is due to us. Whatever it takes. Money is no object. Even if you have to steal it. Understood?"

Wikus nodded. "Of course, Master van Rensburg. I am on my way."

He strode out of the room.

"Honeybee, you're irresistible when you treat the servants like that," Kiara breathed into his ear, and her hand wandered back towards his belly. This time he didn't push her away.

8

MUSEUM DIRECTOR'S OFFICE, BELVEDERE, VIENNA. THE NEXT DAY.

DR. CLEMENS BREUER GAZED ACROSS THE PALACE GARDENS that stretched between the Lower and Upper Belvedere. The man who had built the palaces, Prince Eugene, had designed the gardens across three immense terraces. With its symmetrical blooming parterres, its fountains, stairways, landings, and topiary, it was the epitome of baroque gardens. Although Breuer had been the director of the museum and its exclusive collection for quite a few years, he never tired of the beauty the prince had brought to life in the eighteenth century—an art that modern builders and landscapers seemed incapable of emulating.

In accepting the position of director, he had fulfilled his life's dream. For a leading expert on Gustav Klimt and his work, there could be no higher distinction.

A knock on the door tore him from his daydreams. He absently called "Come in," and his assistant opened the door.

"A Dr. Enno Lüthi from Geneva Reinsurance is here."

Breuer raised his eyebrows and looked uncertainly at his assistant, who knew him well and could practically read his mind. Anticipating the director's unspoken question, he said, "No, Director. We have nothing scheduled with our insurance company. Dr. Lüthi seems to have come unannounced."

Breuer nodded. Geneva Re was the Belvedere collection's primary insurer. It had taken a tremendous effort several years earlier to find an insurer willing to underwrite the priceless paintings in the museum, Klimt's "The Kiss" above all. So, when a representative of one of the world's most important art insurance companies came knocking, something was afoot. He hoped he wasn't in for more of the headaches that the famous Swiss precision had already caused him during the contract negotiations.

"Ask him to come in," said Breuer, interested to hear the reason for the unheralded visit.

A gray man stepped into the office. Everything about him was gray: graying hair and mustache, a gray three-piece suit, gray tie. Even his expression looked gray.

If someone googled "Swiss insurance rep," they would find a picture of Dr. Lüthi, Breuer thought with amusement.

"My dear Director Breuer, I hope I haven't come at an inconvenient time, but what we have to discuss can't be put off."

Lüthi spoke in purest High German; Breuer could detect only the slightest traces of a Swiss accent. The man had obviously gone to a good deal of trouble to rid his speech of the singsong tones of the Swiss dialect.

"Not at all, not at all. I can always find time for Geneva Re," Breuer said, and the two men sat down at the conference table in the corner of the room, overlooking the garden.

"In recent months," Lüthi began, "the incidence of theft from the galleries we insure has grown alarmingly. Some were prevented, of course, and I have been able to recover most of what was actually stolen."

Lüthi momentarily hesitated. He shook his head in annoyance and reached into the inside pocket of his jacket.

"I apologize. What was I thinking?" he said, and he pushed a business card across the table to the director. "I am the new head of security at Geneva Re, and I am visiting all of the venues we cover to talk about a forthcoming change in our security measures."

Breuer did his best to maintain his poker face, but feared he was failing miserably. When an insurance company spoke of "changing security measures," it most likely meant a lot of work and expense. The sigh that escaped him was, fortunately, quiet enough that Lüthi did not notice it, or was kind enough to ignore it.

"Our primary focus is on the physical transfer of works of art to other institutions during loans. Many of our transports have fallen victim to—at least—attempted attacks and robberies. For this reason, I have developed a new procedure that every institution that we underwrite will be expected to follow."

It occurred to Breuer immediately that he would be dealing with exactly the kind of situation Lüthi was talking about in just a few days' time—the loan of his greatest treasure.

"The movement of artworks will now take place according to one of two methods," Lüthi said, retrieving a handful of documents from his briefcase. "This is the addendum to our existing contract, containing the passages that relate to such transfers. We will be using not only the usual high-security armored transports, the kind typically used to transport money, but also a completely unremarkable mode of transport as a variant."

Lüthi grinned, obviously proud of his strategy.

"A vintage VW bus or a similar, ideally run-down, vehicle will be used, something that potential thieves would never believe we would use to transport works of art."

Breuer tilted his head, interested. By Swiss standards, this was incredibly creative.

"Shortly before the actual transfer is to take place, the toss of a coin—which I will personally carry out—will decide which mode of transport is to be used. If the VW bus wins, I myself will be behind the wheel. That will preclude any risk of an employee, potentially in league with thieves, leaking any details of the route or the mode of transport employed." He raised his hands apologetically. "Now, I know perfectly well that your staff are all absolutely above reproach in this regard, but this is now the rule for everybody."

Breuer was visibly relieved. At least the new amendment would not put any additional strain on his already limited budget.

"Please have your legal office peruse the addendum and return a signed copy to us at your convenience."

Breuer nodded. "Of course, Dr. Lüthi. I'll see to it right away."

"Thank you." Lüthi was already on his feet and preparing to leave. "Please excuse me for running off so soon, but I have many conversations like this ahead of me. But we'll be seeing one another soon enough, for the Klimt transfer."

The two men shook hands and Lüthi took his leave. Breuer waited a few minutes, then called in his assistant.

"Send an email to our contact at Geneva Re . . . uh . . . I've lost his name . . ."

"Vito Rüegger," the assistant said.

"Of course. Send an email to Rüegger and ask him about this Dr. Lüthi."

The assistant nodded.

"Also, put through a call to the CEO of Geneva Re. I'll talk to him myself. I want to be on the safe side."

Thirty minutes later, a phone call confirmed everything Lüthi had said, and Breuer received an email affirming that the procedure Lüthi had described was now the insurer's official policy.

9

SIDE ENTRANCE, THE BELVEDERE, VIENNA, AUSTRIA

FRANÇOIS CLOUTARD CROSSED PRINZ-EUGEN-STRASSE TO a house standing opposite the Belvedere. The instant he stepped into the hallway, he tore off the gray beard.

"*Merde*, why are these things always so terribly itchy?" he murmured to himself, mentally running through the plan they were preparing for the hundredth time. He could trust Fábio and Adalgisa, he knew, but there was no room for slip-ups at all.

He'd promised to deliver "The Kiss" to the family in Naples, and lot depended on him doing that—in fact, everything did. If all went according to plan, Cloutard would get his old life back. He'd be back in the game, with his old networks still intact, his safehouses available to him once again—and the people he'd gone to so much trouble to recruit for his art smuggling, grave robbing, and general burglary operations would once more be his. The family would see to it all; Cloutard could rely on them for that. But if he did not deliver on his promise, then he would be dead. If he failed, his execution would be as swift and fatally certain as the reward for his success would be.

Cloutard opened the door to the apartment he had occupied only a short time before, the windows of which conveniently faced the Belvedere. Tom's grandfather, Arthur Julius Prey, lived in an apartment in the building next door. Cloutard had told him he wanted to live in the area himself when he was in Vienna, and Arthur—who, through his former profession as a prize-winning photojournalist, seemed to know half the people on the planet —had helped him get an apartment in the neighboring building. But, sensibly enough, Cloutard did not divulge what he really wanted the apartment for.

From the windows, they could observe all the comings and goings, the routines, every delivery into or out of the museum.

"They called immediately, and we confirmed your story," said Adalgisa as Cloutard entered the living room, which they had transformed into a small operations center. "And I intercepted the email and replied. They've bought the Geneva Re story."

Cloutard smiled. He had never doubted it. Over the decades, he had raised this kind of production to an art form.

"*Mes amis*, where do we stand otherwise? Do we have everything we need? We only have three days," Cloutard said.

Adalgisa nodded. "After tonight, we'll have everything recorded. We've documented everything going in and coming out. There won't be any surprises."

Cloutard slipped his flask out of his jacket pocket, and Adalgisa and Fábio immediately held out their own glasses for a sample of the Louis XIII it contained. They toasted to their success, and to Cloutard, it felt like old times. As much as he enjoyed jetting around the world and hunting down artifacts with Tom and Hellen, that kind of honest work was simply not his calling. Tom was the honest one. Cloutard, was a crook, and he always would be. And he loved it.

"Once we are done with the Klimt, what then?" he wondered out loud.

Fábio, who had tossed back his cognac, grinned mischievously. Cloutard knew his old accomplice—he probably had the next job lined up already.

"Whatever it is, say it," said Cloutard, taking another sip.

"You know the rumor that the 'Mona Lisa' in the Louvre is supposed to be a replica?"

"Certainly. Vincenzo Peruggia stole the painting in 1911, but since it found its way back to the Louvre in 1913, the powers that be have refused to examine it too closely. They are afraid they might discover that their good old 'Giaconda' is not the real thing. You hear the wildest rumors about what Peruggia did with it."

Fábio nodded eagerly, unable to contain his enthusiasm. "I have heard—from very reliable people—that a casino boss at the Venetian in Las Vegas has the real 'Mona Lisa' hanging in his office."

Cloutard screwed up his nose. "*Naturellement.* And you want to steal it from him? A Vegas casino boss? Are you looking for an early grave? And quite apart from that, I believe it is extremely unlikely that it is the real one."

"I'll dig a little deeper, François," Fábio said. Still grinning with excitement, he looked to his wife. Cloutard was not especially surprised that Adalgisa would immediately be interested in a caper like that.

"To be perfectly honest . . . I am a little torn about where to take things from here," Cloutard said pensively. "Being inside Blue Shield has advantages that are not to be underestimated. I have access to information that no one else does."

"But at some point, you have to *use* that information," said Adalgisa reproachfully.

Cloutard's phone rang. He raised his eyebrows. "I have to take this," he murmured, leaving the room. Outside, he answered the call, "*Monsieur*, I have not heard from you in a very long time."

10

BLUE SHIELD HEADQUARTERS, UNO CITY, VIENNA

"NEVER DO ANYTHING LIKE THAT AGAIN!" HELLEN RAILED at Tom, who had just arrived at the Blue Shield offices. "How about, just once, you let me in on what you're doing? You could have been blown to smithereens in the damned Wewelsburg!" She swallowed, struggling hard to hold onto at least a semblance of composure.

"I called as soon as we got out," Tom said in his defense. Hellen shook her head in frustration, pacing back and forth through the Blue Shield reception area. Vittoria Arcano had crept back behind her desk. She looked from Hellen to Tom and back as if she were watching a tennis match.

Edward came out of Theresia's office just then but realized immediately why his daughter was so upset.

"It's all a game to you, Tom, I know that," Hellen said. "But I simply would not be able to handle losing both you and Mother, maybe even on the same day. Think about how it was for you when they shot your Uncle

Scott in Alexandria and Noah turned your world upside-down."

She paused for a few seconds. Tom managed to meet her eyes for only a moment before his gaze dropped back to the floor. He knew he'd left her alone while he'd gone off chasing adventure on his own, yet again. The reproving looks from Edward and Vittoria didn't make him feel any better.

"I thought we could rely on each other. After all we went through together after the attack at the Hofburg and the theft of the Holy Lance, I thought we were moving in the right direction, that we could trust one another."

Tom had never seen her so furious. He thought about saying something but changed his mind. He wanted to give Hellen the chance to let off as much steam as she needed to.

"But what do you do? My mother is lying in the hospital, dying, and you go off with Cloutard, break into the Wewelsburg, and end up blowing the whole place sky-high! It's now or never, Tom. Either you include me in your life from this moment on, or you and I are through. Done. History. I can do without a man who's constantly doing his own thing—and who leaves me stranded when I need him the most."

She took a deep breath and slumped onto one of the chairs in the waiting area.

"You're right," Tom said. "It was wrong of me, and I apologize. It will never happen again. From now on, I won't leave you in the dark."

The anger in Hellen's face gave way to bewilderment, and it was no different for Edward and Vittoria. Tom had always found it difficult to admit a mistake, let alone actually say he was sorry. Normally, he would have tossed out one of his glib and often totally inappropriate remarks to try to save face.

But those days were over. Hellen mattered too much for him to destroy what they had. When they'd found the room with the Grail, he had realized something crucial: he loved her. His days as a lone warrior, a taciturn cowboy riding off alone into the sunset, had come to an end. What they had gone through after their chance reunion in Vienna, and everything that had happened since, had changed him. He had to admit that he was finally starting to grow up. And as an adult, he had to own up to the mistakes he made, had to admit when he'd screwed up and ask forgiveness of the people he loved. It wasn't easy, but it felt right.

"I'm sorry, Hellen. I mean it," he said, now looking at her without flinching. For several seconds, the room was utterly silent. The atmosphere was so charged that Edward and Vittoria hardly dared to breathe.

"Apology accepted," she said.

Tom smiled, relieved to have cleared the air, but he was clearly struggling, too.

"What happened to the Pope is weighing on me," he said grimly. "Did I tell you he tried to reach me? Maybe I could have prevented what happened."

Hellen had rarely seen him like this. She knew Tom well. Deep down inside, beneath the tough exterior and all the dumb jokes, there was a sensitive human being. And it was likely that Theresia's injury, the attack on the Pope, and the fact that he had let Hellen down had all hit him far harder than he wanted to let on.

Hellen looked at Tom. It seemed to take forever, but she finally stood up and went to him. She raised both hands to his face, drew it down to hers, and gave him a long, heartfelt kiss.

And that was when Cloutard threw the door open and marched inside.

11

BLUE SHIELD HEADQUARTERS

"*Mes amis*, it looks as if I have come at just the right time." He stepped in front of Hellen and grinned at her. "I would take a welcome kiss like that any time."

Hellen shook her head with a smile and boxed the Frenchman in the side.

"*Alors*, if I am not going to get a kiss—" He looked across at Vittoria "—then perhaps I could bother you for a decent cup of café au lait? But not that dishwater from the machine in the corridor. I hope Blue Shield has finally seen fit to spring for a respectable espresso machine. If not, I will personally drive to a shop on Wollzeile right now and steal one."

"We have. I'll make you a coffee," Vittoria said, and headed down the hall toward the kitchen.

If the atmosphere up to that point had been fraught, Cloutard had managed to break the ice very effectively. Tom grinned at his French friend and even Edward's expression was noticeably friendlier.

"Well, now that we can all get along again," he said, looking first at Hellen, then at Tom, "perhaps you can tell us what possessed you to go to the Wewelsburg."

"First the most important thing," Cloutard said. "How is Theresia?"

"As well as can be, all things considered. She seems to be on her way to recovery. The doctors want to wake her from her coma in two days."

Cloutard raised his eyebrows and looked at Tom. Vittoria hadn't yet returned, so he took out his flask of Louis XIII and allowed himself a hefty swig. "*Merde*, all the more reason to find out who was behind it," he said, nodding to Tom to take it from there.

"At the Wewelsburg," Tom began, "we found AF's head-quarters. The place was like a situation room from that TV series 24. And we found evidence that AF was controlling practically everything. Not just the missions we've been involved with since the Sword of Peter, either. They're mixed up in far more than that."

"So, you think the attack on my mother was triggered by AF and not the Society of Avalon?"

"One hundred percent. The Pope's murder is on them, too. They'd tried already, in Barcelona, but at least there we were able to stop them." Tom's voice broke, and he struggled to continue. "Their second attempt, unfortunately, was successful."

Cloutard's phone pinged, and his expression changed. Tom and Hellen noticed immediately.

"What is it, François?" Tom asked. He had seldom seen his friend look so concerned.

"You would not believe me," he said. The hand holding the mobile phone sank. "Someone just offered to sell me the Chronicle of the Round Table."

12

BLUE SHIELD HEADQUARTERS

HELLEN TURNED PALE. *CLOUTARD WAS IN TOUCH WITH THE people who were responsible for her mother's condition?* The Frenchman saw the look on Hellen's face and immediately backpedaled.

"The thieves themselves have not contacted me directly, mind you—it has come through an intermediary I have known for a long time, someone trustworthy."

Hellen shrugged. "Sorry, François, but I don't care. Right now, precious Arthurian artifacts come second. I have to be here for Mother." Her voice trembled.

Edward nodded and placed one hand protectively around his daughter's shoulders.

"What matters now is putting a stop to AF. The Chronicle isn't going to run away. It's more important to find out who almost killed Theresia, who murdered the Pope . . ." Tom's own words caught in his throat again, but he pushed onward. "And who really killed my parents. Guerra was just a contract killer. The AF commander-in-chief must have been pulling the strings back then, too. It's time we put a stop to that fucking outfit once and for all. No disrespect intended, but right now I don't give a damn about the Chronicle."

Tom had grown louder as he spoke. Hellen looked at him —she understood his feelings all too well. *Yes, AF has to be stopped*, she thought.

"I was thinking the same," said Cloutard. "Still, my contact has had some work done on the Chronicle. He has given me a little insight into what they discovered, specifically into the parts that you had not yet analyzed, Hellen. According to his experts, it supposedly contains not only the location of Excalibur, but—absurdly—the route to Merlin's Fountain of Youth."

"The arcanum?" said Edward, who until then had kept silent. "The elixir that Paracelsus and the other alchemists were seeking when they weren't trying to turn base metals into gold?"

Hellen spoke up: "There's a legend that Merlin, the wizard and King Arthur's confidant, created a fountain that would bestow eternal youth, and that his Druid friends watched over it back then."

"The Fountain of Youth?" said Cloutard, rolling his eyes. "Hellen, are you serious? If I had not seen the things I have, I would get up and leave right now."

"In the early Renaissance, Paracelsus dedicated himself to the topic and wrote about a substance—arcanum— that cured all disease and gave whoever consumed it eternal youth," Edward added. "And by the standards of the day, Paracelsus was considered a serious physician, so there are many who believe there could be something to it."

"As exciting as that all sounds right now, it's a long way down my list of priorities," said Hellen with finality.

"Especially because it would cost us ten million euros," Cloutard added.

Tom whistled through his teeth. "Ten million? Not bad. Maybe we should have sold it when we had it."

Hellen gave Tom one of the glares she saved for those kinds of situations, but said nothing.

The door opened again, and Vittoria came in. "There's a Wikus de Waal from Cape Town outside. He says Blue Shield is in breach of its contract with his employers."

13

VIENNA GENERAL HOSPITAL, AUSTRIA

CAPTAIN MAIERHOFER, COMMANDER OF THE COBRA special forces and Tom's former superior, ran his fingers through his hair a final time and tugged at the lapels of his jacket. He glanced impatiently at the floor indicator. Throughout his professional career, first as a Cobra himself and later as the CO of the antiterror outfit, he'd faced all kinds of dangerous situations and every kind of stress. But what he was feeling now took stress to a whole new level. The elevator slowed and stopped, and the doors opened with a soft *ding*. He hesitated, looking at the bouquet of flowers in his hand. A moment passed and the doors began to close, but his hand shot forward, and they slid open again.

He stepped out of the elevator. The floor seemed abandoned. He strode along empty corridors, puzzled at the lack of personnel. It was early evening, true, but he would have expected a little more life in a hospital that size. Finally, he saw a single, white-coated doctor, walking quickly toward him.

"Excuse me," he said. "Where can I find Theresia de Mey? She recently had an operation." The man seemed rushed.

"No idea. Ask a nurse," the man said with a strong accent, and he jabbed a thumb back in the direction he'd just come.

"Thank you," said Maierhofer, walking on.

He saw nobody at the next corner, either. *Where is everyone?* he wondered. He suddenly saw a sign that read "Intensive Care." An arrow pointed back in the direction he'd just come from, and he turned on his heel and hurried back along the corridor. At the end, he pushed through the double door through which the doctor had just passed.

Moments later, he found himself in the intensive care ward. In contrast to the regular patients' rooms, the walls of the individual rooms there were made of glass. Maierhofer moved past one after another, feeling a sense of hopelessness as he looked down the row of patients in their little aquariums, kept alive with high-tech electronics and machines. In some of the rooms, curtains were drawn to give at least a semblance of privacy . . . but here, too, there was no one in sight. An uneasy sensation began to grow in the pit of his stomach. Cautiously, he tried one of the curtained doors. Wrong room: a man in his nineties lay on the bed. He moved on to the next room with closed curtains and opened the door.

"Oh, excuse me," he said, and turned to leave again when he saw a doctor in the room injecting something into an IV tube. The doctor turned around, revealing the patient.

Maierhofer's stomach clenched when he recognized Theresia de Mey's pale, drawn face. And now he recognized the man, too. It was the doctor who'd sent him in the wrong direction just a couple of minutes earlier.

He looked more closely now. It was the shoes that gave him away.

"You're no doctor," he said. "What have you done?"

The man froze. As if in slow motion, he placed the empty needle on a side table. The men stared at each other for a few heartbeats, then a shrill, pulse-like beeping broke the silence. One of the medical machines was going crazy.

Quick as lightning, the fake doctor whipped a silenced pistol from under his coat and aimed it at Maierhofer.

14

BLUE SHIELD HEADQUARTERS

HELLEN, EDWARD, TOM, CLOUTARD AND VITTORIA STARED at the South African incredulously. Hellen was the first to find her voice.

"So, you're saying you had an agreement with Theresia to hand over the shield of Joan of Arc to you because your clients . . ."

"Eon and Kiara van Rensburg," the South African said.

". . . excuse me, Eon and Kiara van Rensburg, are the rightful owners?" Hellen said.

Wikus de Wall nodded. From his briefcase, he produced a contract on official Blue Shield letterhead. Hellen and Edward quickly scanned the papers, then both nodded.

"Just so I don't die ignorant," said Tom, "we're talking about the shield of Joan of Arc that was supposed to be auctioned off at that castle in Switzerland? The same shield that you, François, then handed over to AF, and that we recovered together at Lake Como along with all the other stolen relics?"

Hellen nodded. "That's it. And this contract confirms that the van Rensburgs are the rightful owners, and that Blue Shield was supposed to arrange transport of the shield to Cape Town a week ago."

Hellen briefly explained the situation to Wikus de Waal and why Blue Shield had not been able to meet their contractual obligations.

"Theresia didn't say a word to me about the contract," said Vittoria, a little defensively. Edward nodded as if to confirm that Vittoria wasn't to blame.

"The van Rensburgs are opening an exhibition at their private museum two days from now, and the shield is supposed to be the *pièce de resistance*," Wikus de Waal said coolly. "Ms. de Mey also promised that an expert from Blue Shield would be present to provide our guests with a brief historical introduction to the shield."

Hellen sighed. She had done something similar at the auction at Waldegg Castle in Switzerland, when their involvement with AF had really begun. Everything that had happened back then suddenly resurfaced: the first encounter with Cloutard, her kidnapping by Jacinto Guerra and subsequent rescue by Tom at Lake Como, and all the rest of it. And though she was the real expert on the shield, she simply could not bring herself to leave her mother alone now. She looked up at her father.

"Can you take care of it, Papa? I have all the information you'll need in my office. You already know half of it anyway, and you can read the rest during the flight to Cape Town. I don't want to leave mother by herself."

Edward looked sympathetically at her. "Of course. I'll fly to Cape Town, make the presentation, and be back within seventy-two hours."

"Thank you, Papa," Hellen said.

Edward gave his daughter a hug and held her tightly for a few seconds. Tom and Cloutard looked at the floor, a little unsettled—Tom because he could not help Hellen with this at all, and Cloutard because he was reminded that the shield, for him, had been the beginning of the end. That was when he'd fallen into the trap that Ossana and AF had set for him. He, too, wanted nothing more than to help put an end to AF once and for all. And something was telling him they would need the Chronicle for that.

Edward indicated to Wikus de Waal to follow him. "Let's go down to the repository. That's where we keep the things for which Blue Shield is temporarily responsible. All I need is a plane ticket. We still have to sort out the customs red tape and then we can be on our way."

"You won't need a ticket, and customs won't present a problem," Wikus de Waal said, his voice sharp. "The van Rensburgs have a private jet waiting for us at Vienna Airport, and the paperwork has already been prepared."

Edward nodded, impressed.

Cloutard looked intently at their visitor. His employers both seemed to be art collectors, but Cloutard had never heard of them. He would have to make a few inquiries.

"I'll be back soon," Edward said. "Vittoria and I will take care of this while you look after Theresia." He embraced Hellen again and kissed her on her forehead.

"This way, please," said Vittoria, and left the office, followed by Edward and de Waal.

The telephone in the anteroom rang and Tom picked it up. Seconds later, all the color drained from his face.

15

VIENNA GENERAL HOSPITAL, TWO HOURS
LATER.

THE ELEVATOR DOORS WERE OPENING MUCH TOO SLOWLY. Hellen forced her way through them and ran. Ignoring everything around her, she pushed through the double doors that read "Intensive Care. Authorized entry only."

"Hellen!" Tom shouted, racing after her. Cloutard followed as quickly as he could.

"Excuse me!" cried a nurse, hurrying after Hellen. "Wait! You can't go in—"

Hellen froze. Thousands of pieces of shattered glass lay in the corridor in front of her mother's room. The glass wall had vanished, the curtains hung in shreds, and the space in front of the room had been provisionally sealed off. A few loose flowers were strewn among the shards.

The nurse came to Hellen.

"You're Theresia de Mey's daughter, aren't you? Your mother has been moved. They're examining her right now."

"But what . . . what . . ." Hellen stammered, upset.

"What happened?" Tom asked, stopping next to Hellen.

"I'm afraid I can't answer that," the sister said. "But a doctor will speak to you shortly."

"Oh, *mon Dieu*. What happened here? What did the nurse say?" asked Cloutard when he finally caught up. Tom, holding Hellen in a tight embrace, only shrugged. "That explains the police out—" Cloutard said, but he stopped when he saw a doctor coming their way. Before the doctor could open his mouth, all three were bombarding him with questions.

"What happened?"

"How is she?"

"How could this happen?"

"Tell us!"

"Please, one at a time," the doctor said. "Come with me." He led them back through the double doors to a waiting area outside the intensive care ward.

"We've been examining your mother thoroughly since the incident," the doctor began. "But . . . well, frankly, we don't know what's wrong with her. I'm sorry."

"But just yesterday she was on the road to recovery." Hellen's eyes filled with tears and her voice cracked. "You said . . . you said she'd get well again," Hellen sobbed and turned to Tom, her eyes pleading. He took her in his arms, and she sobbed uncontrollably.

"What incident?" Tom asked.

"You should ask the police," the doctor said, and he nodded toward the end of the passage. Only now did Tom see the small group of officers taking instructions from a man in a suit who was standing with his back to Tom. "I haven't been told exactly what happened yet, either," the doctor continued. "But all of Ms. de Mey's counts deteriorated seriously from one moment to the next. We have no medical explanation for it yet. Our laboratory is still running tests, but . . .." Again, he hesitated. "But right now, it looks like only a miracle will help her."

Hellen paled and buried herself in Tom's embrace again.

"I'm terribly sorry. She has a week left, at best, I believe, unless we're able to learn something from the test results."

Each word was like a bullet. Tom's guts twisted.

"Please excuse me," the doctor said softly, and he disappeared back into the intensive care ward.

Tom could see how much the doctor's words had shaken Cloutard, too. The Frenchman and Theresia would probably have become a couple if Hellen's father hadn't returned from the dead. Cloutard slowly lowered himself onto a visitor's chair and took a long draft from his hip flask.

"What does that even mean, 'no medical explanation'?" Cloutard said with a sniff. "There has to be an explanation."

"Maybe I can answer that question," a voice Tom knew all too well suddenly said. Hellen looked up and wiped away her tears. Cloutard rose to his feet and all three looked in disbelief into the face of Tom's former Cobra boss, Captain Maierhofer.

"Whoa," was the first thing Tom said when he saw Maierhofer's black eye and the small lacerations covering his face. "What are you doing here?"

Cloutard leaned close to Tom and whispered, "He has a thing for . . ." and nodded in the direction of Theresia's room.

"Vaaaahgner. Thanks for your sympathy," Maierhofer sneered. Tom winced at Maierhofer's pronunciation of his name—wrong, as usual. But for once he chose to ignore it.

"All right, seriously, what happened to you?"

"Sit down," said Maierhofer, who held an iPad in his hands. He pointed to the chairs in the waiting area, and Tom, Cloutard and Hellen sat.

He explained briefly what had happened, then turned on the iPad. "This is from a camera inside intensive care. The nurses use it to watch the rooms." He pressed Play. "Maybe you'll recognize the attacker."

"I can't watch this," Hellen said, choking back a sob, and she stood up. "It's all right, really," she whispered to Tom, when he also stood up. "Thank you, but I have to go and freshen up a little anyway."

Tom sat again and the three men watched the video together. Through a gap in the curtain covering the glass walls, they had a clear view of the man with the gun. For a moment, nothing happened. Then Maierhofer whipped the bouquet into the man's face and grabbed his gun arm.

"Um . . . wow," Tom said as he watched the two men fight. "You're still pretty good for an ol—" He saw Maierhofer's face just in time and caught himself.

"*Impressionnant*," Cloutard whispered.

"You need to work on your landings, though," Tom added, as Maierhofer was hurled bodily through the glass wall. The assailant fled and Maierhofer struggled back to his feet.

Maierhofer pressed Pause and gave Tom an ill-tempered glare. Tom gulped. *I've really got to learn to control my mouth*, he thought.

"Do you know him?" Maierhofer asked, moving on from Tom's foolish remark. He pointed at the image of the man frozen on the screen.

Cloutard and Tom looked at one another and shook their heads. Disappointed, Maierhofer put the iPad aside.

"Wagner, what hornets' nest have you stirred up now? Why would someone want to kill the head of Blue Shield?"

"That's a complicated question," Tom said.

For a moment, no one said a word. Then Maierhofer, his voice low, addressed Tom directly.

"Vaaaahgner, you know I'm not your biggest fan. But do me a favor: find these bastards and—"

"That's what I plan to do," Tom interrupted his former CO.

"And Wagner, one more thing. Maybe this will help you. I managed to get it from him during the fight." Maierhofer stood up and dug a small evidence bag out of his trouser pocket. He held it out to Tom.

Tom drew a sharp breath, hardly believing what he was seeing.

"*Mon Dieu*. Isn't that . . .?"

Hesitant, Tom took the bag. Inside it was a silver ring with a crest. He hadn't seen that particular crest before, but he knew those rings very well indeed.

"Yes, indeed. It's a signet ring from the Society of Avalon."

16

WAITING ROOM, INTENSIVE CARE WARD, VIENNA GENERAL HOSPITAL

WHEN HELLEN RETURNED FROM THE BATHROOM, SHE SAT and remained silent for a while. Maierhofer had already left, leaving Tom, François, and Hellen behind. All of them were shocked, but Hellen most of all. Tom could see that very clearly. The words "only a miracle will help her" were burned into each of their minds.

Tom knew exactly what Hellen was feeling. His own thoughts took him back to Syria, to the bombing that had claimed his parents' lives. He had carried the pain deep inside for years, and then, suddenly, the man responsible for their deaths was standing in front of him at the airport in Milan. Tom could still remember the fury and anguish, all the emotions that had boiled up inside him.

Hellen wasn't at that point, though. Not yet. Tom was sure of that. Thanks to Maierhofer, they knew that the Society of Avalon was behind the attack on Theresia— and they hadn't lost her yet. Hellen could still hope. Her mother was still alive, even if it would take a miracle to keep her that way.

Tom would do anything he could to make that miracle happen. He owed it to Theresia. And more importantly, he owed it to Hellen. He watched her now as she struggled to speak. She took a breath, attempted to say a word, but then couldn't get it out. She tried three times, and on the third attempt she was able to push it through.

"Then we're going to need that damned miracle," she said almost defiantly, breaking the silence between them.

Tom and Cloutard knew immediately what she was talking about.

"I know how irrational it is to go chasing after a legend more than a thousand years old, but right now I have nothing better to go on," she whispered, and Tom sensed that she didn't really want to put it into words. He looked at Cloutard, who nodded without a second's hesitation.

"You think we should find Merlin's Fountain of Youth, don't you? Paracelsus's arcanum, or whatever the stuff is called."

Hellen managed to dredge up a tiny smile. "I know it's a fairy tale, but what else do we have? It's a minuscule chance, and frankly it seems almost absurd . . . but I don't ever want to accuse myself of not trying it. I can't sit around here wringing my hands, waiting for Mother to die. I have to do something!"

Hellen's voice had risen from a whisper almost to a wail.

"Then we're going to need the Chronicle first," Tom said. "If I've got it right, it contains instructions for how to find the Fountain of Youth, right? If we're lucky, there'll be an 'X' to mark the spot."

"We had the Chronicle in our hands once already. We know how cryptic dear Arthur was and we know how many hands it went through after him, so I doubt it will be as simple as you say, *mon ami*," said Cloutard. "But you are right: we need the Chronicle. Without it, we have no idea where to start."

17

WAITING ROOM, INTENSIVE CARE, VIENNA GENERAL HOSPITAL

As he spoke, Cloutard had crossed to the coffee machine. He bought three coffees and gave one each to Tom and Hellen, then added a dash of cognac to his own.

"Let me have a shot, too. I could really use it right now," said Hellen, holding out her cup.

Tom and Cloutard looked surprised, but Cloutard immediately added a large slug of Louis XIII to her cup. "This stuff is undrinkable without it," he said drily.

Tom sipped at his own, pulled a face, and nodded. He held his cup out to Cloutard, too—he also needed something stronger.

"There's just one catch," said Hellen. "We don't have ten million euros. And we're going to need that much to buy the Chronicle, aren't we, François?"

"I am afraid so. But . . ." He paused, thinking for a moment, then said, "I have an idea." He paused again and took a deep breath. "Maybe you had better have a little more," he said.

Hellen and Tom looked at the Frenchman quizzically, but Cloutard only topped up their cups from his flask. Tom suspected the worst.

"*Alors*, I am not going to beat around the bush." He looked around, then signaled to them to lean in a little closer before continuing in a whisper. "I have been planning for some time to break into the Belvedere in the next few days to steal Gustav Klimt's 'The Kiss.' Or rather, to replace it with a replica."

Tom and Hellen almost dropped their cups.

"Excuse me?" Hellen was struggling to catch her breath. "You were . . . what?"

Tom laid one hand on hers. She understood: this was not the moment for her to lecture on morality.

"I know you are disappointed in me, but I will explain everything later." He gulped back the last of his coffee and cognac, grimaced and continued: "My plan is this: we offer the Klimt—the forgery, I mean—in exchange for the Chronicle. A Klimt as famous as this is worth more than a trifling ten million euros. My contact would have to take it."

Cloutard knew that he was signing his own death warrant. Twice, in fact. The mafia were waiting for him to deliver, and his intermediary would be less than happy when he eventually found out he'd been handed a forgery.

"Won't that get you in deep trouble?" said Tom, apparently able to read Cloutard's thoughts.

"Right now, that is beside the point. We can take care of it later," he said flatly. "But we need a miracle. And for a miracle, one has to be able to accept an occasional risk." Hellen's look of gratitude assured him that he was doing the right thing.

"So, it turns out you're a good guy after all," said Tom, winding the old villain up.

"Shut your mouth and let us go through the plan," Cloutard shot back. "I will contact my man. I will tell him that I have already swapped the Klimt. We make the handover, and we are in business."

"Is your man with the Chronicle here in Vienna?" Hellen asked.

Cloutard nodded. "Yes. We can make this happen very quickly."

Through Hellen's desperation, a tiny seed of hope sprouted. If anyone could make a miracle happen, it was these two lunatics. Tom put his arms around Hellen again when he saw the tears brimming in her eyes.

"We'll do this. We'll find the Fountain of Youth and save your mother."

18

IN FRONT OF THE BELVEDERE, VIENNA

ISAAC HAGEN LOOKED AT THE PICTURE OF THE MUSEUM director on his laptop, which lay open on the passenger seat. Hagen was on the Belvedere website, and the director—Dr. Clemens Breuer, a leading expert on Gustav Klimt—was easily recognizable on the screen. If anyone could tell him whether the painting Cloutard had offered in exchange for the Chronicle was real, then it was Breuer. He checked his watch. He still had plenty of time before the handover. He had parked opposite the main entrance of the palace and was watching the front door.

And there he was. A man wearing a suit and carrying a briefcase left the building, gave the doorman a friendly nod, and walked along Prinz-Eugen-Strasse toward the city center.

Hagen closed the laptop and climbed out. He retrieved his sports bag from the back seat and followed the man, staying well behind and on the opposite side of the street. After a short distance, Director Breuer stepped onto the pavement, intending to cross. Hagen slowed his steps. The director waited for a gap in the traffic, then quickly strode to the other sidewalk, then turned into a side street, the Belvederegasse. Hagen stayed on him, closing the gap now, only about ten paces behind his quarry. Breuer stopped beside a silver Mercedes and rummaged in his trousers pocket for a key. He opened the car and placed his briefcase on the rear seat. Hagen looked around—the coast was clear.

"Stay perfectly calm and do exactly what I tell you," Hagen hissed into Breuer's ear, stepping up close behind him and jabbing his pistol into his back.

"Wh . . . what do you want?" the director stammered.

"For now, just drive." With his left hand, Hagen opened the driver's door. A prod with the pistol made it clear to Breuer that he should get in. At the same time, Hagen climbed into the back seat and closed the door.

"What do you want? Take the car, take my money, but please . . . I have children."

"Don't worry, we're just going for a little drive. I need your expertise."

"What? But I'm just an employee."

"Don't sell yourself so short, Dr. Breuer. And if you do what I say, I promise I won't kill you."

Terrified, the director looked in the rearview mirror at Hagen.

"Drive," Hagen said.

19

BENEATH AN OVERPASS, PRATER PARK, VIENNA

CLOUTARD LOOKED AT HIS WATCH. IT WAS ALMOST midnight. Hagen still had two minutes. As agreed, he'd parked the delivery van underneath the overpass that spanned the Hauptallee, the broad pedestrian boulevard that ran through the center of the Prater park in Vienna. It was certainly an out-of-the-way location. During the day, countless runners, strollers, cyclists, and even horseback riders made the most of the city's sprawling recreational area. Twice the size of Central Park in New York, the forested Prater lay just two miles from Stephansplatz, at the heart of Vienna. But at night, the area was deserted. Not even sex workers or drug dealers strayed along the Hauptallee at night. Cloutard leaned on the back of the van and listened to the steady rumbling of the cars racing down the multilane highway overhead. Dozens of concrete pillars carried the roadway above the treetops, supporting the cars and trucks in their rush past this little patch of nature.

For the hundredth time, he asked himself why Hagen had decided to sell the Chronicle to him, of all people. And where had he gotten it? They had assumed all along that the Society of Avalon had recovered the Chronicle for themselves. Even the police were stumbling in the dark and had filed the case away as the work of professionals.

And now there he was, swapping a forged painting— commissioned by one of the most dangerous *capo dei capi* —for the Chronicle of the Round Table. Once he had this behind him, he would have to disappear for a while. He could not drag his friends any deeper into this mess than he had already.

He heard something and straightened up. A car. A few seconds later, he could make it out in the darkness. As agreed, Hagen had driven along the boulevard with his headlights off, to make doubly sure they wouldn't be seen. The silver Mercedes slowed under the bridge and rolled to a stop beside the delivery van. Isaac Hagen climbed out of the back of the Mercedes, but he was not alone—hands raised, the driver also climbed out. Hagen directed him with his pistol toward the van.

"Monsieur Hagen, what is this?" Cloutard greeted the Briton.

"You said I could bring an expert with me. So, I figured I might as well bring the best man for the job. May I introduce—"

"Dr. Clemens Breuer. I know who he is," Cloutard interrupted him. "Have you gone mad, bringing a man of his standing here? You might as well tell the whole world you have the real picture."

"Let me worry about that. Where's the Klimt?"

"The Klimt?" said Breuer, his voice trembling.

Cloutard immediately turned and opened the back of the van.

"After you," Cloutard said, and Hagen and Breuer climbed inside. Cloutard followed them. Breuer's eyes widened when he saw the large wooden crate, more than six feet square, strapped vertically in the center of the cargo bay.

"Help me, please, Dr. Breuer," said Cloutard politely to the director, who was on the verge of panic. Together they loosened the straps, leaned the crate against one side of the van, and removed the lid.

Breuer gasped when he saw the painting inside.

"That . . . that's impossible. Where did you get this?"

"I will give you three guesses," said Cloutard.

"Tell me if this is the real painting and you can go." Hagen pressed his pistol to the director's head. "But, of course, only if you forget about our jaunt out here forever. If you don't, your family will suffer a little accident one day soon, if you take my meaning."

Breuer nodded. Cloutard handed him a flashlight, and the director, hands trembling, set to work.

20

CHAMBERS OF THE DECEASED POPE, VATICAN CITY

AS IF THE HOLY FATHER WERE STILL ALIVE, THOUGHT Cardinal Taddeo Monteleone, the Pope's former camerlengo, as he entered the room. The furnishings were spartan: a simple, wooden bed; a prayer desk in front of a modest tabernacle, also of wood; a plain table with six chairs, around which the Pope had held intimate discussions with his innermost circle; a wooden cupboard; a narrow bookshelf; and a small cross on the wall above the door. No personal items at all that might reveal something of the individual who had occupied the room. The camerlengo had never understood why the Holy Father had chosen to live as simply as he had. His approach to life had manifested itself similarly at mealtimes and in the other routines of daily life. The Pope had eaten only simple meals—a rarity in the Città de Vaticano. He had insisted that no ingredients be imported from abroad and had drunk cheap communion wine. And by doing so, he had set an example that neither his cardinals nor anyone else in the Vatican had taken so seriously—to say nothing of their other carnal desires.

But now the Holy Father was dead, and many things were about to change. Monteleone had set the necessary steps in motion on the day of the Pope's assassination. At least fifteen days of the *sede vacante*—roughly translated as "vacant seat"—period had to pass before the conclave could begin. Soon enough, white smoke would rise and there would be an announcement of "*habemus papam!*" signaling the election of a new Pope. According to tradition, the Pope's chambers were to be kept sealed until the next Pope moved in. But Monteleone had never been a stickler for the rules.

The door suddenly opened and a priest around thirty years of age entered without knocking.

"Father Quintiliano. I am glad to see you," said Monteleone.

The younger priest carried a laptop under his arm, which he now placed on the table. Then he knelt in front of Monteleone and kissed his hand. Maintaining silence, he stood again and opened the laptop. A few seconds later, the video call connected.

"Your Eminence, I am happy to see you well. Regrettably, several men of the cloth in the Holy Father's entourage also lost their lives in the bombing."

"It surprises me greatly to hear 'Eminence' and 'Holy Father' from the mouth of a Jew. But yes, you are right, Noah. Unfortunately, we had to accept a number of losses."

"To make an omelet, one has to break eggs," said Noah Pollock, unmoved. "Our goal was to cause a stir, after all."

The camerlengo nodded, but he did not respond to Noah's callous words.

"We've completed our part of the deal," Noah continued. "Now it's your turn. You will ensure that our man, the current Cardinal Secretary of State, leaves the conclave as the new Pope. Your position as head of Vatican intelligence will no doubt simplify that outcome," he said with unmistakable admiration.

21

HAUPTALLEE, PRATER, VIENNA

"I hope you realize this makes us square," said Hagen.

Cloutard was surprised but nodded. He'd pushed the deal he had made with Hagen to the back of his mind. AF had sent Hagen to assassinate Cloutard about a year earlier, but Cloutard's mother had gotten the drop on Hagen and held him captive. They had come to an agreement: Cloutard would allow Hagen to go free, and Hagen would owe him a favor. Now he was making good on that promise with the Chronicle, and being very well paid for it in the process. Or at least, he believed he was. Cloutard took a little satisfaction from knowing that he was palming off a forgery on Hagen, and that—if Cloutard was lucky—the mercenary would never get a chance to take revenge. But Cloutard would stay on his toes. It was dangerous to underestimate Hagen.

"If this makes us square, why do you need the painting? You owe me, so why am I giving you anything of value at all?"

"It's simple: after this little swap, I'm going to have to disappear. The AF leader and his thugs will scour the world for me once they find out I had the Chronicle all along and didn't hand it over. But why are you complaining? Be glad I'm willing to trade. A picture this size isn't exactly a check for ten million. I can't just stick it in my pocket."

"All right, we're even," said Cloutard, and he held out his hand to shake. Hagen took Cloutard's hand but gripped tightly and pulled him closer.

"Make sure your mother knows it, too. It's bad enough I'll have AF breathing down my neck. I don't need a mafia widow out to get me, too."

Cloutard chuckled. "Fair enough."

"That old lady . . ." Hagen shook his head. "She even scared the shit out of me."

"Who do you think you are talking to? She did the same to me for decades," said Cloutard, frowning.

"Well, Director? What is the diagnosis? Are we looking at the real Klimt or just a very good copy?" said Cloutard with a wink at the director.

"I . . . yes. The picture is real, there's no doubt about it. But how were you able to steal it from my museum?"

Cloutard ignored Breuer. "See?" he said to Hagen. "I would never try to rip you off."

"Okay. Pack it up again."

Cloutard and Breuer quickly replaced the lid on the crate, returned it to its upright position, and strapped it firmly in place.

"I have showed you mine. Now show me yours," said Cloutard with a grin as all three climbed out of the back of the van.

"Uh . . . excuse me," Breuer stammered. "May . . . may I go now?" He looked pleadingly at the two criminals.

"Just one more little detail. Neither of you move an inch," Hagen ordered. He went to the Mercedes he and Breuer had arrived in and fetched his sports bag from the back seat. He put it on the trunk lid and opened it with one hand, keeping his pistol trained on Breuer with the other. From inside the bag, he took out a second pistol, this one wrapped in a cloth.

Breuer recoiled. Cloutard could see that he was thinking about running.

"But you . . . you promised you wouldn't kill me," Breuer pleaded, tears in his eyes.

"And I'm a man of my word," Hagen said, tossing the second pistol, also fitted with a silencer, in Cloutard's direction. Cloutard, taken by surprise, caught it clumsily, fumbling it like a hot potato. "He's going to shoot you," Hagen added, and he shifted his aim from Hagen to Cloutard.

22

CHAMBERS OF THE DECEASED POPE, VATICAN CITY

"Do we think we actually know more than Mossad or your own organization, AF?" the camerlengo asked.

"The art of lying should come a little more easily to a man in your position, Your Eminence," said Noah drily. "Your intelligence service was at work long before anybody even thought of Mossad or AF, so don't feign innocence now. No one will believe you."

Monteleone nodded again, ignoring Noah's sarcasm. "I will see what I can do. I believe that the right man will be elected Pope," he said.

"I hope so. I don't want to have to take things into my own hands again. The leader would be extremely unhappy if something were to go wrong now and another man as liberal as the last one took the reins there. To really stir things up, we need the Vatican to take conservative positions, even dogmatic ones. Only when the fronts are completely fixed will we be able to exert control more easily. As long as the faithful have a common enemy, they don't see who's really steering the ship. And fear has always been a good tool for keeping the rabble in check."

Monteleone said nothing.

"Very well. Today must be Your Eminence's day of silence. Fine with me. As long as we get the right result."

The connection was broken. The young Jesuit closed the laptop and looked at the camerlengo questioningly.

"I know what you are thinking, Brother, but you're mistaken. I would not countenance having Bonavita in the Papal seat for a second. The election will fall in my favor. I have already put everything necessary in place."

"But Eminence, don't you fear the vengeance of this organization? You cannot have forgotten that AF murdered not only the Holy Father, but also the American president. The new man in the White House is one of theirs. You would be in danger from the first day of your pontificate."

"Maybe so. But that man, Noah, was right about one thing. I am the head of the oldest intelligence service in the world. Which, as it happens, is also the oldest organization of assassins. We have been sending our men into the chambers of emperors and kings for centuries. We can handle these AF jokers, and in any case, I will not bow to them. Even if it means that my Jesuits must once again march out like the heavenly host—even if they must bring me the head of every one of these AF parasites, as John the Baptist's head was once brought to Herod—we will be victorious."

Cardinal Monteleone was on his feet now, and his last words had been delivered like a sermon, as if he were already standing in the pulpit at St. Peter's.

"Quintiliano, you are my best man. Inform our brothers in every country. Tell them to be ready in case a new Crusade is required. We have prepared the files on the cardinals and their transgressions, haven't we?"

Quintiliano nodded. "Our agents have gathered everything we need to ensure you receive the necessary votes in the conclave. There are some truly disgusting stories among them. . ." Quintiliano said with some revulsion, and quickly crossed himself.

"Don't turn soft on me now. You are a Jesuit priest, a warrior of God. Our ends will justify our means," Monteleone said harshly. "To work. And don't forget: there are still many votes to be added, but the result should not be a landslide. There should be at least three rounds of voting, or the world will grow suspicious, and we do not want that."

23

HAUPTALLEE, PRATER, VIENNA

"*TU ES FOU*. YOU CAN'T BE SERIOUS. I WOULD NEVER SHOOT anybody!" Cloutard held the pistol in two fingers by its silencer, like a smelly sock.

"It's your decision: him or you. So decide. We don't have all night."

Cloutard gulped. Trembling, he aimed the gun at Breuer.

"No! Please, no!" Breuer staggered back until he was up against the back of the delivery van.

"Please," Cloutard pleaded with Hagen. "You already have more than you wanted. Take the picture. You will get at least fifty million on the black market. But don't force me to kill anyone."

"Get on with it." Hagen's voice was icy. He stepped close to Cloutard and pressed his pistol against his temple. Cloutard closed his eyes hard. "I'll count to three. One . . ." Cloutard fired once, then again, and Breuer slid to the ground with two bullets in his chest. "There now,"

Hagen said. "That wasn't so hard, was it?" Holding the cloth, he took the pistol back from Cloutard and wrapped it up again. "Just a little insurance," he added, waving the wrapped pistol in Cloutard's face before pushing it into his waistband.

Cloutard did not move. He stared in disbelief at the lifeless body, then whipped out his flask of cognac and took a swig to calm his nerves. Then he looked up, glaring hard at Hagen.

"All right. Let us finish this. Where is the Chronicle?"

Hagen nodded toward the sports bag on the trunk.

"I hope it is the real thing," Cloutard hissed. "If I find out that you have tried to offload my own forgery onto me, my mother will be the least of your problems." He saw in Hagen's eyes that the threat had hit home. He checked the contents of the bag.

"Don't sweat it," Hagen said. "It's the real deal. I took it from the hands of one of those unconscious Avalon fools in the elevator right outside your Blue Shield offices, at the UNO City."

"You were there?"

"Oh, yes. Noah sent me to get the Chronicle, but those morons beat me to it. I put them out of commission with a fentanyl-derivate grenade, then just walked out the front door with the Chron—"

"Shh!" Cloutard interrupted him. He nodded along the boulevard. A hundred yards away, a police car crossed the Hauptallee at a crawl.

"I thought no cops came this way?" Hagen whispered.

The patrol car stopped. Hagen didn't dare to move. Suddenly, it turned along the boulevard in their direction.

"The keys!" Hagen snapped, holding out his hand.

"In the ignition."

"Okay, my dear Frenchman. Then this is goodbye."

Hagen jumped behind the wheel of the van and started the motor. He rolled down the window and turned back to Cloutard one last time.

"By the way, drive carefully. The car is stolen. I wouldn't get pulled over with it if I were you," he said with a laugh as he drove away. The patrol car crawled closer until it stopped directly beside Cloutard.

"Hands in the air and don't move," said Adalgisa through the side window, grinning broadly.

"Fábio, he is gone. You can get up," Cloutard said.

"Next time, you be the one who gets shot," Fábio groaned as he sat up, grimacing with pain. He opened his shirt to reveal shredded pouches of fake blood over a bulletproof vest. "Next time, I'm sticking to hacking websites."

Cloutard reached down and helped him to his feet.

"On the other hand, you could have earned an Academy Award just now," Cloutard joked.

Fábio gave him a pained smile, handed him the key to his Mercedes, then climbed into the patrol car beside Adalgisa. "One day, you're going to have to tell me why you swapped that picture for a pile of old documents and put yourself on the wrong side of the mafia. And that crazy Hagen, too, the moment he finds out you double-crossed him."

"You are right. And one day, I will tell you."

24

CONFERENCE ROOM, BLUE SHIELD HEADQUARTERS, UNO CITY, VIENNA

"THAT'S AMAZING!"

Hellen's face lit up. She was in her element. Tom had seen her like this many times: all her cares, her doubts, her fears simply fell away from her. She was completely focused.

Vittoria Arcano was demonstrating a new software package that Theresia had recently ordered for Blue Shield. About a year earlier, together with leading museums around the world, Blue Shield had placed an order with a company that specialized in the development of artificial intelligence. Hellen was aware, of course, that AI played a key role in many kinds of software, and that such programs were already producing astonishing results: They could perform tasks as simple as writing texts or as complex as translating entire libraries, or predicting terrorist attacks by analyzing the behavior of nations. So much was already possible. Explaining the software to Hellen, Vittoria had uploaded an image of a large wall in an Egyptian temple, covered in hieroglyphics. Seconds later, the program produced an array of possible interpretations. The software had caught the world's attention when, at its introduction, it had decoded the Voynich manuscript—a medieval text that had puzzled science for centuries—in just fifteen minutes. Unfortunately, the contents of the manuscript had turned out to be less exciting than the AI's speed in cracking the code.

Hellen was as excited as a kid at Christmas. "I can only begin to imagine how useful this software will be for us. This is going to change everything!"

Tom smiled. He loved to see Hellen lose herself in her enthusiasm. This would distract her from the seriousness of her mother's condition, at least for a while.

"Personally, I don't think it's that amazing," he said. "It's just Google Translate for old stuff, right?"

He knew he could really rile Hellen up with comments like that. But he was just pulling her leg a little, cheering her up, and she knew it. She jabbed him playfully in the ribs, then glanced at her watch.

"Where's Clou—"

That was as far as she got, for at that moment the Frenchman threw open the door and stepped into the room. He held a large sports bag in his hand. Hellen inhaled sharply. "Did you get it?"

"*Naturellement, mon chére.* What did you think?" He swung the sports bag onto the conference table and opened it. Hellen pulled the bag over and carefully lifted out the three leather rolls inside.

"And your middleman took the bait, just like that? He didn't spot the Klimt as a fake?" Tom asked, his forehead lined with concern.

"Do not insult me, please," said Cloutard, with feigned earnestness. "I am a crook, or had you forgotten? The power of suggestion and the Oscar-worthy talents of Fábio were enough to convince him."

Tom raised his hands placatingly. "La, la, la, I don't want to hear any more," he said, sticking his fingers in his ears for a moment. "And don't say another word about what your contacts are still capable of," he added, a little reproach in his voice.

"Tom, remember that François's talents have saved our skins several times," Hellen chided, not looking up from the rolls as she carefully spread them out on the table.

Tom raised his eyebrows in surprise. Hadn't Hellen always been the one to protest against Cloutard's methods? Right now—now that he was helping her mother—she understandably thought a little differently. The end justified the means, it seemed . . .

"Enough discussion. I'm going through this thing from cover to cover right now. With a little luck, the software will be able to help, otherwise it'll mean night shifts. Time we don't have." Hellen sighed and shooed Tom and Cloutard out of the conference room. Vittoria began scanning the individual parts of the Chronicle, putting them into a form the program could work with.

Two hours later, the door opened, and Hellen emerged.

Cloutard and Tom jumped from their seats and looked at her eagerly, but she only screwed up her face. "It's tough, but the software has given us a few bits of useful information, and I've been able to analyze some of it myself."

"*And?*" said Tom and Cloutard, almost in unison. They looked at here impatiently. "Come on, the suspense is killing us!"

25

FORTRESS OF THE SOCIETY OF AVALON, MATTERHORN GLACIER, SWISS ALPS

TRISTAN DISMOUNTED FROM THE SNOWMOBILE AND GAZED up at the fortress. It took his breath away every time. Strictly speaking, the structure should not even have existed. Every time he came here—in the midst of this rugged landscape of mountains and glaciers, the literal high point of which was the Matterhorn, at almost 15,000 feet—he wondered anew how the enormous fortress had come to exist at all, and who had built it.

Years before, more or less by chance, he had joined the Society of Avalon. Even as a young man he had been a seeker, delving into various religions, the philosophies of the Far East, the mythologies of many different cultures. He had joined a number of sects and had experimented with some very dangerous designer drugs.

A normal life, one that stayed within the usual bourgeois boundaries, had never been comprehensible to him. He had gravitated toward criminality at a young age, but he had never been just another craven, small-time crook— he saw himself as something better. He took care to always look his best. He ate well, kept himself in good physical shape, and spent a lot of time expanding his spiritual horizons. And after experimenting with various activities early in his criminal career, he had settled on the strictest discipline of all: assassin.

And then, one day, a man appeared in his life who could have been an older version of himself. Educated, cultivated—and cold-blooded when it came to making his plans a reality. They had crossed paths during a job for the mafia on the French island of Corsica, and had immediately developed a mutual regard.

Once the man had thoroughly checked his background and he, Tristan, had completed several smaller assassinations at the older man's behest, he had been invited here, to this breathtaking fortress, for the first time. And it was here that he had learned all there was to know about the centuries-long history of the Society of Avalon, a company that saw themselves as the spiritual descendants of the Knights of the Round Table. The man who had so impressed him the first time they met on Corsica turned out to be the head of the society, a direct descendent of King Arthur himself. He had thus been accepted into the fellowship of the Round Table and given the name Tristan. Ever since, he had traveled the globe in search of artifacts from the original Round Table and its first great king.

Why they were searching, he did not know. But the pay was good, and he led an exciting life. That was all he needed.

He looked around, a little surprised. At previous meetings, he had never arrived alone. There had always been other knights in the helicopter, and the snowmobile convoy had become legendary. Roaring through the high, alpine landscape, he felt like a modern-day knight through and through. Today, however, he was alone. The mighty doorway opened automatically as he approached, and he stepped through into the enormous entry hall. But it was deserted as well. A normal man would have been feeling nervous by now, but Tristan's pulse stayed steady. He was wary, certainly, but he could not imagine that the fortress had been taken over. Who would even be capable of such a thing? Apart from that other organization, Absolute Freedom, which he had heard about before joining the Society of Avalon, no one could present a danger to them. His chest swelling with pride, Tristan entered the room that contained the Round Table itself.

Except that it, too, was empty today. But for one man, the society's ruler, the man he knew only by his codename: King Arthur. He was sitting at his usual place at the table, and a single candle cast its feeble light around the hall. The scene might have been ghostly if Tristan had believed in anything as ridiculous as ghosts. Arthur looked up, and Tristan strode to him, knelt before him, and offered a humble greeting.

"Sit, Tristan. I have a special assignment for you."

26

CONFERENCE ROOM, BLUE SHIELD HEADQUARTERS, UNO CITY, VIENNA

"First the good news. The Chronicle really does talk about Merlin's Fountain of Youth and the arcanum associated with it. The Chronicle was written hundreds of years before Paracelsus even existed, but the wording about the arcanum is mostly the same. I compared it to his old writings—he copied some of the passages word for word."

"Plagiarism? So, it's not just modern-day politicians, but Renaissance doctors, too? The guy was really ahead of his time, wasn't he?" said Tom.

"Now the bad news," Hellen continued, ignoring Tom's observation. "The Chronicle doesn't say much about where the Fountain of Youth actually is. Either it's only vaguely described, or the software and I are both on the wrong track. All I've found so far is something about a magic forest."

"Fangorn?" said Tom with a grin, making Cloutard and Hellen shake their heads.

"But I *have* discovered that we need three specific artifacts to get to the fountain. So, as long as we don't know exactly where we should be looking, I suggest we focus on finding those things."

"What do we need?" Cloutard nipped at his hip flask, then held it out to Hellen and Tom.

"You're going to turn us all into alcoholics," said Hellen, turning down the offer. Tom was about to allow himself a swig, but he saw Hellen's frown and shook his head instead. Hellen said, "We need Caliburnus, Pendragon's shingle, and the Druid's amulet."

Tom and Cloutard narrowed their eyes.

"Uh . . ." Tom began. "I mean, excuse my ignorance, but what the actual f—?"

"That part, I'm happy to say, was easy," Hellen cut him off. "Caliburnus is the Latin name for King Arthur's sword, Excalibur. Pendragon is another name for the king, but I haven't yet worked out what the 'shingle' part means. As for the Druid, that can only be Merlin."

"Piece of cake," said Tom. "We need Excalibur, Merlin's amulet, and a shingle from the roof of Camelot," counting on his fingers to add a little emphasis to his words. He cuffed Cloutard playfully in the chest. "We can do all that before lunch, right?" But a second later, his smile turned to a frown. "Seriously, where do we even begin?"

Cloutard also looked glum. He stared at the floor, pondering.

"One step at a time," said Hellen, and Tom was amazed at

her confidence. "Of course, we're not going to be able to just snap our fingers and, poof, we've got what we need. We'll start with Excalibur—I found another clue to that in the Chronicle."

She pointed at the monitor. The software had just finished analyzing another page of the Chronicle.

"*Per tot discrimina rerum*," Tom read at the line Hellen was indicating. "Hmm. I guess that's Latin, right?"

"'Through so many perils,'" Cloutard murmured. "The motto of Maximilian I."

Hellen nodded. "I'm impressed, François. Emperor Maximilian I apparently had some kind of direct connection with the Knights of the Round Table. He stole the motto from them, and he was also known as the 'last knight.' He is supposed to have been Excalibur's guardian for a while, and he would have been accompanied by the Black Knights."

"In *Ivanhoe*, Richard the Lionheart was known as the Black Knight, *n'est-ce pas*?" said Cloutard.

"Yes, but I don't think they're talking about Richard the Lionheart here. I think it must be referring to the 'Schwarze Mander.'"

"Schwarze Mander? What's that?" asked Tom.

"Maximilian I's tomb is in the Hofkirche, or Court Church, in Innsbruck. The sarcophagus is huge, and it's flanked by twenty-eight bronze statues that protect the tomb. And perhaps Excalibur as well. The statues are colloquially called the 'Schwarze Mander,' meaning 'black men.' And you'll never guess who one of those twenty-eight figures is supposed to represent." She looked up at their curious faces and smiled. "King Arthur."

"So, there's a King Arthur statue at the Hofkirche in Innsbruck. And you think we'll find Excalibur there?"

"Honestly, I have no idea. But Maximilian I is a lead we should certainly follow up, even if all we find is another clue."

"It's not great, but if it's all we've got . . ." said Tom.

"Well, then, what are we waiting for? Next stop, Innsbruck!" Hellen spoke cheerfully but instantly grew serious again, aware of how much was at stake. Tom and Cloutard hurried out after her.

27

FORTRESS OF THE SOCIETY OF AVALON, MATTERHORN GLACIER, SWISS ALPS

TRISTAN DID AS ARTHUR BADE AND SAT DOWN. HE KNEW that something extraordinary was happening.

"As you may have heard, we recently lost our first knight, Lancelot."

Tristan stiffened. Was the honor of first knight being passed to him?

Arthur, on his feet now, crossed through the darkness to the wall beside the fireplace. He slid a stone plate aside and pressed a button. From the ceiling, a large panel began to descend, which Tristan soon realized was a huge screen. Arthur returned to his seat and activated a recording from an app on his phone. Seconds later, Tristan saw a conference room and several people talking.

"Lancelot's mission was to retrieve the Chronicle of the Round Table from Blue Shield Headquarters in Vienna. Unfortunately, he failed, and a short time later he perished in Jordan. Considering his incompetence of late, that would have been on my agenda soon anyway."

Arthur peered grimly at Tristan. It was clear that the Society of Avalon did not tolerate failure. Tristan maintained his neutral expression and waited for him to continue.

"Although he failed to obtain the Chronicle, he did manage to install a surveillance camera and microphone in the Blue Shield offices." Arthur was on his feet again now, leaning on the table with both bands and staring with cold eyes at Tristan. "From that, we have learned that Blue Shield, with the aid of the Chronicle, is hunting down our most important artifacts. One of those, at least, you are already familiar with, because we have been looking for it ourselves since the beginnings of our brotherhood: the sword of the king, the mighty Excalibur."

Tristan inhaled audibly. He stared at the screen and listened attentively as the Blue Shield team discussed the contents of the Chronicle.

"So, it is quite simple: we need only stay on the trail of these Blue Shield people, and they will present the sword to us on a silver platter."

Arthur pushed a leather folder, on the table beside him, toward Tristan.

"In there you will find everything we know about the sword. You will have time to study it as we go."

"As we go?" Tristan asked, following his king now to the main door.

"You will accompany me, and help me to finally obtain the last of our outstanding treasures. If you prove yourself worthy, you will be the new first knight of the Society of Avalon. And if, in the process, you manage to get rid of the Blue Shield team—Wagner, de Mey, and Cloutard—for good, I will be especially pleased. They have been a constant thorn in our side." He stopped for a moment, then added, "And then, perhaps, I will let you in on our final secret as well."

Arthur had whispered these last words, as if he feared someone might be listening.

Tristan had suspected from the start that Arthur was a far more powerful man than even his position as head of the Society of Avalon suggested. And he, Tristan, was ready for whatever lay ahead.

28

OVER INNSBRUCK, AUSTRIA

JUST HOURS LATER, TOM, HELLEN AND CLOUTARD WERE sitting in the Lockheed C-130 Hercules transport plane. The plane, as well the Humvee it contained, were essentially spoils of war. After the battle with the Society of Avalon's "knights" in Jordan, Tom had peremptorily seized the Hercules and flown it to Vienna himself. Happily, it had been fitted out with numerous add-ons that could prove extremely useful to them, things that Theresia de Mey would never have authorized them to purchase.

For its inaugural flight for Blue Shield, Tom had handed the controls over to their trusted pilot, Walter T. Skinner. Skinner had flown for them numerous times, ever since the adventure that began with the auction of Joan of Arc's shield and Hellen's kidnapping, and he had been excited about his first flight in the behemoth as a kid on Christmas morning. Tom had seen that instantly and had chosen to sit in the cargo hold with Hellen and Cloutard for the duration of the flight. He checked their equipment and inspected the Hummer in preparation for its first mission in Blue Shield's service.

"We have not exactly chosen the best time to be searching Innsbruck for Excalibur," said Cloutard.

"The storms, you mean? Yes. It won't be easy," Hellen said.

"Don't worry. This baby is perfect for the job," said Tom, slapping the hood of the huge vehicle. "The Society of Avalon didn't hold back with it—it even has a deep-water fording kit."

"A what?" said Cloutard.

"A snorkel. We could drive this thing through five feet of water."

Hellen rolled her eyes.

"Boys and their toys," she said. "That's not what I meant. Do you really think we can just drive into a flooded disaster area after the worst storm this region has ever seen? Hundreds of thousands of people had to be evacuated. Innsbruck will be crawling with army, police, firefighters, and hundreds of helpers. Half the city is underwater. The River Inn is a raging torrent, and half the mountain is threatening to turn into a massive mudslide. If it does, it will bury the entire northern section of Innsbruck—and if we're out of luck, the cathedral and the Hofkirche as well. And you think having the right *vehicle* is our biggest problem?"

Tom gulped.

A sudden jolt made Hellen start nervously. She was buckled into a jump seat against the wall and clutched at the cargo net stretched along the side of the fuselage.

"Sorry, folks," came Skinner's voice over the loudspeakers. "Take your seats and put your seatbelts on, please. The weather's going to make this a little bumpy."

"Tom, where are you going?"

Tom ignored Skinner's instructions and headed for the cockpit instead, staggering through the plane like a drunken sailor and up the narrow ladder to the cockpit.

"What's going on?" he asked Skinner.

"The tower's not giving us permission to land. Too dangerous, they say. The runway isn't visible and it's under a foot and a half of water."

"Shit," Tom swore, banging his fist against a side panel.

"Hey! Easy, man. Don't hurt my baby," Skinner said.

"Your baby?" Tom said with a grin, but he raised his hands apologetically. He thought for a moment. "Couldn't you just drop us?" he suggested. Skinner's eyes widened and he was about to reply, but Tom went on: "Isn't this thing made for that? The Humvee's strapped to a skid that was built for low-level drops, right? You fly as low as you can, and the parachute will pull the Hummer and the skid out together."

"Oh, you'd like that, wouldn't you, Mr. Adrenaline? Sorry, there's no way in hell we're doing that."

"Then land without permission. We'll deal with the consequences later. Can you do that?"

"Hey, who do you think you're talking to? Of course I can. This machine was designed to land on even the crappiest surfaces. But go back and buckle up. It's gonna be a real splashdown."

Tom clapped Skinner on the shoulder and headed back to the cargo area.

"What did he say?" Cloutard asked as Tom took his seat and pulled his seatbelt tight.

"It'll be an interesting landing. Hold tight."

"Sorry I snapped at you earlier," Hellen said to him. "I'm just frazzled. I'm doing my best to stay focused on the mission, but I keep thinking of Mother and how I might lose her. It's driving me crazy."

Tom placed his hand on hers and squeezed gently.

"We'll save your mother, I promise," said Tom, gazing lovingly at her. Deep inside, however, he wasn't so sure. They were feeling around in the dark on this mission, and their chances of success were slim at best.

"Hold on, we're coming down," Skinner's voice rasped through the speakers.

Hellen tightened her grip on Tom's hand and closed her eyes tightly. The bumping and rattling increased steadily as the raging storm knocked the colossal plane from side to side. It was all Skinner could do to hold it on course.

"*Merde*, one of these days one of your ideas is going to go very, very wrong. I hope I am not around when it does," said Cloutard, taking out his flask. He took a swig and offered it to Tom, but Tom just shook his head.

The Hercules touched down heavily, and a thunderous rush joined the earsplitting roar of the propellers.

"It's going to be close, people," Skinner said. "Hold tight!"

29

INNSBRUCK AIRPORT, AUSTRIA

THE PLANE PLOWED THROUGH THE TORRENT, SPRAYING sheets of water on both sides. Skinner did everything he could to keep it straight. In the back, Tom, Hellen and Cloutard were being shaken and tossed around. Hellen's fingers clawed into Tom's hand. Normally, a C-130 could land on three thousand feet of runway, but the flood made it impossible to estimate how much they would really need. But at last came a final shudder and the Hercules came to a stop, just a little too close for comfort to the buildings bordering the small airport.

Tom jumped to his feet.

"All right, no time to lose. I don't feel like dealing with the authorities here."

"What? Why? What have you done?" Hellen asked.

"Let's just say that I find it easier to ask for forgiveness than permission."

Tom went to the control panel on the wall and lowered the rear ramp. The rain instantly began to whip inside through the widening gap.

"Come on, climb in!" he shouted, and Hellen and Cloutard quickly clambered into the Humvee.

Just as Tom was getting in behind the wheel, Skinner came hurrying back from the cockpit. "Hey! The tower just ordered us not to disembark. Someone's on their way."

"Thanks. If they arrest you, I owe you a favor," said Tom, and he closed the door and threw the Hummer into reverse.

But he didn't make it to the end of the ramp. Two Puch G300 off-road vehicles with Austrian Army plates pulled up at the end of the ramp. Four uniformed men jumped out of the first car and were instantly up to their knees in water. All four looked furious. They rushed up the ramp.

Tom climbed out again.

An officer stepped forward. "What do you think you're doing here? Who the hell are you?" he barked. Tom slammed the Humvee's door behind him and went back to the soldiers.

"Lieutenant Colonel, we—" Tom began, checking the soldier's rank badge. But Hellen had also climbed out. She pushed in front of Tom and cut him off.

"I'm Dr. Hellen de Mey, deputy head of Blue Shield. We're part of UNESCO and responsible for protecting cultural heritage worldwide." She held her official ID up for the officer to see.

"I don't give a damn who you are. Do you have any idea what we're dealing with here? And you fly this thing in and land—without permission!—potentially putting even more lives at risk. What are you doing here?"

"We're the first responders, so to speak—we're here to inspect the situation of local cultural assets in the current emergency. We'll report to UNESCO on the situation as quickly as possible to ensure the well-being of Innsbruck's irreplaceable treasures."

Tom and Cloutard shared a glance, then both smiled and looked at the floor. Neither of them had heard Hellen lie so shamelessly before.

"How do you see this going, ma'am?" The soldier nodded toward the Humvee. "I can't just let you drive off into the city with your fancy gear. Too many buildings have already been swept away by mudslides and water, and dozens more are on the verge of collapse."

"Lieutenant Colonel, Blue Shield reports directly to UNESCO. That means to the United Nations. With respect, we don't have to ask your permission. I hope that's clear to you."

"We'll see about that." With a curt signal, he waved his men up to join him. The soldiers planted themselves in front of the four newcomers.

"*Quel connard*," Cloutard whispered. "Asshole."

"For now, you're coming with me. I'll be confiscating your plane and that car with pleasure. We don't have enough useable vehicles as it is," the lieutenant colonel said with undisguised fury. "Take them away."

"But you can't do that!" Hellen protested.

"I can and I will." The soldiers took Hellen, Cloutard, Skinner, and Tom by the arm to escort them off the Hercules.

"Easy there," Tom snarled, pulling free of one of the soldiers' grip. But he knew that resistance was useless at that moment. He couldn't shoot his way out of this one.

"Can we at least bring our things?" Hellen asked.

The lieutenant colonel nodded, and they fetched their backpacks and rain gear from the Humvee.

"Off to a great start," Hellen muttered, taking her place in the back seat of the Puch.

30

AIRPORT BUILDING, INNSBRUCK, AUSTRIA

THE DOOR FLEW OPEN, AND THE OFFICER STORMED INTO the room where they were being held. Hellen, who had been using the time to continue studying the data scans, looked up. Cloutard and Skinner had made themselves comfortable in a corner. Tom, who had been pacing back and forth restlessly the whole time, paused and looked up.

"Lieutenant Colonel, when can we leave?" asked Hellen, standing up. "You can't keep us locked up here forever. We have to get to the Schwarzmander Church."

"We've done some checking. It seems you are from Blue Shield, but UNESCO doesn't know a damned thing about any 'first responders' inspecting the situation here in Innsbruck."

"I can explain that—"

The lieutenant colonel raised his hand. "I wasn't finished. Your plane and the Humvee are registered to a company called Avalon Inc. and are not Blue Shield property. I'll be interested to hear your explanation for that one."

"Funny story, actually," Tom began. "We were in Jordan, and—" But Hellen grabbed him by the arm.

"Lieutenant Colonel, you're right, we're not here on official UNESCO business. But we have to get to the Hofkirche without delay. There's something there that we need to check. Please. It's a matter of life or death."

"Life or death, is it?" the officer said skeptically. "Spare me the theatrics. That church is five hundred years old. What's in it that all of a sudden can't wait? Besides, it could collapse any minute."

Hellen's eyes widened.

"What? Why? What happened?"

"A crane doing renovations on the building next door fell over and damaged the church roof badly. You can't go inside. It's too dangerous."

"Listen," Tom cut in. "We don't have time for Q-and-A. We have to get into that damned church, and you don't have the authority to hold us."

"And you, Mr. Wagner, should tread lightly. I looked you up as well—I have to say, *your* file makes very interesting reading. Car chases through the center of Vienna and Salzburg, a shootout in the Hofburg and another on the Spanish Steps in Rome, damage to public buildings, et cetera, et cetera."

Tom was furious now. He'd always had a problem with authority figures, but this was no time for an argument. He had to play the only trump he still had.

"If you've read my file so closely, then you also know I saved the chancellor's life. One call from me and you're out of a job," he growled. "But things don't have to go that far, do they? We're all sensible people here."

Cloutard let out a laugh but stopped instantly when Tom shot him a scathing glare. Without giving the officer time to reply, Tom went on: "Here's a suggestion: Blue Shield will put our Hercules and our pilot at your disposal for the duration of the emergency. In return, you look the other way for a few hours and let us finish what we came here to do. What do you say?"

31

AIRPORT BUILDING, INNSBRUCK, AUSTRIA

THE LOOK LIEUTENANT COLONEL GAVE TOM SPOKE volumes. Clearly, no one had ever talked to him like that in his entire career.

"That's your suggestion? Bribery?" he said, unnervingly calm.

Tom swallowed hard. He looked at Hellen. Tears were brimming in her eyes, and the disappointment and reproach in them stung. Had he gone too far? Had he just made an already complicated situation worse? Had he just sunk any chance they had?

"All right," the officer said, after a long moment. "We really could use your plane."

Hellen looked up at Tom with relief, and he smiled broadly back. Cloutard shook his head in disbelief.

"Pack your things and get out of here before I change my mind. And don't come crying for help if the roof falls on your heads."

"Thank you, sir. Thank you very much," said Hellen, repacking her backpack.

Tom turned to Skinner, who was glaring at him unhappily. "I owe you one," Tom said.

Half an hour later, Tom guided the Humvee through the old part of the city and turned onto Burggraben, a street that led directly to the Hofkirche—or "Schwarzmander Church," as it was known locally. The waters of the overflowing Inn River had inundated every corner of Innsbruck. The necessary evacuation had taken place days earlier, and the streets of the beautiful city center were left to the thundering hail- and rainstorms still raging on all sides. The local situation was beyond critical.

The Humvee forged ahead slowly through the deep water. Parked cars were submerged up to their windows. Hellen, Tom, and Cloutard looked around in disbelief, but no one spoke. None of them had ever experienced a catastrophe like this. The bridges over the Inn that hadn't been washed away were marked only by the streetlamps jutting from the water.

The Burggraben, a pedestrian zone, was a dead end, but a breezeway at the end led through the neighboring building and beneath the Silver Chapel, part of the Hofkirche, to the main entrance.

Tom stopped the car. Hellen sighed. As the officer had said, a huge crane set up on the Burggraben had toppled onto the church. The ground beneath the crane had given way and its shorter end, with the counterweights, had crashed directly onto the bell tower, causing it to collapse.

"No way to get past that," said Tom, and he began backing up. They drove around the church and the former Franciscan monastery beside it, now a museum, and managed to reach the front of the church that way.

Tom stopped the car.

"How do we get inside?" Hellen asked.

They looked around. From their research, they knew that the only way to reach the church was through the museum. But all the windows at street level were secured with heavy iron bars. Tom looked up at the building. "I've got an idea," he said.

32

OUTSIDE THE HOFKIRCHE, FLOODED CITY
CENTER OF INNSBRUCK.

"GOD PRESERVE US," CLOUTARD SNIFFED. "WHAT ARE YOU
planning to do now?" Exchanging his usual three-piece
suit and hat for functional outdoor clothing had left him
feeling a little out of sorts.

Tom parked the Hummer close to the wall directly
beside the museum entrance, then opened the car
window and climbed out onto the roof. The rain slashed
mercilessly at his face, and he was soaked to the skin in
seconds. Above the entrance hung an ornate, wrought-
iron sign that read "Tiroler Volkskunstmuseum." He
pulled himself up on the sign and was able to reach the
windows on the first floor, which were not barred. He
used the butt of his pistol to smash the glass, pushed his
hand through, and opened the window.

"What are you waiting for? Come on up," he shouted
down.

Hellen was the next to climb onto the Humvee's roof,
with Cloutard close behind. Hellen pulled herself up on

the sign, and Tom reached out and pulled her up the last section and through the window.

"I would have welcomed a little help myself. I am not as young as I once was," said Cloutard, gritting his teeth and struggling through the window by himself.

They quickly ran downstairs to the ground floor, where Cloutard put his lockpicking skills to work and opened the entrance to the church.

The sight before them was at once breathtaking and dreadful. Eight red marble columns rose more than thirty feet from the floor, supporting the vaulted ceiling of the magnificent triple-nave church, built in honor of Maximilian I by his nephew, Ferdinand. Two of the columns had fallen directly onto Maximilian's sarcophagus, which was surrounded by elaborate wrought-iron panels with gold ornamentation. Tom, Hellen and Cloutard looked up past the small waterfalls cascading from the gaping hole in the roof. The rubble from the bell tower and the vaulted ceiling had buried Maximilian I's superb—but empty—tomb. The heavy, counter-weighted end of the toppled crane protruded through the roof, dangling ominously overhead.

Hellen waded slowly through the central nave and past several of the twenty-eight figures in dark bronze, the "Schwarze Mander," which surrounded the tomb in groups of four between the marble columns. On the opposite side of the tomb, Tom and Cloutard moved laboriously through the high water, climbing over rubble, beams, and fallen statuary.

"Hellen, watch your step," Tom warned. "Everything here is extremely unstable" The splintered timbers of the roof creaked in the storm winds overhead.

"How are we supposed to know which of these "Mander" is King Arthur?" asked Cloutard, searching in vain for a nameplate or label.

"It should be on the west side, somewhere in the middle," Hellen shouted back. "Wait, I'll come around."

"I've got bad news," Tom said, as Hellen turned the corner to join them. "Not all of the statues survived."

Hellen's optimism took a blow as she looked across the fallen pillars to Tom. She climbed cautiously over a broken section, which had smashed into the two figures standing closest to it. Their upper halves were sunken face down in the olive-colored water. All that could be seen were their legs on the pedestals.

"That one is 'Ernest the Iron,' one of the Habsburg dukes of Austria," Hellen said, pointing to the third figure of the group of four, still standing. "Which means the one lying here is King Ferdinand I of Portugal." She pointed to the figure lying in the water to the left of it. "And this must be Arthur."

"Okay, what now?" said Tom.

"I do not think we are strong enough to get him back on his feet," said Cloutard.

"This would be an excellent time to tell us how you actually managed to steal the Gloriosa Bell from Erfurt Cathedral," Hellen said sarcastically. "We could really use some logistics like that."

"How did you know . . . Edward, that old rat!" Cloutard said, but only shrugged and shook his head. "However," he went on, "the Humvee has a winch, correct?" He looked up, and Hellen and Tom followed his gaze. The rear section of the crane hung directly overhead.

Tom got it. "I'll be right back."

33

HOFKIRCHE, INNSBRUCK, AUSTRIA

TWO MINUTES LATER, AN EAR-SPLITTING CRASH MADE Hellen and Cloutard jump as Tom crashed the Humvee straight through the church's main entrance. He came to a stop just in front of the tomb, sending a wave of water sloshing over them. Tom's grin faded when he saw his friends' withering glares.

"Have you finally gone completely out of your mind?" Hellen snapped.

"Don't sweat it. This church has had it anyway; the door doesn't matter anymore," Tom said brashly as he unrolled the steel cable. He joined his friends and swung the end of the cable like a grappling hook over a steel strut on the crane.

"I'll get this secured. Start the winch on my command," Tom said to Cloutard in the commanding tone he always used for this kind of situation.

"Are you sure it'll hold?" Hellen asked grimly, retreating a few steps.

"We'll see." Tom took the hook, dived underwater, and wrapped the cable around Arthur's neck. Meanwhile, Cloutard had waded back to the car and was ready to activate the winch.

Tom stood up again and signaled to Cloutard. The winch began to turn. The cable scraped and squealed over the steel strut as it tightened. Tom swung his arm in a circle, signaling to Cloutard to keep going. The roof timbers, already holding most of the weight of the crane, creaked alarmingly, but the heavy bronze statue gradually rose out of the murky water.

"Help me," Tom said to Hellen. Between them they guided the figure upright again.

Done. Cloutard shut down the winch.

Hellen immediately set to work examining the larger-than-life-sized statue closely. Not even the slightest detail of the ornate figure escaped her. The statue was dark brown, almost black, and shimmered in the watery light coming through the gap in the ceiling. After a few minutes, she took a step back and, looking confused, inspected the statue of King Arthur in its entirety.

"Something's wrong. Something's missing," she said, and before Tom or Cloutard could say a word, she had already dropped underwater in front of the statue.

Then it happened. A crack. A crash. Tom looked up.

"No! Hellen!" he screamed.

A heartbeat later something knocked him off his feet. Cloutard had leaped at Tom and pushed him clear at the last second as a shattered beam, broken free by the shifting weight of the crane, fell vertically like an immense spear. Slamming into the church floor half a yard from Cloutard and Tom, it tipped and began to fall exactly where Hellen had dived. A fraction of a second later, she resurfaced.

"Hellen! Look out!" Tom cried.

She reacted instantly, jumping back and taking cover under the toppled marble column. The beam crashed against the red marble.

"Are you all right?"

"I'm fine. I'm okay."

Tom sighed with relief and hurried over to her, but she had already crawled out from under the beam before he reached her. Tom threw his arms around her. "I'm sorry. I nearly killed you with that stupid idea," he said, crushing her to his chest.

"Don't exaggerate. I'm fine. Now give me a hand." She pointed to a spot on the water.

"What are we looking for?"

"Pendragon's shingle," Hellen said proudly. "When I stood back and looked, I saw the strange position of Arthur's right arm, and I realized something was missing."

"What? His sword's hanging from his belt."

"His shield. He was supporting himself on his shield, but it was missing. Strictly speaking, it's his father's shield. Uther Pendragon was Arthur's father."

"What does that have to do with a shingle?" Tom asked. They felt around in the water and lifted the bronze shield to the surface between them.

"Easy: the word 'shield' comes from the Old High German *scilt*, which meant 'shingle.' So, Pendragon's Shingle just means Arthur's father's shield, that's all."

"But this can't be Arthur's father's *real* shield," said Tom.

"Of course not, but it could still give us a lead to—" Hellen suddenly fell silent as they propped the heavy shield against the statue's legs. Tom and Hellen turned silently and looked at each other. Cloutard, standing behind them, also stared at the shield.

"*Messieurs*," he said, "I do not know about you, but I believe that shield bears a remarkable likeness to—"

"Joan of Arc's shield!" said Tom and Hellen together.

Hellen's hand glided over the ornate decorations.

"But not exactly," she said. "It's a mirror image. The three lions are facing the other way, and that changes their meaning completely. Help me turn it around." Hellen and Tom lifted the shield and rotated it. "Damn. But it's just as I thought," Hellen said.

"What is it?"

"A few years ago, I studied Joan of Arc's shield in the minutest detail, but there was this one little thing about it that always bothered me: the engraving on the back of the shield. And if I've understood the clues in the Chronicle correctly, not only do we have to figure that out, we also need to have the shield physically with us to find the Fountain of Youth."

"Which means going to Cape Town and somehow getting Joan of Arc's shield back from the diamond guy?" said Tom.

"I'm afraid so, yes," Hellen said, thinking hard. Then she straightened up and all three returned to the Humvee.

"By the way, François, thanks for saving my skin," Tom said.

"*Pas de problème.* I had to pay you back sometime," Cloutard replied.

Hellen took out her phone. "Vittoria? We need three tickets to Cape Town, the sooner the better. From Munich, if possible. Getting back to Vienna now would take too long."

"Why? What happened to the Hercules?"

"Don't ask."

34

HANGKLIP SUMMIT, NEAR CAPE TOWN, TWENTY-FOUR HOURS LATER

TOM EASED THE RENTAL CAR THROUGH THE SMALL TOWN OF Strand, situated directly on False Bay, east of Cape Town. After following Marine Drive for a while, they turned onto the R44 coast road just past the village of Gordon's Bay. A little over an hour later, they had reached their destination.

Pringle Bay lay on the edge of the Kogelberg Nature Reserve. The reserve covered just eleven square miles, and nowhere else on the planet were so many plant species concentrated in such a small area. At one time it had been a popular day-trip and hiking area, but now it was the private garden of one of the richest men in the world.

With Pringle Bay behind them, they followed a narrow road that wound through the unspoiled landscape for a few minutes.

"More proof that you can buy anything with enough money. Even a nature reserve," Hellen said irritably when she spotted a sign marking the area as just that.

Tom eased the car to a stop. Ahead of them was a checkpoint. It looked like a small border crossing, and heavily armed guards were checking a black limousine. With a mirror attached to a telescopic pole, one of them moved around the car, inspecting the underside, while another checked the occupants' invitations.

"We can only hope that Vittoria got us on the guest list in time," Cloutard said. He plucked a few bits of lint from the linen jacket lying across his lap and smoothed it with his hands.

"Finally back in your fancy threads and still so grumpy? Or are you worried about the Klimt?" said Tom, who'd been watching Cloutard in the rearview mirror. "You know we're not going to leave you alone with that. You can count on us."

"I know, I know. It is not that. To be honest, my mother's reaction when she finds out frightens me more than any killer the mafia could send after me. But for now, at least, I am out of harm's way." He smiled, but it wasn't very convincing.

When the limousine in front of them passed the checkpoint, Tom rolled forward slowly.

"Invitation, please," the grim-faced guard demanded.

"We don't have an invitation, but we're supposed to be on a separate guest list. We're from Blue Shield. Tom

Wagner, Dr. Hellen de Mey, and François Cloutard," Tom explained, handing the man his Blue Shield ID.

"Mister van Rensburg's personal assistant, Wikus de Waal, is expecting us," added Hellen, leaning across from the passenger seat to Tom's window.

The sentry did not reply. He took a step back and murmured something into his two-way radio.

"The van Rensburgs seem to be just a tiny bit paranoid. These guards are better equipped than some special forces I've seen," said Tom in a low voice, his military instincts on the alert, taking in every detail. Hellen's eyes followed the other sentry, who was circling the car and searching the chassis for bombs and anything else that shouldn't be there.

The guard stepped up to the driver's door again and leaned down to Tom.

"Follow the road about a mile. Mister de Waal will meet you at the end of the parking area." The guard gave the interior and its occupants a final once-over, then handed back Tom's ID and waved them through.

At the end of the private road, at the top of the Hangklip—a small, wedge-shaped mountain that jutted toward the ocean like a ramp—rose the enormous estate. The sprawling, multistory Victorian-style manor had been built close to the edge of the almost vertical cliff. Tom drove the car to the rear parking lot as instructed, where dozens of limousines, sports cars, and other luxury vehicles were already lined up. A man in a tuxedo emerged from the building and came toward them as Tom nosed the car into an empty space.

"Mr. de Waal, thank you for meeting us on such short notice," Hellen said in greeting, doing her best not to stare at the man's scar, which only accentuated his sinister appearance.

"Welcome to Hangklip Summit," said de Waal, shaking their hands. "Master van Rensburg will arrive shortly. I have been instructed to make you as comfortable as possible in the meantime. Follow me, please," said de Waal with no emotion whatsoever, and he turned toward the villa.

35

VAN RENSBURG ESTATE, HANGKLIP SUMMIT

"Master van Rensburg," Tom mimicked soundlessly, when de Waal was walking ahead, facing the other way. Hellen rolled her eyes and jabbed him in the side but could not suppress a smile.

"Ms. de Mey, may I?" said Tom, with a sparkle in his eye, holding his elbow up for Hellen to take. "I have to say, that dress looks incredibly good on you."

As Hellen took his arm, Tom's eyes wandered down the deeply cut back of the dress to her rear.

"Eyes front, Mr. Wagner," Hellen said with a laugh. "And you don't look too bad yourself."

"Indeed. You should wear a suit more often," Cloutard joked. "It would add an extra touch of class to our little troupe. Why always jeans and T-shirts?"

"Mr. de Waal, where can I find my father?" Hellen asked as they entered the house.

"Dr. de Mey is preparing his talk, I believe."

De Waal led Tom, Hellen and Cloutard through the large entrance hall to an elevator. Like a British butler, he stepped aside and ushered them ahead before stepping into the elevator after them.

When the elevator doors slid open, de Waal led them out and past a guard post, to a security door. Muffled party noises came from the other side. A nod from de Waal sufficed—the guard behind the desk pressed a button, and the door swung open with a soft hiss.

"Please make yourselves comfortable. I must attend to my other duties." A barely perceptible nod and de Waal disappeared.

"Oh, yes, with enough money, one can buy anything at all," said Cloutard a little wistfully as they gazed around the private museum.

An endless glass wall stretched from one end of the extensive room to the other, offering an unparalleled view of the ocean. A hundred or so guests were strolling through the museum or chatting in small groups. Young, uniformed women moved among them, serving drinks and hors d'oeuvres.

"Missing your old life?" Tom asked.

"How could I not?" Cloutard answered, throwing his arms wide, almost knocking a tray of champagne glasses out of a hostess's hands.

"*Excusez-moi,* madame," Cloutard apologized. "But it is good that you are here. Would you happen to have a small glass of Louis XIII for a clumsy old Frenchman?"

The hostess smiled. "Of course, monsieur. I will back in a moment."

Cloutard returned her smile happily.

"Look at this!" said Hellen, hurrying over to a display cabinet. "It's the second volume of Aristotle's *Poetics*. It was thought to be a myth. And here . . . and here . . ." she said, moving to the next cabinet. For a few moments, she forgot everything around her.

"Hellen?" Edward's voice brought her back to reality. "What are you doing here? De Waal just told me."

"Papa!" said Hellen, throwing her arms around him. "Mother is . . ." she began, her voice faltering.

"No . . ." Edward stammered.

"You were already on your way here when we found out."

"Hellen, what's happened?"

"Some . . . someone poisoned her and . . ."

Edward's face shifted through an array of emotions as Hellen described everything that had happened in the last forty-eight hours: disbelief, fury, hatred, and finally a shimmer of hope. For a moment, he said nothing. Then, looking at Tom and Cloutard now, he whispered, "And now you're here to steal the shield from van Rensburg? Forget it. This place is a fortress and he's got a private army."

"We aren't here to steal it. We were hoping he would lend it to us," Hellen said.

"What's going on over there?" Tom said. People were drifting toward the wall of windows.

"The van Rensburgs, I guess. They love making dramatic entrances," Edward said, and they also went to witness the arrival of their hosts.

A dark helicopter was heading for the house and soon touched down on the designated landing platform. Tom turned pale as his eyes scanned the ocean beyond the helicopter. A gigantic, pearl-white yacht lay at anchor just off the coast.

36

MONTE CARLO HARBOR, ON BOARD A YACHT, ONE YEAR EARLIER

NOAH WAS FEELING CONFLICTED. ON THE ONE HAND, HE had a lot to thank the leader for. He had done something for Noah that he never dreamed would be possible: an experimental operation carried out by AF surgeons and scientists had given him back the use of his legs. Noah once again felt himself to be a complete man, and the gratitude he felt toward the leader was boundless.

And yet he still feared him. Greatly. He had seen the lengths to which he was willing to go to achieve his ends. He knew how many people had died on the leader's account. Many times, he had seen not only how cold-blooded he could be toward his adversaries, but also how harshly he could deal with his supposed friends and allies. For years, a deep friendship had existed between the leader and Count Pálffy, who had been loyal to the leader for years and had even saved his life more than once. After the botched mission in Barcelona, however, he quickly fell from favor and found himself on the leader's hit list.

But that was all beside the point. The count had failed, and he had paid for his failure. And Pálffy was just one example. Nobody was safe from the leader's wrath if they fell short of his expectations.

Noah knew that the leader's goal was their prime concern. Everything and everyone else was second to that. Regardless of how close to him you were, any failure would put you at risk.

Noah had never understood why all the artifacts mattered, nor had he understood the mania with which the leader searched the world for them. At first, he thought his goal was world domination of a sort through AF—undermining governments, bribing industry and business magnates, manipulating the masses—in order that one day, like a puppeteer, he would hold all the strings in his hand.

Now, however, Noah was starting to feel as if all that was just incidental, that the leader was actually pursuing deeply personal goals, something like a vendetta or egomania. In truth, no one knew what was really going on in the leader's mind. All of them, Noah included, were no more than chess pieces he moved around his board, ready to sacrifice every single one of them if it brought him closer to winning. Noah would not have been at all surprised to discover that the leader was running other, parallel, endeavors, about which neither he nor anyone else in AF's upper echelons had the faintest idea.

Noah boarded the yacht and made his way to the sundeck, where the leader usually met with those who worked for him. As always, he smiled, stood up, and came to meet Noah, greeting him warmly.

"Good morning, sir," Noah said. A stranger looking on would probably think that the leader was truly happy to see him, but Noah knew better. Everything was a front. The man had a thousand faces. Noah had seen him slip into countless roles, his attitude and mood shifting from one second to the next. In his presence, Noah was always on guard.

"I don't know what's good about it. Your wonderful German sniper failed miserably in Rome. All he managed to do was get Wagner on YouTube."

37

HANGKLIP SUMMIT, PRESENT DAY

"WHAT IS IT? YOU LOOK YOU'VE SEEN A GHOST!" HELLEN asked, noticing Tom's sudden transformation. Her took her by the arm and drew her to one side, away from the curious guests. "Tom, you're scaring me! What's going on?"

"I think we've just walked into the lion's den."

"What do you mean?"

"See that yacht out there? Ossana kept me prisoner on a boat just like that. Ossana was originally from South Africa, she always called the big boss 'daddy,' and now here are all these artifacts that aren't even supposed to exist. You get the mega-rich all gathered in one place, and suddenly this van Rensburg guy sends his 'personal assistant'"—Tom made air quotes with his fingers—"to take back a shield that allegedly belongs to him. If Scarface is just his personal assistant, I'm Mickey Mouse."

"Tom, what are you telling me? That van Rensburg runs AF?"

"Sure, why not? He fits the profile: he's stinking rich and literally has his own private army."

"But his papers were all in order. He really is the rightful owner of the shield," Hellen said.

"Are you sure about that? Documents can be forged. Also, why did your mother take so long to approve the contract and arrange transport? Why didn't she say anything to any of us? You yourself told me how she said 'they'll kill us all.' Maybe she found something out and someone tried to kill her because of it."

"But that was the Society of Avalon."

"Which brings me back to my theory that AF and the Society are one and the same, or that the Society is just part of something much bigger, at least. In any case, we're talking about a terrorist organization with a taste for antique artifacts. In the Wewelsburg, we got a glimpse of the just how far-reaching the organization is. There are dozens of cells."

"Tom, I don't know. For now, it all sounds a little too far-fetched. My mother had a lot to deal with; she might have just forgotten. And van Rensburg isn't the only one with a megayacht and a weakness for antiques. I think we have to look a little deeper and try not to jump to conclusions. We want something from the man, after all."

"So this is where you all disappeared to. What is going on?" Cloutard asked, joining them now along with Edward.

"We'll tell you later," said Tom. He wasn't entirely convinced, but neither could he ignore her arguments entirely. But he wasn't ditching his theory just yet.

The clink of a glass rang through the exhibition hall, and the assembled guests fell silent. Then Eon van Rensburg and his wife stepped out onto the stage to thunderous applause.

"Hello, my friends, and welcome to my humble retreat. Today we have a very special artifact for you, and we will unveil it at eight o'clock sharp. To make the event even more special, Kiara and I"—Eon pinched his wife's bottom fondly—"have flown in a leading expert, Dr. Edward de Mey, to tell you all about this legendary piece of antiquity. Until then, make yourselves at home and let our enchanting hostesses spoil you. Thank you, and enjoy!"

"Papa?" Hellen asked. "Where is the shield now?"

"Over this way," said Edward.

They went to the end of the exhibition hall. In a section marked off with red cords stood a high, covered glass case.

"Hellen, now that you're here, perhaps you could make the presentation?" Edward asked as they stood before the concealed shield.

"I hope it won't come to that at all. We don't have time for presentations or to spend the night partying. We have to examine the shield as soon as we can and find the next clue. Mother's life depends on it."

38

VAN RENSBURG'S PRIVATE MUSEUM, HANGKLIP SUMMIT, SOUTH AFRICA

"I THOUGHT MY EARS WERE DECEIVING ME, BUT IT SEEMS they were not." Berlin Brice, better known as the Welshman, had appeared from nowhere behind them. "Almost the entire de Mey family is here. All except . . . Edward, where did you leave your enchanting wife?" But Brice ignored the hostility radiating from Hellen and Edward and turned instead to Tom and Cloutard. "Mr. Wagner, I believe you still have to return my private jet, the one you borrowed in Cairo." Tom could not hide his grin. "And François Cloutard, of course. My old friend. Amazing who you run into at events like this." Brice let out a mocking laugh.

Taken by surprise, the team was speechless, but even if they had wanted to speak, Brice did not give them the chance. He went on without pausing: "May I introduce my companions? The captivating Katalin Farkas and my right-hand man, Morgan T. Wright."

Tom eyed the "right-hand man." He was built like a tank, almost a head taller than his boss, and he stood half a step behind him. *Like an ex-soldier or private bodyguard*, Tom thought.

"I know you," Hellen said spitefully. "You were the cleaning lady for my old boss, Count Pálffy."

Katalin glared at her. Then she leaned close to Brice, whispered in his ear, and walked away.

"I would not have expected that from you, Ms. de Mey. From Wagner, sure, but from you? I'm disappointed," the Welshman said with a shake of his head.

"What are you even doing here?" Tom said, his eyes boring into Brice's.

"I assume the same as you. Looking for Pendragon's Shingle, of course."

Hellen drew a sharp breath and her eyes widened. The tension was palpable. Tom could see in Hellen's eyes that Brice's words had caught her unawares. So, Brice knew about the three artifacts they needed to find the Fountain of Youth. It was not a complete surprise—he'd had part of the Chronicle in his possession for a while, after all.

Just then, Wikus de Waal approached the small group and cleared his throat. Tom turned away from Brice and looked at the "assistant."

"Master van Rensburg will see you now. This way, please."

Without another word, the team left Brice and followed de Waal out of the museum.

"Wagner showing up here changes everything," said Brice. "They're a step ahead of us again. That can't be allowed to happen with Excalibur. See to it. Get me the sword, whatever it takes."

"And the shield, my king?" Morgan—otherwise known as Tristan—asked, bowing slightly before the man he believed to be descended from Arthur.

"The shield isn't going anywhere. We know exactly who has it. And when the time comes, Wagner will take it exactly where we need it to be."

39

EON VAN RENSBURG'S OFFICE, HANGKLIP SUMMIT

The diamond magnate's office was close to the helipad. A doorway led from the landing zone directly into the circular room, which offered an almost 360-degree view. The office was cantilevered, hovering like a small UFO beyond the edge of the Hangklip Summit cliff. De Waal stood patiently by the entrance to the sparsely furnished room. There was an enormous desk, a conference table, and a sideboard that curved away to the left and right, following the glass façade and adorned with a few smaller works of art. On one side stood the typical collection of small, framed photos: the van Rensburgs with heads of state, with the Pope, and with a few entertainment industry A-listers.

Eon van Rensburg leaned back in his armchair, arched his fingertips together, and said nothing. The story Hellen de Mey had just told him seemed to have left him momentarily at a loss for words. He seemed tense, but contemplative.

Tom and Hellen exchanged a questioning glance. Was his silence a good sign? A bad sign? Finally, he broke the silence.

"Ms. de Mey, Mr. Wagner. Ever since you recovered my shield more than a year ago, I've been following your careers very closely. And I have to say, you've both impressed me very much indeed. The Florentine diamond, the Library of Alexandria, the Philosopher's Stone, Mayan gold . . . my God, you even found the Ark of the Covenant. But even you must admit that the story you've just told me sounds as incredible as a Tolkein tale. There's really only one thing I can say."

Hellen's confidence sank. She reached for Tom's hand.

"I love it!" Van Rensburg sprang to his feet. "It's the best thing I've heard in ages."

Hellen let out a shocked laugh. Eon van Rensburg had transformed right before her eyes, turning from worldly businessman to euphoric schoolboy in a moment.

"I'm terribly sorry to hear about your mother, of course." For a moment, his euphoria faded. "And of course I'll help you save her life. Those rich morons out there wouldn't know a shield from a sword. I'll find something else to wow them with this evening. I've certainly got enough old junk in my vault."

Hellen, Tom, Cloutard and Edward could hardly believe their luck as they watched their host pace excitedly through his office. Then he paused for a second.

"What I'm trying to say is that of course you can borrow the shield." He looked directly at Hellen now and, for a fraction of a second, his expression mutated into some-thing dark and cold. "On the condition that you bring it back." A moment later, he added, "And one more little thing: once you have your Fountain of Youth project behind you and your mother is back on her feet, I'll have a favor to ask of you. Do we have an agreement?"

Tom hated these kinds of deals. He knew only too well that the favor, when called upon, would mean nothing but headaches for them. But before he could object, Hellen had already shaken hands with van Rensburg and sealed the deal. He could only hope it wouldn't come back to bite them.

Eon van Rensburg let out a laugh as he shook Hellen's hand. He turned to de Waal.

"Wikus, bring the shield. Then dig something out of the vault, something we can show off at eight. Maybe the gold from Lake Toplitz."

"Gold from *Lake Toplitz*?" Edward gasped.

Van Rensburg turned to him. "You still owe me a lecture, and I intend to have it. I've already announced you, and I won't be made a liar in front of all my guests."

Edward only nodded.

A few moments later, de Waal returned with the shield in a soft, padded case and laid it on the conference table in the center of the room.

Hellen rose to her feet. "May I?" she asked.

Van Rensburg nodded and gestured invitingly. He emerged from behind his desk and joined her at the conference table.

Hellen quickly unzipped the case and carefully lifted the shield out of its padding. Three lions filled the upper right corner, with three more in the diagonally opposite quadrant. Three fleurs-de-lis decorated each of the other two segments.

"I spent a long time studying the shield a few years ago, but I was never able to figure out the engraving on the back of the shield." She turned it over and placed it face down on the case. Her fingers traced the thin lines that, starting in the upper corner, stretched back and forth across the back of the shield all the way to the bottom.

"I know exactly what you mean," said van Rensburg. "The shield always makes me think of Richard the Lionheart. His coat of arms also shows three lions passant, though they are a mirror image of these. But I never got any further than that either."

Tom, Cloutard, and Edward sat across the conference table and watched as Hellen and van Rensburg lost themselves in the details of the shield and the stories that surrounded it. Even Tom's confidence grew as the two chatted. He was feeling a little guilty—after all, he'd initially doubted that their search would get them anywhere at all. Any sane person would have. But now the first step had been taken.

Hellen's phone pinged. She glanced at it and smiled.

"Melk! It fits perfectly with Richard the Lionheart," she said.

"Melk?" Tom asked.

"Vittoria has made some progress decoding the Chronicle. She's found a section about Richard the Lionheart, and that matches perfectly with our shield here. I know where we have to go next."

40

KANDAHAR, AFGHANISTAN, 1999

NIKOLAUS III, COUNT PÁLFFY VON ERDÖD, CLIMBED OUT of the Humvee and peeled off the flak jacket that had been crumpling his beige three-piece suit. He tossed the jacket onto the passenger seat, removed his tactical helmet, and smoothed his sweat-soaked hair. Then he turned to his private jet, which was parked twenty yards away. Its engines were already warming up. The second they stopped, the hired soldiers had set up a defensive perimeter around the Humvees and formed a human corridor to the steps of the private jet. Medics were waiting with a stretcher at the foot of the jet's airstair, and Pálffy waved them over. Assisted by one of the mercenaries, he helped the unknown man—a man whose freedom they had bought from terrorists in the mountains northwest of Kandahar just hours before—out of the back of the Hummer. The medics lifted the frail, injured man onto the stretcher and carried him to the plane.

"Daddy, daddy, daddy!" Pálffy suddenly heard the overjoyed voice of the twelve-year-old African girl who had appeared in the doorway of the jet. She ran down the steps. The expression of the man on the stretcher instantly brightened when his adoptive daughter threw her arms around his neck. Then the medics carried the stretcher into the plane and immediately set to work tending to the man's injuries.

"Guerra." Pálffy turned to the mercenary chief and handed him a well-stuffed envelope. "Pay the men. We'll meet at headquarters in Paderborn, two days from now." The man nodded, then whirled his forefinger in the air over his head, a signal to move out. The Humvees drove off in a cloud of dust as Pálffy closed the hatch behind him.

"Thank you, my friend," said the man. He lay in the rear of the plane, in the makeshift medical area they had set up. The medics had already cleaned and dressed his wounds and set up a saline infusion. The young girl sat beside him and held his hand.

"Did you find what you were looking for?" Pálffy asked.

"Ossana," said the man, and the girl looked up. "Go up front and get yourself something to drink. I have some important business to discuss with Uncle Nikolaus."

She trotted away obediently, and Pálffy shut the cabin door behind her.

"I was so close to finding a clue about the Holy Weapon, and then those bastards caught me and dragged me off into the mountains." He sat up, his face twisting with pain. "They tortured me for weeks on end. And I was almost ready to give up when I had a revelation." He paused for a moment. "I had a lot of time to think, as you can imagine, and one thing became clear to me. The world out there is going to go to the dogs if we don't do something soon. We must expand our influence. And when we're ready, we can shape the world into what we want it to be."

Pálffy studied the man before him warily, wondering if that was a trace of madness in his eyes. What had they done to him? This wasn't the friend and boss he knew. Then again, a year in the hands of terrorists—men who had done God-knows-what to him—might break even the strongest mind . . . "I'll inform the council as soon as we reach headquarters," the man said. "My plan will take a few years, certainly, but in the end, we will change the world. And you and your organization, Blue Shield, will help."

41

MELK ABBEY, ATOP A HILL ON THE BANKS OF THE DANUBE, AUSTRIA

"I can honestly say, all this rain is starting to get to me," said Cloutard.

Tom, Hellen and Cloutard had just climbed out of the Humvee, which they had parked at Munich Airport for their brief visit to the southernmost tip of Africa. The four-hour drive from Munich to the abbey had not been easy. The wild storms that had already caused them severe difficulties in Innsbruck had only grown worse in the meantime. Now, the Danube River had joined the Inn in bursting its banks.

Cloutard opened his umbrella and looked up from the abbey parking lot to the bastion of the Benedictine monastery: the original Latin designation was *Abbatia SS. App. Petri et Pauli apud Melk*; today it was simply known as Melk Abbey. Originally founded in 1089, the abbey, built by Jakob Prandtauer between 1702 and 1746, had been described by its admirers as "the most emblematic, dominant baroque building" in the world. Its magnificent halls, Imperial Wing, High Baroque abbey church and the beautifully designed gardens had made the abbey a unique witness to the centuries of its existence. It also housed Austria's oldest school and a library containing more than a hundred thousand books and manuscripts.

Around the abbey, the storms had wrought visible damage, but there was still worse to come for the locals: floodwaters were already inundating the surrounding town of Melk. Only the abbey, situated high on a rocky outcrop, was safe for the moment. Thanks to the Hummer, the team had made it from the highway to the abbey without serious problems.

Tom looked at Cloutard with sympathy and pointed at the umbrella, which was intended more than anything to protect Cloutard's Panama hat.

"*Un parapluie, tu es sérieux?*" Tom said.

Cloutard shuddered as if he'd just bitten down on a lemon. "Your accent is abominable. I would thank you not to mutilate my divine language like that."

"Do you think your German sounds any better, you Francophone snob?" Tom countered.

"When you two are done sniping at one another, can we focus a little?" Hellen's voice was icy. There was too much at stake. "We have to get to the abbey library. According to the Chronicle, Richard the Lionheart destroyed the Austrian banner with a 'very special sword,' which angered the emperor and eventually led to Richard being imprisoned here in Austria."

"If I remember correctly, Richard was held at Dürnstein Castle, and that's not much more than a pile of rubble these days. What are we expecting to find here?" Tom asked. Cloutard was also looking at her dubiously.

"Returning from the Holy Land after the Third Crusade, Richard the Lionheart suffered a shipwreck and caught malaria. He was forced to travel by land instead of by sea, which was naturally extremely dangerous because his route took him through the Holy Roman Empire. And the Austrians, as I said, were not exactly fond of him."

As they talked, they descended the long stairway that led from the parking lot to the abbey's main entrance. The winds had already turned Cloutard's umbrella inside out a dozen times and after it had been nearly torn from his hand yet again, he finally tossed it aside angrily and held onto his hat with both hands.

"Not exactly the most stylish look, François," Tom said with a smile.

They passed the splendid gardens and entered the abbey proper, Hellen inquiring at the entrance as to whether she could meet with the abbot. All three shook themselves like wet dogs, expelling at least the worst of the water they'd accumulated. Hellen introduced herself as a representative of UNESCO, which should have opened every door in the place. The abbey, after all, was on UNESCO's list of world heritage sites—the monuments, buildings, and natural wonders that received special support from the organization.

"I'm afraid I have to disappoint you, Dr. de Mey," said the abbot's secretary, appearing after a few moments. "The entire staff are on their way to Rome as we speak, accompanying the cardinal to the Pope's funeral. I'm afraid I can't help you any further." She paused briefly, and her tone took on a note of reproach. "Apart from that, a friendly visit from UNESCO, considering the impending state of emergency we're facing here in Melk, seems more than a little ill-timed. Now I must get back to work. I'm sure you understand." And with a final nod, she left.

42

MELK ABBEY, ENTRANCE AREA

"Stupid cow," Hellen hissed after the departing secretary, and Tom and Cloutard raised their eyebrows. Hellen's nerves were clearly frazzled.

"I'll ask again," said Tom. "What are we looking for here? We were talking about Richard the Lionheart's imprisonment."

"Of course. Richard travelled through Austria in disguise, accompanied by just a handful of close allies, among them Philipp of Poitou, who later became Bishop of Durham. Philipp's diaries are supposed to be somewhere here in the library. They're not in the official catalogue, of course, because if they were we'd be able to study them online. But they *are* supposed to be here. An old university friend of mine knows Melk well."

She looked around. The abbot's secretary had disappeared, but the man at the ticket counter was still watching them distrustfully. Hellen stalked over to the counter and bought three tickets.

"Let's go in," she said to Tom and Cloutard, and she was already leading the way. "I'll explain what we have to do as we go." They crossed the Prelate's Courtyard, and at the far end made their way up the Imperial Staircase to the first floor.

Cloutard frowned and nodded, impressed. "*Mon ami*, now your girlfriend is showing you how it is done. Normally, it is you setting the pace. But Hellen is in charge of this mission."

"I always knew she had it in her. The possibility of losing her mother is really driving her. Let's hope she doesn't do anything rash," said Tom following Hellen upstairs.

"Ah, yes. That is rich, coming from you," Cloutard murmured.

Hellen had set her bag down on a bench and was rummaging inside it. She took out her iPad and checked her email.

"Andrzej Łukowski, a fellow student from when I was studying with Professor Van der Loos, spent years researching Melk. I wrote to him as soon as I saw '*Abbatia SS. App. Petri et Pauli apud Melk*' in the Chronicle."

"Van der Loos?" Cloutard looked inquiringly at Tom.

"Before your time, François," Tom explained. "That was when we were chasing the Florentine diamond in Amsterdam and at Schönbrunn. It was the first time we crossed paths with our British friend, Isaac Hagen."

"The Florentine diamond . . ." Cloutard said almost rapturously. "I wish I had been part of that."

"Of course you do. You would have put it in your pocket and made a run for it."

"*C'est possible*," the Frenchman grinned, and he took a sip from his flask.

They went into the sumptuous Marble Hall, framed by salmon-pink marble pillars ornamented with gold. A door at the end led outside to the Altane, a semicircular balcony that connected the hall with the library and offered a breathtaking view over the river—or normally it would. Today was not a day for taking in the view. Tom looked around. Directly below, at the foot of the hill atop which the abbey stood, a street called Nibelungenlände ran alongside a small branch of the Danube. They quickly followed the Altane to the library entrance at the far end.

Hellen, entering first, strolled close to a gaggle of visitors and eavesdropped on their guide, who was explaining a few details about the library to his tour group.

"In the 1920s, the abbey found itself in financial difficulties. Many of the books, some of which were very valuable indeed, had to be sold. From today's perspective, the most painful to lose was an original Gutenberg Bible, which now resides at Yale University."

The man was visibly distressed as he related the anecdote, but his expression brightened quickly. "However, there is also a legend"—his voice grew softer and he signaled to his group to move a little closer, adding some drama to the moment—"that the librarian at the time managed to spirit a number of valuable books to safety. He did not want them to be sold. Unfortunately, though, it seems to be no more than a legend, because to this day his secret hiding place has not been discovered." He paused thoughtfully for a moment before continuing. "The legend goes on to say that there is a secret passage leading through the catacombs below the abbey to the town of Melk. It seems the monks back then built the tunnel so that they could secretly take part in the worldly life of the town."

"Nice way to put it," Tom whispered to Cloutard. "The clergy were real party animals back then. Some things never change—the priest at St. Stephen's Cathedral once lost his driver's license for drunk driving," Tom said with a grin.

"Yes! Thank you, Andrzej," Hellen suddenly exclaimed. Several of the tourists turned to check what the commotion was, but just as quickly returned to their own business. Hellen swiped enthusiastically over the display of her iPad, on which Tom and Cloutard could see a series of plans.

"These are maps of the Melk catacombs," Hellen explained. "I'll forward them to you in a minute. Andrzej stumbled across them just recently in the Polish abbey at Tyniec, which is also a Benedictine monastery beside a river, even older than Melk. The catacombs under Melk were modeled after the ones in Poland. Our only hope now is that the diaries weren't sold and that they're still in the old librarian's hiding place."

"So, you want to go hunting around the catacombs for a hiding place that probably doesn't exist on the off chance that maybe, possibly, you might just discover the diaries of Philipp of Patootie or whatever his name is?" said Tom.

"If you've got a better idea, Tom, I'm all ears," Hellen snapped at him.

"She's got you there," said Cloutard.

"François," Hellen said, waving Cloutard closer, "I could use your help. There's a young woman in the other room who's there to make sure that visitors don't do anything they shouldn't. You need to distract her so that Tom and I can get downstairs to the catacombs. The stairs are closed and off limits to visitors," Hellen said.

Cloutard peeked into the adjoining room and saw the attendant in question. He smiled mischievously.

"*Mignon et adorable*. Finally, a task befitting my talents."

He adjusted his tie, pulled his hat a little lower over his face, smoothed his mustache with his fingers, and headed for the young woman.

43

LIBRARY, MELK ABBEY

THE LIBRARY CONSISTED OF TWO ROOMS, ONE LARGER AND one smaller, with bookshelves that rose from floor to ceiling around the periphery. Thousands of leather-bound books and folios filled the gold-embellished wooden shelves. Ten feet up, a gallery ran around all four sides of the larger hall, allowing access to even more volumes. But everything was cordoned off with red velvet ropes—the books could only be admired from a distance.

Through the open double doors, Tom and Hellen were able to watch as Cloutard bewitched the young attendant. The guided tour, meanwhile, had moved on, and there were only a few couples still strolling among the shelves.

Hellen had asked Cloutard to lure the young woman into the large hall: access to the lower levels was via a spiral staircase in the smaller room, guarded by an ornate accordion gate.

"Hey, Hellen, check this out," said Tom, pointing to a section of a bookshelf. "There's a hidden door behind these books. I can see light on the other side."

"I know. There's a ladder back there that leads up to the gallery. There's another one over there," Hellen said, pointing to a shelf on the other side of the room without taking her eyes off Cloutard. "Or did you think the monks could fly?"

"Oh," said Tom, seeing only now that there was no other visible way of reaching the gallery.

"Let's go!" Hellen said. Cloutard had finally managed to lure the library attendant away, and Hellen grabbed Tom by the sleeve and pulled him with her into the smaller room.

The gate, reminiscent of the latticed door of an old elevator, was, as expected, locked. An oval sign with the words "No Entry" made it doubly clear that visitors were not welcome to go that way. In a tight recess in the wall behind the gate, a stone stairway spiraled down into the darkness. Tom looked around quickly. Covered by Hellen, he rapidly picked the simple lock and slid the gate open. Hellen scurried through and he followed, closing it quietly behind him.

44

CATACOMBS, MELK ABBEY

"This reminds me of Valletta, somehow. When we went down that creaky old wooden staircase," said Tom. The beam from his flashlight lit the cold stone walls around them.

"At least this one's not rotten. It's not going to collapse," Hellen replied.

"Watch your step," Tom whispered, when they were one floor lower. "End of the line." A horizontal wooden hatch reinforced with iron prevented them from going any lower, although the stairway obviously continued downward. Tom heard a sound from inside the room and abruptly pushed Hellen back against the wall.

"I heard we'd probably close earlier today," a museum staffer said.

Tom raised a finger to his lips and peeked around the corner. Then he signaled to Hellen that there were two people.

"That's good news, at least. If this rain keeps up, we'll be facing the same mess here that they're dealing with in Innsbruck," a second voice said. Cigarette smoke wafted to where Tom and Hellen hid in the stairway, directly into Hellen's nose. She slapped her hand over her nose and mouth, struggling not to cough. Then a phone buzzed, and one of the museum attendants took the call.

"Shit, we're closing right now. Come on, we have to get all the visitors out," said one of the men, and he crushed his cigarette out underfoot. Their footsteps receded into the distance and finally faded completely.

Hellen inhaled with relief but could not completely stifle a small cough. Tom immediately tackled the small padlock that secured the trapdoor under their feet. He lifted the hatch and shone his flashlight into the shaft below.

"This definitely goes down to the catacombs," he said, climbing through. Hellen followed close behind. The steps were old and worn, the walls crumbling and moist. When they reached the bottom, they found themselves standing on a very wet floor.

"Looks like we're at ground level. There's water getting in somewhere," said Tom, shining his flashlight around. They were inside a low, vaulted chapel, only about ten feet by six. In the end wall was a small niche with a rotten prayer bench in front of it. A broken statue of Mary leaned against the wall of the recess. "Dead end."

"No. According to Andrzej's plans, there should be a way into a hidden passage somewhere here." Hellen took out her iPad again and studied the plans. "See? It's starts just behind the chapel." She pointed at the map and went to the end of the room. "We probably just have to find the mechanism that opens the entrance." They checked the prayer bench and the small niche with the Mary statue. Hellen put her iPad away and grasped the statue.

"What are you doing?" Tom asked, when he saw Hellen straightening the figure. "I thought you weren't a believer."

"I'm not, but that's no reason not to respect the faith of others." They heard a click when the figure was once again upright. "See? A little respect can work wonders," she said, grinning broadly.

"You probably have to turn her," said Tom.

Hellen held the small statue in both hands and twisted it with all her strength. They heard another click, followed by the grinding scrape of heavy stone. Dust trickled down from the ceiling as the entire niche slid backward.

"I get it now," said Tom. "A quick preventive prayer before heading out to party with the sinful peasants."

Hellen smiled. "Nobody's perfect." She switched on her own flashlight now, ducked, and disappeared into the opening. When Tom had also slipped through, they again heard the all-too-familiar scrape of stone.

"No! Goddamnit," Tom muttered, trying in vain to stop the stone block from closing. There was no way back. They were trapped.

45

LIBRARY, MELK ABBEY

THE YOUNG WOMAN'S CELLPHONE RANG.

"Excuse me a moment," she said to Cloutard, and she stepped away and took the call. Until her phone rang, she had fallen completely for the Frenchman's charm and practically forgotten her job. Her smile gave way to an increasingly earnest frown. She ended the call and slipped her phone back inside her jacket.

Before Cloutard could ask what had happened, the young woman raised her arms and spoke in a loud voice.

"Ladies and gentlemen! I'm sorry, but the museum is closing. We have been instructed by the disaster management office to evacuate all visitors. Please make your way to the exit as quickly as possible."

Cloutard shuddered. Slowly, he followed the other visitors into the smaller room. At the head of the spiral staircase with its latticed gate, he paused and looked down. *What about Tom and Hellen? If the museum closes, they have no way of getting out of the catacombs*, he thought. Should he try again to play the Blue Shield card that had failed Hellen earlier? Could he persuade someone to help him?

"You really have to leave now," the young woman said, and with outstretched arms she herded the remaining guests into the next room, where more staff were waiting to guide them out. Cloutard gave in reluctantly and followed the small crowd down the stairs and through the abbey church, then back to the Prelate's Courtyard.

Only when he stepped outside did he realize how serious the situation had become.

"*Merde*," he whispered, flipping up his jacket collar and holding onto his hat. The rainfall had increased exponentially. As if in a monsoon, vast quantities of water were falling from the sky. The visitors ran for the exit as fast as they could, fear spreading among them.

Cloutard was still standing in the arched church entrance, wondering what to do. Ice-cold rain whipped into his face. He looked grimly up at the sky as if cursing God. He was soaked to the skin, and his beloved Panama hat hung over his ears like an old fisherman's cap. He began to run. Crossing the Prelate's Courtyard, he ran through the Benedictine Hall and the Gatekeeper's Courtyard to the main entrance, and from there past the restaurant to the visitors' parking lot. He jumped into the Humvee and slammed the door. The rows of trees planted between the parking spaces to shade parked cars had turned dangerous. They flailed wildly and broken branches whirled through the air. Here and there, visitors were still running to their cars and driving away.

Runnels of water were pouring down from everywhere where the ground was higher, and within minutes the streets and footpaths were transformed into raging torrents.

Then Cloutard saw a man run onto the parking lot, and he had an idea.

46

CATACOMBS, MELK ABBEY

THE LIGHT FROM THEIR FLASHLIGHTS SWEPT THE TUNNEL floor, the roughly hewn walls, the ceiling. There were two paths in front of them: one leading east, the other south.

"Which way from here?"

"This one's a dead end," Hellen said, pointing to the eastern branch. "But this one is supposed to lead to the village on the south side of the abbey."

"Which one do we take?"

"Let's try the dead end. It runs about a hundred and fifty yards to the east," Hellen suggested. "If he hid the books anywhere, it would be here. That's where I'd hide them, anyway."

"How exactly do you think we'll find the old librarian's hidey-hole? The plans only show the passages, and they're anything but accurate," said Tom, studying them on his phone. The display cast a ghostly light on his face.

"I don't know. It'll definitely take some time."

"No kidding. We can't just knock on every square inch looking for a hollow space."

"I don't know if he hid them in a niche and walled it up or simply buried them in a hole. No idea. He certainly didn't put anything in the plans," said Hellen, getting upset.

"So, it's another needle-in-a-haystack search. Wow. Well, whatever we do, we'd better do it fast. The floor's getting wetter and wetter. Water's coming in somewhere. If they're already closing the abbey, the situation outside must be getting serious."

"Don't you think I know that? But this is about my mother's life—I'm not doing it for fun. This whole thing was chancy from the get-go, but I'll be damned if I don't use every second I have to find those diaries."

Tom stopped and turned to her. A tear slid down Hellen's cheek.

"Hellen, I'm sorry. I'll be by your side until we've found the fountain and saved your mother's life, I promise." He hugged her, and for a moment she wrapped her arms around him and squeezed him with all her strength. Then she pushed herself free again.

"Come on, let's start looking," she said, wiping her tears away and pushing past Tom.

They swung their flashlights over the walls and passage floor, but all they saw was roughly chiseled rock and stony ground. No bricked-up niches. Nothing at all.

Suddenly, though, a loud creaking sound made them both start.

"Stop!" Tom shouted. "Don't move a muscle." As if in slow motion, he crouched, pulled out his knife, and probed his way inch by inch toward Hellen, jabbing the blade into the floor as he went. When he was about three feet from her, they heard the creaking again, and his knife dug into wood through the dirt. He quickly retreated a short distance.

"Tom, what is it?"

"You're standing on wooden planks. Very, very old wooden planks."

Hellen gulped. Cold sweat dappled Tom's forehead. Hellen was standing on wooden slabs, probably rotten, and they had no idea how deep the hole beneath was.

Tom slowly knelt and began carefully clearing aside the soil and stones at Hellen's feet. Unconsciously, she shifted her weight from one foot to the other, and the wood groaned softly beneath her shoes. Then there was a loud "CRACK" and the wooden panel—covered in dirt and debris and slowly rotting for decades—broke. Hellen shrieked and fell.

Fast as lightning, Tom pitched forward onto the floor and reached out to catch her.

47

PARKING LOT, MELK ABBEY

CLOUTARD HAD RECOGNIZED THE MAN THE INSTANT HE SAW him. Wading as fast as he could, the museum guide battled his way through the waters streaming from the abbey park across the parking lot and down toward the village. He was heading for a car parked by itself some distance away. Cloutard jumped out of the Humvee and hurried after him. The man was fumbling with his car keys, trying to get in and flee the floodwaters.

"Wait!" Cloutard called out, making the man drop his keys in shock.

"What do you want?"

"Sorry, but I need your help," Cloutard said. This was no time to beat around the bush, so he said, "My friends are trapped in the catacombs, and I need your help to get them out," he said, puffing himself up before the tall, thin man. The guide, who had been telling wide-eyed visitors the story of the secret passage only shortly before, was taken aback and looked at Cloutard in disbelief.

"What? Are you crazy? Is this a joke?"

"I assure you, it is no joke. We are from Blue Shield, which you may have heard of. We were following a clue that we hoped would lead us to the old librarian's lost books. But the abbey management was not particularly cooperative, so we had to take matters into our own hands and get creative."

He had piqued the man's interest. "You're looking for the old librarian's books? But they are just a legend. A number of manuscripts vanished back in the 1920s, it's true, but—"

"Oh, *mon Dieu*, just come with me," Cloutard said, out of patience. He grabbed hold of the man's arm and pulled him along toward the Humvee.

"Hey!"

"I have no time to explain all this in detail. I have to show you something."

The museum guide went with him grudgingly, and they climbed into the huge vehicle. The rain pounded on the roof.

Cloutard took an iPad from his backpack and called up the plans Hellen had forwarded earlier. "Here. These are plans of the catacombs and the notorious secret passage used by the wayward monks." Cloutard handed the iPad to the man, who studied the plans with fascination. "I need to know how I can help my friends."

48

CATACOMBS, MELK ABBEY

HELLEN LET OUT A BURST OF SHOCKED LAUGHTER. TOM, who had only managed to grab her by the hips, lay stretched out in front of her in the mud. His face was spattered with the gray-green water splashed up by Hellen's plunge.

"I think I've found the hiding place," Hellen said with a grin. She had dropped only about two feet and was standing in a hole about a yard across, filled almost completely with water.

Tom looked up a little sheepishly. He wiped the muck from his face and they both laughed.

"Help me out of here," Hellen said, holding out her hands. He scrambled to his feet, grasped her hands, and pulled her out of the hole. They were face to face, standing close together now. Very close together. Their eyes met. Hellen wiped a bit of grime from Tom's cheek and kissed him fleetingly. "My hero," she said.

Tom pulled a face. "How was I supposed to know it was only knee-deep?"

"You've seen too many Indiana Jones movies. What did you expect? A pit filled with spears and crocodiles?" Hellen said. She shone her flashlight into the hole. Chunks of broken wood floated on the grimy water.

They knelt and broke away the remaining timbers, enlarging the hole, then reached into the chilly water and felt around.

"I can feel something," said Tom. "A handle."

"Me too."

They gripped the handles tightly and between them hauled a heavy box out of the water. They heaved it away from the hole and set it down again. The box was made of steel and closed with a rusty lock almost a hundred years old, which proved no match for Tom's knife: he pushed the blade behind the lock and pulled it off easily with a sharp jerk. But the lid was still jammed closed, as if someone had sealed it specially to protect the books from moisture. Tom went to work with his knife again, scraping around the edges of the lid, and they soon managed to open it.

"Jackpot!" they said in unison.

Hellen didn't hesitate. She pulled out one book after another and began leafing through them. "You read," said Tom. "I'll see if I can find a way for us to get out of here." Hellen responded with no more than a small wave of her hand.

A quarter of an hour later, Tom returned, splashing through ankle-deep water.

"I think I've found a way out," he said. He sounded a little out of breath and looked soaked. "Pack whatever you need and let's go. We have to get out of here fast."

Hellen did not react. She hadn't noticed that the passage floor was no longer just damp, but submerged under two inches of water. And it was getting deeper.

"This whole story is starting to get very strange indeed," Hellen said, poring over a page in one of the ancient folios.

Tom frowned down at her. "Hellen, we have to—"

"Remember how Guerra gave me an unknown version of the *Chronicle of the Morea* to analyze?" she said, cutting him off. "When they were holding me prisoner at Lake Como?"

"Sure. That was that old Knight of Malta's story. His Grand Master gave him the task of getting the Sword of Peter from Constantinople to the Knights, and he ended up parking it underneath the church where all the Grand Masters are buried, right?"

"Yes. We learned from the writings of Robert de Clari, the knight's brother, how the Sword of Peter found its way to Malta."

"Wait, wait. I remember this. Joseph of Arimathea left Israel and, according to the legend, went to England with Mary Magdalene. To Glastonbury, right? Where King Arthur is supposed to be buried. Somehow, in all the confusion of the Crusades, the Sword of Peter somehow found its way back to Solomon's Temple and was taken from there to Constantinople by the Knights Templar when they fled Jerusalem. And that's where our Knight of Malta came in.

"Exactly right."

Tom and Hellen were so absorbed in the story that they forgot about the rising water.

"But what does all that have to do with us, here, now? I thought we were looking for Excalibur," Tom said.

Hellen rapidly scanned another section of the old folio. "I am so glad this is in French and not Aragonese, like Guerra's version. I can work with old French much better."

"I thought you were looking for the diaries of that guy Philipp, the one who was held prisoner here with Richard the Lionheart."

"Yes, but this is even better. It says here that Richard the Lionheart was also accompanied by Robert de Sablé, who was the Grand Master of the Order of Malta back then. And Richard was said to have mutilated the Austrian flag by cutting it up with a 'special sword,' as I mentioned before."

"Hellen, sorry, maybe I'm a little slow today or maybe I'm just tired, but you've lost me."

"We were always wondering how the Sword of Peter got from England back to Jerusalem, right? Robert de Sablé took Excalibur from Richard the Lionheart and took it back to Solomon's Temple in Jerusalem."

But Tom was only more confused than ever. "Huh? Aren't you mixing up apples and oranges? One minute you're talking about the Sword of Peter, the next about Excalibur. What are you trying to say?"

Hellen looked at Tom and said nothing, waiting for him to connect the dots himself. Slowly, what she was saying dawned on him. But he didn't get the chance to share his epiphany. A loud rumbling not far away made them both look up in fright. Tom ran back in the direction from which the noise had come.

49

PARKING LOT, MELK ABBEY

"Where did you get these plans?" asked the guide.

"They were found somewhere in a Polish abbey in Tyniec."

"This is fantastic!" The man looked out the window to get his bearings, then turned the iPad to orient the plan correctly.

"According to this, there are two passages. One runs south to the village and ends beneath one of the oldest buildings in Melk—it's a butcher shop now. I doubt anyone could still get out through there. These buildings have been rebuilt and renovated so many times in the last five hundred years. If the tunnel still existed, someone would have found it by now."

"And the other?"

"Also not promising. It ends underneath the side arm of the Danube, east of the abbey."

Suddenly, the Humvee tipped sideways and began to

slide. The surprised museum guide let go of the iPad and braced his feet between the center console and the dashboard. "What's happening?"

"What do you think?" Cloutard shouted to make himself heard over the increasing roar of the rain. "We are losing the ground beneath our feet, literally." Thinking fast, he started the engine, swung the wheel around and stepped on the gas. With a jolt, the heavy off-road vehicle pulled clear of the sinkhole forming beneath it. The concrete surface of the parking lot had begun to collapse, and part of the pavement was sliding away. The windshield wipers were running at full speed, but Cloutard was still driving practically blind. He looked quickly right, then left.

"Look, look!" shouted the man beside him, hitting him repeatedly on the shoulder. When Cloutard saw what the man was so excited about, he could hardly believe his eyes. The trees surrounding the parking area were tumbling like dominoes, one after the other. A section of the hill on which the parking lot stood was sliding into the valley, burying buildings as it went.

Cloutard thought for a moment.

"Go! Drive! We have to get out of here," the man beside him screamed in panic. Cloutard made a daring choice.

50

CATACOMBS, MELK ABBEY

"COME ON, PACK QUICKLY—WE HAVE TO GET OUT OF HERE" Tom shouted, running back. Just a few steps past the intersection of the passages, his fears had been confirmed. The route to the village had collapsed. Boulders, rubble, and earth blocked the tunnel. Tom could see no light coming from the surface, but muddy water was pouring in from countless cracks and gaps.

"But the books . . ."

"We're out of time! Take what you need and let's go."

Unable to decide, Hellen stared at the contents of the case. A sudden surge of water around her ankles dragged her out of her thoughts. She grabbed the *Chronicle of the Morea*, sealed it inside a large ziplock bag and slid it into her backpack. Then she slammed the lid on the metal box and forced it down as hard as she could, hoping that the books might somehow survive.

Tom took her by the hand and pulled her with him down the passage.

"But it's a dead end," said Hellen, stopping and holding Tom back.

"The passage to the village has caved in. We can't go that way. And if you remember, we can't get back to the abbey, either."

"But the monks had to be able to get back in somehow. There must be a way to open the door from this side."

"Maybe. But by the time we've found it, the catacombs will be full of water. We've got one chance, and it's at the end of this tunnel."

"But it's a dead end," Hellen repeated. Tom grabbed her by the shoulders and looked into her fearful eyes.

"Trust me. We've always found a way out."

Tom took her hand, and they ran on.

More and more water was filling the catacombs. Their steps grew slower and their progress more difficult as they sloshed through water up to their knees.

"Come on, we're almost there."

"Tom, what are you going to do?"

"I've got an idea, but you're not going to like it."

Ten yards from the end of the passage, Tom stopped.

"Here's our exit." Tom shone his flashlight onto the ceiling, where water was seeping through countless tiny cracks and dripping to the floor. He took off his backpack and began searching through it. "I made a mental note about this spot earlier. There's a small branch of the

Danube that flows just in front of the abbey. If I've calculated correctly, we must be right underneath it."

"And?" Hellen was slowly starting to realize what Tom had in mind.

"Remember Nizhny Novgorod? Remember when the roof collapsed and the lake above it completely flooded the cave?"

Hellen's eyes widened and she looked up.

"And do you remember that we were inside a submarine back then? How do you—"

"Got it!" Tom announced.

Hellen breathed in sharply when she saw what Tom was planning.

"Now I know why Cloutard didn't want to be around when you got it wrong."

51

PARKING LOT, MELK ABBEY

CLOUTARD STOMPED ON THE ACCELERATOR. THE HUMVEE'S powerful motor roared and the vehicle shot forward. Cloutard was able to swerve clear just in time as another section of the parking lot broke away in front of them. He swung the steering wheel hard and rammed a traffic sign, but the pole snapped like a twig when the two-and-a-half-ton beast hit it. They roared across the bus parking area beside the visitors' parking lot.

The man beside Cloutard grew pale. "What are you doing? You're insane!"

"Hold tight!" Cloutard shouted as he steered the Humvee through the fence surrounding the parking area and its nose dropped sharply.

Water sprayed, branches broke, and leaves flew as the Humvee rode the landslide down the overgrown hillside. Cloutard and his involuntary passenger were tossed around wildly inside. At the bottom of the hill, they just missed the last house on Wiener Straße. The wooden fence surrounding the grounds wouldn't pose much of a problem, but a three-foot-high fieldstone wall lined the street at the bottom of the hill down which the Humvee was riding the landslide. A drop from there might be difficult.

Cloutard, gripping the steering wheel tightly, closed his eyes. But the wall, too, was no match for mass times speed. The layered stones of the old wall practically exploded ahead of the Humvee and it plunged into the torrent pouring through the idyllic village. Cloutard slammed on the brakes and whipped the wheel around, sending water surging into the house across the street. The vehicle slid sideways into a parked car and finally came to a stop.

The two men turned and looked at each other for a few seconds in shock, then they both burst into relieved laughter.

"Who did you say you worked for again?" asked the man, straightening himself in his seat.

"Where to now?" Cloutard asked.

"That way. Follow the road beside the abbey."

They drove on. The Humvee, outfitted with its snorkel, trundled unfazed through the floodwaters. The torrent was now hip-deep, rendering normal cars useless. Local residents were fleeing the storm on foot or in small boats. The only other car they saw was a Tesla, rolling past in water up to its windows. People carried belongings on their heads, whatever they could quickly pack into a sports bag or plastic sack.

Cloutard steered the car at walking speed around the base of the hill on which the abbey stood until they reached Nibelungenlände, the street that ran parallel to the side arm of the Danube.

"What now?" Cloutard asked, stopping the car and climbing out. "Where does the tunnel end?"

"I don't know exactly. According to the plan, somewhere just ahead." The man pointed out over the masses of olive-green water. The small pedestrian bridge that crossed the branch of the Danube to the Wachau Arena was all that was left to show where the river actually was.

Cloutard's shoulders sagged. All he could do was hope.

A loud report suddenly sent water shooting high into the air in the middle of the flood, making Cloutard and the guide jump. The water came splashing back down, and when the surface had settled, he saw them.

"Here!" he cried, waving his arms joyfully and wading through the flood.

Tom and Hellen had bobbed to the surface like two corks and swam toward Cloutard. When they had solid ground under their feet again, Cloutard threw his arms around Hellen. But Tom just stood and stared at the battered Hummer.

"What the hell did you do to my car?"

52

MELK

"Pretty straightforward, really. We took cover, and I detonated a small charge on the tunnel ceiling. The passage filled with water, and we swam to the surface," Tom explained when they were back in the Humvee. The museum guide had left them—he had enough problems of his own to deal with.

"I am so glad you made it out. I felt so helpless," said Cloutard. "And now that I know you are both in one piece, what did you find out?"

Tom and Hellen exchanged a glance.

"The Sword of Peter and Excalibur are one and the same!" they said together, more excited than ever.

"But . . . but . . ." Cloutard gasped. "How in God's name is that possible?"

"This folio seems to be the only complete version of the *Chronicle of the Morea* in existence." Hellen took the ziplock bag containing the book out of her backpack. "I was only able to glance through it down there, but it must have happened something like this: Joseph of Arimathea took the Sword of Peter to England, where according to legend it became the magical sword of King Arthur. After the Norman Conquest, the sword fell into the hands of a Frenchman, Gottfried von Bouillon, who knew about the power of the sword and who carried it with him into the First Crusade. Then it stayed in the Temple of Solomon until it passed into the hands of Richard the Lionheart. When he was taken prisoner, the Grand Master of the Knights Templar rescued the sword and took it back to the temple. When the Templars were forced to flee Jerusalem, they took the sword with them to Constantinople, and when the Turks took Constantinople, one of the Knights of Malta spirited the sword away to St. John's Co-Cathedral in Valletta, where we found it and took it to Rome."

"Incredible. So we actually found Excalibur and did not know it."

"Indeed we did."

"But that also means—" The words stuck in Tom's throat.

Hellen nodded with resignation. Her enthusiasm suddenly faded, and her thoughts returned to her mother. "Yes. It means we have to get the sword out of the Vatican if we want to find the Fountain of Youth."

"Which wouldn't be a problem if . . ."

All three knew what Tom was getting at. If the old Pope, whose life Tom had saved in Barcelona, were still in Rome, it would be easy. But now the Pope was dead, and his camerlengo, who was not well disposed toward Tom at all, was in charge until a new Pope was elected.

"The camerlengo will never willingly give us the sword," Hellen said sadly.

"Then we'll just have to steal it," said Tom. "And you, my dear François—you are going to have to outdo yourself."

53

ON BOARD A YACHT IN MONTE CARLO
HARBOR, ONE YEAR EARLIER

THE LEADER'S TONE HAD BEEN GRAVE BEFORE, BUT NOW IT
turned icy. Even in the Mediterranean climate of Monte
Carlo it made Noah shiver. His pulse accelerated and his
voice grew thinner.

"I told you we shouldn't underestimate Wagner."

"I did not underestimate him. But I clearly *over*estimated
you."

The leader was on his feet now, and Noah shrank
another inch in his chair as the man stalked toward him.
He placed his hand on his shoulder, too close to Noah's
throat for it to be a coincidence.

"You know how important these artifacts are to our
mission. We need all of them; only then can our quest be
a success. If even one is missing, we will be left quite
literally empty-handed. "I gave you back your legs, even
though you and my darling daughter here failed me in
Ethiopia." Standing beside him, Ossana gulped in fear.
"Do not let me down again. We are preparing a new plan

right now, one that involves the gold of El Dorado. The last thing we need is more interference from that half-witted James Bond. I want you to get rid of Wagner once and for all. Eliminate him. I don't want him getting in our way again."

His hand was touching Noah's throat, now, his thumb resting in the notch below his larynx. The leader's hands were warm, but a chill ran down Noah's spine. All he had to do was press, and it would all be over for Noah. The leader could not abide failure.

Noah, his voice faltering, said, "As you've noticed, that is not an easy task. The man has the luck of the devil." But that was all he got to say.

"No excuses, no explanations. I don't want to hear about how hard it is to kill him. Take all the resources we have and finish the son of a bitch! You know me, Noah. So you should also know that all these justifications . . ." his hands suddenly squeezed Noah's throat, and from one moment to the next, Noah couldn't breathe. He fell backwards from the chair and banged his head hard on the sundeck. The leader knelt over him, both hands tight around his neck. Ossana stood by indifferently, a cold smile on her face. The leader pressed as hard as he could. "All these justifications simply don't interest me. I want results, not flimsy evasions. I want Wagner dead, do you understand me?"

He had not raised his voice at all. He spoke with the same calmness as a moment before. The only difference was that he was in the process of choking Noah to death.

Fear entered Noah's eyes. His life could be over in seconds, but he did not dare to defend himself. If he did, the leader's wrath would know no bounds. He resigned himself to his fate . . . and then the leader's grip slackened. Air found its way back into Noah's bronchial tubes, then into his lungs. Noah sucked in a gust of air. Without warning, the leader's personality had shifted again. He helped Noah to his feet and back onto his chair before returning to his own.

"Kill Wagner. I don't care what it takes. I don't care what sacrifices you make. Wagner dies. He *dies*!"

Noah stood up, still gasping for breath. He nodded curtly and left the yacht. His mind was racing. He didn't have the slightest idea how to do what his master was demanding of him. Or whether he could do it at all.

54

BASILICA DI SAN CLEMENTE, ROME, ITALY

"It says here that the church and the cloister have belonged to Irish Dominicans since the seventeenth century," said Tom, who was killing time with a quick visit to Wikipedia. "Have our four sisters switched from communion wine to Jameson and Guinness, or why are we meeting here?"

As usual, Hellen ignored Tom's attempt at humor. The inner courtyard around her was surrounded on all four sides by arcades. And it was empty, although they were supposed to have met Sisters Lucrezia, Alfonsina, Renata und Bartolomea there fifteen minutes earlier.

They had first met the four nuns when they had given Tom a ride in their van on their way to Barcelona, after his first encounter with AF mercenaries. They had also played an important part in rescuing the Pope shortly afterward, and their paths had crossed several times since.

Hellen had a bad feeling—it wasn't like Sister Lucrezia, the Mother Superior, to be late. Hellen paced back and forth nervously. The Basilica di San Clemente was not far from the Colosseum, situated between Via Labicana, which followed the same route it had since antiquity, and Via di San Giovanni in Laterano, at one time the historical pilgrimage route from Lateran to the Forum Romanum.

"This place looks less like a church and more like a barracks, somehow," said Cloutard, strolling around the small well in the center of the courtyard.

"You're right, François. It's believed that the church used to be part of the gladiatorial barracks of Ludus Magnus, which were just a block from here," Hellen said.

"Gladiators? Maximus? Ben Hur?"

"Yes, Tom."

Hellen's reply was distracted, because as she spoke, she saw the four nuns hurrying through the gate and into the courtyard. It made her smile to see the four nuns approaching, arranged in order of height, like the pipes of a church organ.

The four sisters greeted them, and Lucrezia embraced Hellen and immediately inquired about her mother's health. Hellen gave them a quick update, and Lucrezia looked all three of them up and down with a critical eye.

"You don't look good. Exhausted. *Stanco*," she said.

"*Molto stanco*," said Cloutard, wiping his forehead wearily.

Hellen nodded, too. "We've been on the move for days, we've hardly slept, and we've been through some dangerous situations. So, yes, we're pretty drained. But we have no choice. We have to keep going. My mother's life depends on us."

Lucrezia nodded. "Please excuse us for being so late, but all Hell has broken loose in the Vatican, if you'll pardon the expression," she said, crossing herself. "The Pope's funeral is in two days, and they believe that revenge attacks are likely."

"Apart from that, the camerlengo has really been getting on our nerves lately," Sister Alfonsina added. "They're watching our every step. He was a tyrant even before the Holy Father's death, and now that he's in charge it's gotten worse."

Sister Renata spoke up next. "But now he has his hands full with preparations for the Holy Father's funeral and the conclave. We can only hope that he himself isn't elected Pope. That would be a nightmare."

Tom looked at the Mother Superior, expecting her to scold her junior nuns. He had come to know Sister Lucrezia very well indeed: she set great store in propriety and, above all, showing respect when talking about others. He was all the more amazed when no reprimand came. She clearly shared her sisters' opinion of the camerlengo.

"But I thought he administered the voting. I didn't think he could be elected at all?" Tom asked in surprise.

"He has already delegated that task, and many cardinals are backing him," said Lucrezia. "I would not be surprised at all to see him break with tradition and somehow get himself elected. Basically, it is possible for any baptized man or ordained priest to be elected Pope, but as with everything else in this world, the reality is that only the powerful have any real chance. And Cardinal Taddeo Monteleone is certainly one of the most influential men in the Vatican."

"The extra security worries me," Cloutard said. "It will make things far more difficult."

"Things?" Lucrezia asked. "Signor Tom, now would be the right moment to tell us why you're here and how we might be able to help."

Cloutard lowered his eyes and looked at the ground. He obviously didn't want to be the one to reveal their plan to the nuns. Tom also hesitated for a moment, expecting a diatribe from Sister Lucrezia.

Hellen shook her head impatiently. "We don't have time for this," she said, and turned to the four nuns. "We're searching for the Fountain of Youth, which is used to make the panacea, Paracelsus's 'arcanum.' We want to use it to save my mother's life. To find the fountain, however, we need to gather a few specific artifacts. We have one already."

"What do you still need?" Lucrezia asked.

Hellen swallowed but steadied herself. "We need the Sword of Peter."

Complete silence settled over the courtyard for several long seconds. The only sound was the little bit of traffic noise the penetrated from outside. The four nuns looked first at Hellen, then at Cloutard, and finally at Tom. It was like a scene from an Ennio Morricone film. Each looked into the others' eyes. No one dared to speak.

It was the diminutive Sister Bartolomea who finally broke the silence. "What exactly do you mean by 'need,' Signorina Hellen?"

The four nuns were slightly hunched, as if they were afraid of the answer. Tom was back to his old self.

"It's like this: we need you to help us break into the Vatican, get inside the Necropolis, and steal the sword from Peter's tomb."

55

BASILICA DI SAN CLEMENTE, ROME

AGAIN, THE SILENCE. THEN ALL FOUR NUNS CROSSED themselves in perfect unison.

"Hey, cool," said Tom. "Ever thought about taking up synchronized swimming? Then again, do they even make swimsuits for nuns?" Tom's grin was so disarming that none of them could stay serious for long, although the situation certainly warranted it. Everybody smiled. Lucrezia scratched her chin.

"I'm going to ask a stupid question, I know, but . . . what do you need the sword for?"

"The Sword of Peter, as we've only recently discovered, also happens to be King Arthur's sword, Excalibur," Hellen began.

"And together with Joan of Arc's shield and Merlin the wizard's amulet, it is possible to find the Fountain of Youth, at least according to legend . . . although we do not yet know exactly how or where. *En fait, c'est très simple*," said Cloutard. Tom and Hellen nodded in eager assent.

The nuns all looked at Cloutard. Silence fell a third time.

"Of course," said Lucrezia. "We should have thought of that ourselves. Silly of me even to ask." But her face and the look she gave her fellow sisters was clear enough.

They must think we're totally crazy, Tom thought.

"I know it sounds absurd," said Hellen, although her voice failed her several times as she spoke. "But it's our only chance to save my mother's life. Her doctor says it will take a miracle."

Sister Renata looked up at the sky. "If it's a miracle you need, then you're in the right place." And it was instantly clear that the four nuns would help any way they could.

Lucrezia spoke again: "If I know you, you already have some idea about how to do this, and what our role will be." She paused for a moment before continuing. "I should, however, point out that ever since the incident when the Cross of Kitezh was placed on Peter's tomb without anybody noticing, the Swiss Guard now watches over the grave twenty-four hours a day."

Hellen and Tom looked expectantly at Cloutard, whose mind was clearly working overtime.

"I hope you've got something worked out for that, François," said Tom.

"*Naturellement.* Of course I have." He grinned triumphantly, as if they were already holding the sword in their hands. "Here is what we do: with your esteemed assistance"—he indicated the four nuns and bowed a little—"we borrow a Swiss Guardsman's uniform for a few hours. Tom enters the Necropolis dressed as a guardsman, relieves the sentry on duty, takes the sword, and leaves. As I said: *En fait, c'est très simple.*"

Tom nodded and smiled. He liked that plan. The four nuns, of course, saw things a little differently.

"Signore Cloutard, that is anything but simple," Sister Bartolomea said, not only imitating Cloutard's voice, but trying also to imitate his expression. Tom had to grin— she had some talent. "Such uniforms are not simply lying around for anyone to take. They are stored away as securely as anything else in the Vatican, inside the Swiss Guards' barracks. I have been there to deliver a message several times. It is not a place we can simply stroll into."

"Madame, it disappoints me a little that you do not trust me to have thought of that. You are talking to François Cloutard, master thief. That is a minor hurdle, no more."

At the mention of "master thief," the nuns crossed themselves again. Burglary was not among the seven deadly sins, of course, but it certainly broke one of the Ten Commandments.

"*Calmez-vous*, we are not stealing, just borrowing," said Cloutard placatingly, and with a mischievous smile. "I would suggest we find somewhere that serves espresso, and I can explain my plan in detail."

56

SANT'ANNA DEI PALAFRENIERI, A CHURCH
ON THE EASTERN BOUNDARY OF VATICAN
CITY

"DIDN'T SIGNORE CLOUTARD SAY THAT ONLY ONE OF US
should be doing this?" whispered little Sister Bartolomea
when the four nuns had finished praying a rosary.
Cloutard had inducted them into the art of lock picking,
at least as much as he could in the little time they had.
The four nuns had then given Tom a crash course in the
changing of the guard, having seen the ritual themselves
hundreds of times. Now it was the middle of the night,
and the mere fact that they would go to the church to
pray at this time of night would arouse suspicion.
Although the entire Vatican was asleep, they had to be on
guard. The camerlengo had eyes everywhere.

"Do you really want to try it alone, Bartolomea?"
Lucrezia, the Mother Superior, looked questioningly at
the junior nun, who shook her head. "None of us proved
herself especially skilled in lock picking, so we need to go
together. I'm sure one of us will get it."

The other three nodded.

"Then let's go," said Lucrezia, though she was not very confident herself. The four nuns stood up hesitantly from the pews.

Alfonsina and Renata picked up the two trays, each holding a large pot of coffee, a few cups, and several pieces of cake. They had prepared them in advance, on Cloutard's advice, to give themselves a viable excuse if worse came to worst.

They left the small church building through the side entrance to avoid being seen by the guardsman on sentry duty at the Saint Anna Gate, an official border crossing between Italy and the Vatican.

They crossed Via Sant'Anna quickly and turned into a dead-end alley at the Nicholas V Tower, which housed the Vatican bank. On their left, opposite the bank, was the rear of the Swiss Guards' barracks. At the end of the alley, they passed through a narrow passage that led to the inner courtyard. They peeked carefully around the corner, checking for guardsmen in the courtyard, but the coast was clear. Lucrezia crept to a rarely-used door—the main barracks entrance was directly beside the Saint Anna Gate.

While her three fellow nuns waited in the passageway, Lucrezia set to work with the lockpicks, fingers trembling. The lock had clearly not been opened for years, perhaps decades. It was badly corroded, and even getting the first pick into the lock was tricky. Once she had managed that, she tried all the tricks Cloutard had taught them just hours before. But the lock would not budge.

Minutes passed. She was getting nowhere. She tried all the tools she had, but she couldn't get it. She hurried back to the passageway. Sister Bartolomea tried next, but also soon returned. Like the Mother Superior, she had also failed. Suddenly, they heard several voices ringing through the courtyard. All four jumped, thinking they'd been caught. But the voices receded, and the courtyard grew quiet again. Renata was next to try.

"Monsieur Cloutard would probably have gotten inside in a few seconds," Lucrezia murmured in frustration when Renata also came back.

"We are simply not Arsène Lupin," said Renata. Alfonsina was the last to try the picks, but her luck was no better than the others'. "If this fails because of us, Signorina Hellen will never forgive us," she said, looking forlornly at her fellow nuns.

"Which is why we have Plan B," said Lucrezia. "Come with me."

57

SWISS GUARD BARRACKS, COURTYARD

THEY EXITED THE COURTYARD AND HEADED FOR THE MAIN barracks entrance, where the Swiss Guardsman was on sentry duty at Saint Anna Gate. Of course, he also had a good view of the barracks entrance.

Generally, only guardsmen on their break made use of the guardroom. Lucrezia took a deep breath and knocked, and a moment later a sleepy-eyed guardsman opened the door. When he saw the four nuns smiling brightly, he quickly straightened his uniform.

"*Pronto*," the guardsman said.

"Good evening. With all the extra stress you boys are dealing with right now, we thought we'd surprise you with a little midnight snack to make your shift a little more bearable."

The young soldier's expression brightened on the spot, and he ushered the nuns inside.

Three more guards jumped to their feet as the nuns entered. Inside the sparsely furnished break room was a large table with four chairs and a not very comfortable looking sofa, nothing else. Shift schedules hung on the wall beside a small crucifix. Two doors led out of the room, one to the adjoining office of the sentry on duty and the other into the barracks building itself, which included the "*armeria*"—the Swiss Guards' armory, where their uniforms were also stored.

The guardsmen, taken by surprise, stood stiffly. No one said a word for several seconds. The guards' eyes turned to the table and then to the two nuns carrying the trays. At a nod from Lucrezia, they quickly began clearing away playing cards, ashtrays, and drinks from the table. Then Lucrezia glanced at Alfonsina, who immediately set her tray on the table and stepped back.

A little unsure of themselves, the guardsmen sat down again at the table. Sister Bartolomea leaned across the table, picked up the Thermos, and poured coffee for each of them. And then it happened: with a clumsy slip, she knocked over one of the cups, spilling coffee across the table. Lucrezia was beside herself.

"Can't you watch out!" she snapped at the junior nun.

"It's not so bad," said one of the young men.

Lucrezia picked up a cloth and hurriedly wiped up the mess that Bartolomea had made. Red-faced, Bartolomea set the coffee pot back on the table and stepped away, but in passing, she accidentally yanked a uniform jacket from the back of one of the chairs.

"Sister!" Lucrezia barked.

Her face now bright red, Sister Bartolomea picked the jacket up, smoothed it inside and out, and replaced it on the back of the chair.

"I'm so sorry. I don't know what's gotten into me today," she said.

"Don't worry about it," said one of the guards.

Another looked up at Renata, who was still standing motionless with her tray in her hands and pointed to the half-empty table. "There's still some room here," he said.

"No need for greed, young man," Lucrezia chided. "That is for *Comandante* Lorenzo da Silva. We've brought a little snack for him, too, of course," she explained. "Is he in his office?" She nodded casually toward the door that led into the barracks.

"Yes. Go on up. I'm sure he'll be happy to see you," said one of the men, biting into a piece of cake.

"Then we'll be on our way. Enjoy the coffee and cake!" said Lucrezia, shooing her nuns ahead of her.

58

SWISS GUARD BARRACKS

"How did you know the commandant was still here?" Renata asked the Mother Superior once they were out of the break room.

"I didn't. It was just a guess. But as Signor Tom always says, you have to take a little risk. Only then will fortune smile on you." Lucrezia turned to Alfonsina. "Did you get it?"

"Of course," said Alfonsina. During the performance Lucrezia and Sister Bartolomea had put on, she'd quickly searched the jacket of one of the guardsmen, which was hanging on the back of his chair, and proudly presented a keycard and a set of keys. She quickly crossed herself.

"We will have to say a few extra Ave Marias this evening," Lucrezia said firmly. "Now all we need is the uniform."

The barracks was completely still. With all the increases in security, many of the guardsmen were on duty. The rest lay in their beds, catching up on sleep—they would get little enough in the days ahead.

Lucrezia quickly found the key she needed, and the four nuns' faces lit up as they entered the armory, which contained the weapons and uniforms of the Swiss Guard. With the others acting as lookouts, Sister Renata started going through the uniforms, and seconds later, she lifted one of the coat hangers with its colorful uniform from the rack.

"Signor Tom wears German size fifty-four. This should fit him well," she said. Renata had worked with the Vatican tailors and had once even had the opportunity to assist Stefano Gammarelli, the legendary tailor to the Pope, so none of the other nuns questioned her choice. Each took part of the uniform and tucked it out of sight beneath her habit.

"We're lucky the guards don't have to wear their helmets in the Necropolis," said Alfonsina. "That would not be so easy to smuggle out."

They hid the tray away in a closet and quickly left the barracks again. "Now off to the train station," said Lucrezia, looking at her watch. "Twenty minutes' walk to the Stazione Vaticana."

59

PLAZA, SAN PIETRO RAILWAY STATION, ROME

WHAT IS IT WITH ITALIANS AND THEIR TRAINS? TOM thought as he entered the San Pietro railway station in Rome. In his mind, he returned to his first encounter with AF's mercenaries on board the high-speed Italo Treno to Milan. He could still picture the train racing through the countryside at close to 150 miles per hour, and how he was able at the last moment to prevent a disastrous derailment that would have left dozens dead and injured. It was just after that incident that he had met the four nuns. Their Alfa Romeo Autotutto van had suffered a flat tire on the long drive to Barcelona, and he, gentleman that he was, had offered to help. A lot had happened since then, much of it not pleasant at all. Tom had asked himself many times if it was all worth it, but now was not the time to rack his brain about that.

The small station was practically empty at this time of night, so nothing stood in the way of his plan. He strolled along the platform, looking around, and at the end of the roofed platform he discovered a high, free-standing vending machine. Like a parkour *traceur*, he vaulted from the back of a bench onto the top of the machine. He jumped again, swinging his legs up, and landed on the platform roof. Slowly, staying low, he crept back to the other end.

He looked down at the tracks. He had never jumped onto a moving train before. He checked the time: the freight train should be coming through in about three minutes, heading for the Stazione Vaticana, the Vatican train station. The Pope rarely used the papal station, and when he did, it was usually just a symbolic visit for pilgrimages. Tourists used it more often, however, as did a train that traveled once a week from the Vatican to Castel Gandolfo, the Pope's summer residence—and goods were still transported regularly into and out of the Vatican by rail. Tom checked the time again. One minute. He kept looking for the three-light signal typical of an approaching locomotive but saw nothing. *Fingers crossed it slows down going through the station*, he thought.

Another glance at his watch. Still nothing. Apparently, the freight trains in Italy were also far from punctual . . .

He sat on the edge of the roof and ran through the changing of the guard in his mind once more. Lucrezia had been through the process with him countless times. Usually, three guardsmen were involved. One would step up in front of the sentry at his post, run through the traditional ritual, then escort the man back to the guard-house, where the relieving guardsman would already be waiting. The escort would then lead him back to his post.

This meant that, going to the Necropolis alone, the guardsman he was relieving might get suspicious, which would leave him with no choice but to improvise a little. Nevertheless, he ran through the process mentally over and over, practicing the *kommandi* that the guardsmen exchanged during the handover and working on his Swiss accent at the same time. *This could really work*, he thought. Suddenly, the approaching freight train brought him back to the present. He got to his feet and readied himself for the jump. His plan was to run along the roof beside the train, reducing the speed differential as much as possible before he jumped. *It'll work,* he told himself. *At least in theory. Why did the Cobras focus so much on rappelling down walls headfirst? Why didn't they ever train us to jump onto a moving train?* He would have to suggest that Captain Maierhofer when he got a chance. The captain would be far from enthusiastic, of course, which only made Tom smile more.

The train rolled into the station, and when the locomotive drew level with him, he began to run. Gaining as much speed as he could, he jumped just before he reached the end of the roof and landed hard on top of a freight car. Rolling on impact, he came to a stop inches from the edge. He was out of practice. He'd banged his shoulder hard in the roll and it hurt like hell.

He didn't have much time to collect himself. San Pietro was just a few hundred yards from the Vatican City entrance. The train lumbered up a slight uphill grade, heading for the viaduct crossing Via di Porta Cavalleggeri. Just beyond that, Tom saw the entrance gates open, and the train slowed to walking speed as it pulled into Stazione Vaticana. Tom quickly climbed down out of sight between two rail cars, then jumped clear as the train passed through the gate, taking cover behind some bushes next to the station building. He looked around. There were only two workers at the station, and they began unloading the train.

He left his hiding place and quickly—but not too quickly —crossed the road behind the station building. The trick was *not* to try not to be seen. You had to act as if you belonged where you were: confident, upright, sure of yourself. He passed several parked cars and headed straight for a small church, the agreed-upon meeting point. The four nuns, visibly nervous, were already there.

60

BEHIND ST. PETER'S BASILICA, VATICAN CITY

TOM RAN THE LAST STRETCH TO THE FOUR IMPATIENTLY waiting nuns, who steered him hastily into the bushes beside the church. Surrounded by trees and bushes, the Church of St. Stephen of the Abyssinians, was practically invisible from the train station. "Camouflage and deception," Tom whispered. "You all would have done great in the special forces."

The nuns quickly produced the pieces of the guard's uniform from beneath their robes and Tom began getting changed in the cover offered by the bushes. Blushing brightly, the nuns turned away when Tom dropped his trousers.

"I know this sounds disrespectful," he said, looking down at himself as he fastened the final button, "but this uniform makes you look like a clown. Didn't Michelangelo design this thing? All I can say is, it seems like he tried a lot harder with the Sistine Chapel."

"That is a myth that refuses to go away. Michelangelo had nothing to do with the uniform," Sister Lucrezia said, her voice almost harsh. "They were designed and introduced by Commandant Jules Repond in the early twentieth century. And it is no clown's outfit. You are wearing the traditional colors of the House of Medici."

I'm away from Hellen for five minutes and already I've got another woman teaching me history, Tom thought, but he excused himself for his faux pas.

"All right," said Sister Alfonsina, handing Tom the keycard she'd filched from the guardsman. "Signor Tom, this should get you into the Necropolis, but we don't know how long it will still work. When the guard finds that it's missing and reports it, it will be canceled."

"Good luck," said Sister Lucrezia, and the other nuns nodded their support. "Signor Tom, we'll be waiting for you on Via delle Fondamenta, behind the Sistine Chapel. We'll be able to smuggle you out of the Vatican from there." Tom raised his hand in thanks and watched as the nuns melted away into the darkness.

He went through everything in his head again, for what felt like the thousandth time. If he screwed up now, he'd be behind bars for a very long time—not to mention the political shitstorm he'd unleash. Breaking into the Vatican and the Papal Necropolis to steal the Holy Weapon from St. Peter's tomb . . . that would *not* look good on his already highly questionable résumé.

He'd always been an adrenaline junkie, an adventure hound, ever since he'd joined the Austrian Cobra anti-terror unit. But what he'd been through in the previous two years was getting to be too much even for him. *Careful what you wish for*, he thought grimly.

Not that he was about to back out now. What they were trying to do here was far more important than anything else he and the team had ever attempted. But he sensed that he was getting tired. For the first time in his life, he longed for a little peace and quiet. Stability. Less adventure, fewer bullets whistling past his head, fewer situations that put him and the people who mattered to him in mortal danger. When this one was over, he was going to need a break, whether he'd brought down AF and its commander-in-chief or not.

"Discipline, Wagner. Discipline!" he whispered aloud to himself. He swept his gloomy thoughts aside, adjusted his beret, and went through the changing-of-the-guard ritual a final time in his head. Reaching St. Peter's Square, he passed the mighty basilica and walked beneath an archway that connected the basilica with the Museo del Tesoro di San Pietro, an art museum. Below a second archway, he turned toward a door with a sign reading "Ufficio Scavi"—the entrance to the Necropolis.

61

IN THE VATICAN NECROPOLIS

THE NECROPOLIS WAS A STRANGE PLACE, TOM THOUGHT. ALL of the closely packed mausoleums had once been in the open air. When Emperor Constantine began building the first St. Peter's, 324 years after Christ, the Necropolis had been filled in to allow the basilica to be built directly over Peter's tomb, which, tradition held, was located in this Necropolis. In 1940, under Pope Pius XII, a search for Peter's grave had begun and the excavations had unearthed dozens of other mausoleums that had survived through the centuries. Now, Tom stopped beside one of these and looked across toward Peter's grave.

When Tom saw the Swiss Guardsman at his post at the right of the tomb, he recalled that he had no real idea of what time the changing of the guard took place. The nuns had hammered the ritual into him, but they hadn't had time to find out the regular schedule.

A welter of thoughts ran through his mind when he saw the sword atop the grave—Peter's Sword, the "Holy

Weapon" with which everything had begun, the very sword that Peter had used to cut off the servant Malchus's ear on the Mount of Olives when Jesus was arrested.

"They that take the sword

shall perish with the sword."

Jesus had spoken those words to prevent his apostles and acolytes from causing any more people to suffer by the sword. And in doing so, he was said to have touched Peter's sword, imbuing it with his proverbial power—the same power that crusading knights like Richard the Lionheart had planned to exploit for themselves in reconquering the Holy Land.

It wasn't enough that Hellen and he, around two years earlier, had rediscovered the sword and actually had it in their hands—now they had learned that King Arthur's sword Excalibur and the Sword of Peter were one and the same. And that it incorporated another fateful secret: it was one of the keys to the Fountain of Youth.

Everything he'd experienced in the last few years and everything that still lay ahead roiled in Tom's head. He would brazen it out, he decided, whether the sentry on duty was expecting it now or not. He began the guard-change ritual, quickly modifying the process for only two guards. He could only hope that his counterpart would play along.

"Sentry, acknowledge!" Tom rapped at the man from some distance away, raising his left hand to his waist and angling his left arm. The guard on duty was taken by surprise but reacted to the order.

"Attention!" Tom continued, dropping his left hand again so that his arm now lay vertically against his side. "Shoulder arms!"

The guard shouldered his halberd and Tom grinned inwardly. The man was doing exactly what he was supposed to. This would work!

"To post, march!," Tom barked sternly, marching forward and coming to a stop in front of the sentry.

"Post and orders remain as directed," the man said, and he held his halberd toward Tom in outstretched arms. Tom took it from him. The man was certainly confused and was no doubt wondering why he was already being relieved, but the ritual did not allow for conversation. Only when he was back in the barracks would the guard discover the irregularity and be able to sound the alarm. Tom would have to use that brief window of time to make his escape from the Vatican. The man stepped aside, and Tom took his place.

"Sentry, march!" he snapped.

The guardsman whipped his hand down, turned his back to Tom and marched away. Tom's heart was beating so loudly that he was afraid the man would hear it. He didn't dare to move. Seconds felt like hours as the measured steps of the departing guard faded into the distance. Then the Necropolis fell utterly silent. Tom wasted no time. He leaned the halberd against the wall and lifted the sword carefully from the stone. He studied the antique weapon for a moment. The polished steel gleamed, silvery in the twilight. He thought of the last time he had seen the sword in action, when Jacinto

Guerra, his parents' killer, had accidentally impaled himself with it. He unfolded a sack from inside his jacket, carefully pushed the sword inside, and slung the sack over his shoulder. He looked around a final time, and with a last apologetic glance at Saint Peter's tomb, he made his way back to the surface.

62

VIA DELLE FONDAMENTO, BEHIND ST. PETER'S BASILICA, VATICAN

MAKING HIS WAY QUICKLY AROUND THE BASILICA, TOM found the nuns at the end of Via delle Fondamenta, in the cul-de-sac in front of the Sistine Chapel. The streets inside Vatican City were still practically empty. He saw one or two early risers, but they took no notice of him at all. He was in a Swiss Guard uniform, after all, which allowed him access to almost anywhere in the Vatican. At least, it would until the theft was discovered. Cloutard's plan meant that he had to get rid of the uniform as quickly as he could. Swiss Guards rarely wore their uniform outside the Vatican and going out dressed like that would set alarm bells ringing—if they weren't already—and Tom would be caught.

"Did you get it, Signor Tom?" Sister Lucrezia whispered. Tom nodded breathlessly and looked around. The guardsman he relieved would return to the barracks any moment, and all hell would break loose.

Alfonsina handed Tom a bundle containing his clothes and the folded robes of a Benedictine monk, and he practically snatched them from her hands. "Thanks. You've done enough, all of you. Get yourselves to safety. You can't be seen with me."

The nuns nodded, murmured a final "God be with you, Signor Tom," and moved away swiftly to the west, toward the Palace of the Governate.

He looked after them for a moment before heading north, past the Vatican Archive, then turning left and crossing the square in front of the Vatican Art Gallery.

In the dim light of the streetlamps, he could make out a small patch of woods ahead. The park stretched from the Radio Vaticana building to the city wall in the northwest. Concealed among the trees and bushes, Tom quickly changed clothes, folding the uniform neatly and pulling on the brown monk's cowl, keeping the hood as low as possible over his face. And that was when it happened. Life returned suddenly to the sleeping city. All around, strategically placed floodlights flared, and from one moment to the next the Vatican was bathed in dazzling light. The ruse had been discovered.

63

VIALE DEL GIARDINO QUADRATO, NEAR
VILLA PIA, VATICAN

BUT HE WAS NOT SAFE YET, NOT BY A LONG SHOT. WHEN the lights came on, he ducked back deeper among the trees. Vatican City was a labyrinth, but he'd memorized his escape route and rehearsed it countless times in his head. He could not afford to take a wrong turn or suddenly find himself in a dead end.

Hidden by the trees, he hurried to the city wall and turned east. He skirted the Art Gallery and continued along the wall, passing behind various museum buildings until he reached the Fontana della Galera o Galea, the Fountain of the Galley. This was going to be the trickiest part by far. He headed south toward the Via Sant'Anna, alongside the area of the city that housed the Vatican Printing Office, the post office, and the offices of the Vatican daily paper, *L'Osservatore Romano*. When he turned left toward the exit, he could already see the commotion at the Saint Anna gate. He crossed the street, skirted Nicholas V's Tower and pressed close to the wall behind the Swiss Guards' barracks. A quick peek around the corner revealed a group of Swiss Guardsmen and men from the Corpo della Gendarmeria, the Vatican police force, involved in a heated discussion in front of the barracks. Lorenzo da Silva, Commandant of the Swiss Guard, was among them. *I'll never get out here*, he thought. But the Saint Anna gate opened just then, and a small delivery van entered. Tom's command of Italian was just enough for him to see that it was the daily delivery of bread and baked goods.

Now or never. At first slowly, with the hood pulled low over his face, he moved toward the gate. Then he lifted the robe and broke into run. The guardsmen were so immersed in their quarrel that Tom almost slipped past the delivery van unseen. But he was too anxious to get outside. The sprinting monk caught Lorenzo da Silva's eye.

"*All'armi!*" Tom heard the commandant's sudden shout just as he got outside. He turned around and looked da Silva in the eye. The commandant recognized him instantly and began to run. Tom did the same, sprinting away along Borgo Pio. At the corner of Via del Mascherino, he spotted a mounted Roman police officer just leaving a McCafé with an espresso. The officer had tied his horse to a road sign at the end of a row of parked cars. Behind him, Tom heard da Silva bellow: "*Fermo! Polizia!*"

The cop looked up, saw da Silva, and then the running Benedictine monk.

"*Fermare il Monaco!*" da Silva shouted.

The cop glanced down at his espresso and hesitated a second too long. Tom jumped and sprinted over the roofs of the parked cars. From the hood of the last one, he launched himself into the saddle. The policeman, taken completely by surprise, dropped his coffee.

"*Molte scuse*," Tom called, then he yanked the reins from the road sign and kicked the surprised officer aside, even as the man tried to fumble his pistol from its holster.

Tom jabbed his heels into the horse's flanks and took off at a gallop. He knew he couldn't stay on horseback for long. A monk galloping through Rome at night was simply too easy to spot, and he didn't want yet another of his exploits to end up on YouTube. But he had to put some distance between himself, the Vatican, and the raging Lorenzo da Silva.

He rode down the Via del Mascherino—usually clogged with traffic but now, thank God, almost empty—then swung right onto Borgo Angelico and left again onto Via del Falco. Then he jumped down and slapped the horse on the rump, and it galloped on while he went in the opposite direction, toward Piazza del Risorgimento. He pulled off the monk's cowl as he went, tossing it aside as he entered the square. At the bus station, he saw Sister Lucrezia's old Alfa Romeo Autotutto van, which Cloutard had borrowed. The Sword of Peter in his bag, Tom ran to it and jumped in. Cloutard grinned and stepped on the gas.

64

ALFA ROMEO AUTOTUTTO, STREETS
OF ROME

HELLEN KNEW RIGHT AWAY THAT HE'D SUCCEEDED. SHE took his face in her hands, pulled him close, and gave him a long, intimate kiss.

"You're the best," she said, and kissed him again. It was as if a stone had been lifted from her heart. Now, with the sword in their hands, they had taken the second step.

"What are you waiting for?" Hellen said impatiently. Tom slid the sword out of the bag and passed it to her, and she accepted it joyfully.

"*Parfaitement*. My plan and my crash course seem to have borne fruit," said Cloutard, glancing back over his shoulder to see the sword for himself.

Hellen looked up. Tom smiled proudly and their eyes met. And in that moment, both returned to the moment they discovered the sword together in the catacombs of Valletta. Tom had saved her life then, and everything that had happened since had only brought them closer. Hellen knew without a doubt that Tom would do whatever was needed to save her mother's life and that he would put his own on the line without a second's hesitation. They gazed into each other's eyes, both sensing the gravity of the moment. Tom was there for her. Always and in every way. She had never felt as close to him as she did just then.

But she noticed something else, too. She weighed the sword in her hand. The balance was off. She had never noticed that before. Her eyes narrowed and traced the blade to the wooden grip and the pommel. The hilt was supposed to balance the sword and was attached to the tang that ran out of sight through the middle of the grip.

"Something's loose," said Hellen, running her fingers over the hilt. "Was it always like this?"

"It might have happened just now, when I was running with it," Tom said.

Hellen gripped the hilt more firmly, and one half of the pommel came loose under her fingers, revealing a hollow cavity.

"Oh my God!" she suddenly cried, so loudly that Cloutard almost crashed into a parked car in shock.

"*Merde!* Do not frighten me like that. What is it?" he snapped over his shoulder.

Hellen pointed mutely to the recess in the pommel. Her other hand was clamped over her mouth, and she was breathing heavily. It took Tom a moment to understand what had caused her outburst of emotion, but slowly it dawned on him.

"That looks like the recess on the Grand Master's grave in Valletta, where your—"

"Where the amulet my grandmother left me fitted perfectly." Hellen looked at Tom in disbelief. The only sound was the chatter of the motor and the rumble of the tires on the ancient cobblestones of the Roman street. Tom and Hellen held their breath as they realized what it meant.

"You're kidding me," said Tom, almost irritated, when he'd regained his composure. "Could your grandmother's amulet and Merlin's amulet really be one and the same? Is it really part of Excalibur's hilt?"

Hellen nodded silently, still stunned by their discovery.

"Are you seriously telling me we already had all of the things we need now back then? The shield, the sword, and your amulet?" Tom paused, shook his head in disbelief, and let out a laugh. "And now we have to go through the whole circus again to get them all back?"

"I'm not certain about the amulet," said Hellen. "Yes, this recess looks like my pendant would fit, but how could my grandmother have gotten her hands on Merlin's amulet? It's absurd." She shook her head. "Besides, mine's gone. Pálffy took it in Valletta."

"Which suggests that it is extremely important," Cloutard said from the front. Tom nodded.

"What do you know about the amulet?" Tom asked Hellen.

"Not much at all, actually. As far back as I can remember, my grandmother always wore it, and just before her death she gave it to me. That's all I—" She stopped suddenly in mid-sentence. "Father Montgomery . . ." she whispered, her voice almost inaudible.

"Who?" Cloutard asked.

"Father Montgomery. The British Orthodox priest I went to visit in Glastonbury. He was supposed to have information about the sword but when I got there, I found him dead. When we were looking for the Chronicle of the Round Table, I found his notebook with him in his grave. I didn't think much of it at the time, and I wanted to find out more about Father Montgomery from the Seraphim of Glastonbury."

"Who?" Tom asked.

"The Seraphim of Glastonbury, the metropolitan, head of the British Orthodox Church," Cloutard said, pleased with himself, and he took a swig from his hip flask.

"I'm impressed, François," said Hellen.

"I remember," said Tom. "He was the guy you wanted to talk to about the dead priest, but he wouldn't give you an audience." Tom suddenly faltered and looked at his friends. No one said anything—each knew only too well what had happened next. Hellen had been attacked by Society of Avalon thugs, who had shot her and left her for dead. She'd survived, but it had been a close thing—a dark moment, and one she would have loved to be able to forget.

Hellen gulped. "I was certain at the time that he knew important things about Father Montgomery and that he was just trying to slow me down."

"Man, we should really start collecting frequent flyer points if we have to go to London now, too. If the Seraphim really knows about Father Montgomery, we need to talk to him as soon as possible."

"We do not have to go to London," said Cloutard. "The Seraphim is coming to us."

Hellen and Tom looked at Cloutard curiously.

"Would I really have known who the Seraphim was just now? I just happened to read about him in the newspaper while we were waiting for Tom." Cloutard picked up a copy of *La Repubblica* lying beside him on the passenger seat and handed it back to Hellen and Tom. "This Seraphim, like many others, is on his way here for the Pope's funeral. Fábio will be able to find out when he is landing in Rome."

Tom rubbed his hands together. "And then we'll have a little chat with him."

None of them had noticed that a motorcycle had been following them since they left the Vatican.

65

PARKING LOT, OUTSKIRTS OF ROME

"Parfait, merci mon ami," said Cloutard. He hung up and slipped his phone into his pocket.

"So, what did the old hacker say?" Tom asked.

"The Seraphim is landing at 10:30 this morning at Leonardo da Vinci International. His assistant is accompanying him, and he has booked a limousine service to pick him up."

"Fantastic. That's our chance. We only have to find the right driver. There must be dozens of passengers getting picked up by chauffeurs at the airport."

"I've got an idea," said Hellen. "What's the name of the company?" She quickly looked up the name and address of the limo service and held her phone out to Cloutard. "Take us to this address. It isn't far."

"*Oui, ma chère,*" said Cloutard. "I told you. She is definitely in the driver's seat this time," he whispered to Tom as he pulled away.

Hellen dialed the number.

"What are you going to—" Tom began, but Hellen silenced him with a raised finger.

"Good morning, my dear," Hellen began in a rather awkward-sounding English accent. "This is Sister Mary." Tom rolled his eyes at Hellen's extremely unimaginative alias, but she just shrugged and went on. "I'm calling from London, from the office of the British Orthodox Church."

"How can I help you, Sister?" said the woman on the other end.

"One of your drivers was supposed to pick up the Seraphim of Glastonbury at ten-thirty this morning from Leonardo da Vinci Airport. He's not the youngest anymore, but he is making the journey to be present at the Pope's funeral. Unfortunately, I made a mistake with the arrival time when I made the booking. He isn't landing at ten-thirty, but one hour earlier. Would you be able to do me a huge favor and have a driver there at nine-thirty?"

"A terrible thing, what happened to the Pope, Sister," the woman said. "Let me have a look . . . ah, here it is. Hmm, all our drivers are booked up. It's hell out there right n—" She pulled up short. "I beg your pardon, Sister."

"Don't worry about it. You're perfectly right. It's really hell on earth just now."

Tom had to smile.

"Ah, I do have something. I see that one of our cars has just come back. I'll find a driver for you as soon as possible. He should be ready to leave in about thirty minutes; that should work."

"Oh, thank you. You're an angel," Hellen said, and it took all her willpower not to laugh, especially when she how hard Tom was trying to keep himself under control. "God be with you," Hellen threw in just before she hung up. Tom couldn't hold back any longer and all three burst out laughing. For a moment, they all felt a lightness they hadn't experienced in a long time. For a brief second, everything was forgotten.

"God be with you, my angel!" Tom said, and they burst into laughter again.

Hellen's phone rang, interrupting the moment of fun.

"It's Vittoria," said Hellen, taking the call. "Hi," she said with a laugh, making an effort to be serious again. "Sorry, we just had a funny ..."

When Hellen heard what Vittoria had to say, the color drained from her face.

66

ALFA ROMEO AUTOTUTTO, STREETS
OF ROME

"MOTHER'S HEART STOPPED. SHE'S . . ." HELLEN stammered when the call ended.

"She's what?" said Tom. He tried to put his arms around Hellen, but she held him off.

"She . . . she went into cardiac arrest, and they had to revive her," Hellen began again. She was completely composed, no tears, no visible emotion. Her face was a mask.

No one said a word. Minutes passed as they waited outside the exit from the limousine company's garage. As promised, a car drove out, right on time. Cloutard, who had parked the Autotutto opposite the company's offices, pulled in behind it. After a few minutes, the limousine turned into a quieter side street.

"We have to stop that car and put the driver out of commission," Hellen said coldly.

"Do you have an idea how to do that?" Tom asked cautiously.

"We could—" But she got no further. A loud *bang* and the van's abrupt halt interrupted her. Cloutard had driven into the back of the limousine, without braking at all.

"François, you're going to have explain that to Lucrezia. She's not going to be happy," said Tom, realizing right away what Cloutard was up to. "This thing's vintage."

The limo driver climbed out and came back to the Autotutto. He knocked on the side window with a closed fist and began railing at Cloutard in Italian as soon as he rolled down the window. Cloutard climbed out and began shouting back at him in French.

Tom made use of their quarrel to creep out through the back door of the van. He came up behind the agitated Italian, who fell silent instantly when he felt the pistol in his back.

"*Merda, non di nuovo,*" said the man.

Tom led the chauffeur around the van to the side door. Hellen was sitting inside with a roll of gaffer tape in her hands and a look on her face that would have made even the toughest mafioso tremble.

"*Spogliare.* Get undressed," she ordered.

White as chalk and without a word, the man pulled off his jacket and trousers and threw them onto the back seat.

"*Il cappello*," Hellen added, pointing at his chauffeur's cap. He rolled his eyes upward, took the cap off, and added it to the pile.

"Please not to hurt me," the man stammered in broken English as Hellen bound his hands with gaffer tape. She finished by taping his mouth closed, then turned to Cloutard and handed him the chauffeur's clothes.

"*Andiamo*," said Tom, and he opened the back door and pointed inside. Perplexed, the chauffeur just looked at him, but when Tom pressed the gun under his nose, he did what he was told. "Terribly sorry about this," Tom said when the man had one foot in the back of the van, and he cracked the man on the back of the head with the pistol, heaved his unconscious body into the back of the van, and closed the door.

67

LEONARDO DA VINCI INTERNATIONAL AIRPORT, ROME

"Terrible! I love Italian clothes, but this fabric is simply the worst!" Cloutard moaned.

"Don't tell me the chauffeur doesn't use the same tailor as you," Tom mocked through the open partition. He was sitting with Hellen in the back seat of the limo, invisible from outside through the tinted windows.

"I miss my Brioni," Cloutard murmured. "Next time, one of you will get dressed up."

"Just keep your eyes on the road," Hellen snapped.

Tom and Cloutard fell silent. Cloutard parked the car at the airport arrivals hall. He took the sign with the Seraphim's name on it from the passenger seat, climbed out without a word, and disappeared into the hall. Minutes later, he reappeared leading the priest and his assistant, who carried two small suitcases. They headed for the limousine.

"We're on," Tom said to Hellen when he saw them approaching.

"You can put the cases in the trunk," said Cloutard to the Seraphim's assistant, with a nod toward the back the car. Cloutard waited until the man was at the trunk, then he opened the rear passenger door.

"*Grazie*," said the Seraphim, climbing in, and Cloutard quickly shut the door behind him.

"Sorry, the trunk is still locked," said the assistant, trying to open it.

"One moment, sir. The catch is here in the front," Cloutard said, and he pointed across to the driver's side. He hurried around the car, climbed in, started the engine, and hit the gas.

"Who are you? What do you want from me?" the Seraphim stammered when he'd recovered from the first shock. He was staring down the barrel of the gun Hellen was pointing at him. The cleric's anxiety was understand-able—the head of a church probably didn't get a gun in his face every day.

"Your assistant should go to confession tonight," said Tom. "I think he used some pretty bad words just now."

Cloutard widened the distance between them and the Seraphim's furious assistant, and Hellen glared scathingly at Tom.

"We've got a few questions to ask you about Father Mont-gomery," Hellen said. Her voice was ice, and Tom could feel her determination. Her mother was on her deathbed and Hellen was prepared to go to any lengths, even the most extreme, to save her. For the first time, Tom was going to have to be the prudent one. He had to make sure Hellen didn't overdo it.

When the Seraphim heard the name "Montgomery," he turned even paler.

"Please, don't kill me," he stammered in terror.

"Then tell us everything you know about Father Montgomery," Hellen snarled. She leaned forward and pressed the pistol so hard against his forehead that the skin around the barrel turned white. Sweat beaded on the Seraphim's brow.

"But I don't know any more about him than your organization already knows," he spluttered.

"Our organization?" Hellen asked, growing more impatient. "Why would Blue Shield know anything about Father Montgomery?"

The Seraphim's face showed only confusion, and he was breathing hard. "Blue Shield? But . . . but aren't you from the Society of Avalon?

Hellen and Tom shared a questioning frown.

"Why would you think that?" asked Tom, sensing that he should take the helm. In her emotional state, Hellen might shoot the poor Metropolitan dead. He placed his hand on the arm still holding the pistol to the priest's head and gently pushed it down. The Seraphim let out a relieved sigh. "Let's let the man talk," said Tom placatingly.

"You're not from the Society of Avalon?" the Seraphim asked again.

"No. And I'll ask you again, why would you think we were?"

Slowly, the man began to breathe normally again. He dabbed at the sweat on his forehead with a handkerchief, then looked first at Tom, then Hellen. He was clearly struggling to find an answer.

"Father Montgomery once told me that, if anyone ever came asking questions about him after he died, I should watch out. The Society of Avalon will kill anyone who knows they even exist."

"Well, we're still alive," said Tom defiantly. "They're not as good as they think they are, I can tell you that." Tom smiled sympathetically at the man. He had to win his trust. "What else did Father Montgomery tell you?"

The Seraphim shook his head with determination. "I'm afraid I can't tell you." His eyes widened as Hellen's fingers tightened around the grip of the pistol. The Seraphim raised his hands defensively and quickly went on, "he told me in confidence, in the confessional. I can't tell you anything."

Tom knew that Hellen was about to explode, and he held her hands tightly as he spoke again. His voice took on a more menacing tone.

"Father, as much as I respect your sacraments, you're going to have to overcome some of your priestly inhibitions. This is a matter of life and death, and not just one life. As you know perfectly well yourself, the Society of

Avalon is a mob of insane killers and we're trying to stop them. More immediately, the life of Ms. de Mey's mother"—he nodded toward Hellen—"is on the line. So, you're going to have to open up a little more."

The Metropolitan's expression suddenly changed.

"You . . . you're Hellen de Mey?" he asked in astonishment.

"Yes, but—" Hellen was as surprised as Tom. The mention of her name had obviously changed something. The Seraphim hesitated. He glanced for a moment heavenward, almost as if to excuse himself for what he was about to do.

"Father Montgomery was your great-uncle," he said softly.

Hellen did not think she had heard correctly. "He was . . . what?"

"He was your grandmother's brother. And he was also a member of the Society of Avalon."

The priest slowly reached beneath his soutane and withdrew a chain, from which a signet ring dangled. He unclasped the chain and handed the ring to Hellen, whose eyes widened with disbelief. Tom held his breath.

"You mean, my grandmother knew about the Society?"

The Seraphim was about to say something, but then sighed and wiped the handkerchief over his sweat-covered face.

"What? Tell me!" Hellen's nerves were as frayed as they could get.

"The Society of Avalon was not always the band of murderers they are now. When the Society's methods grew more extreme, your great-uncle wanted out." He looked Hellen in the eye. "And . . ." He hesitated, sighed again, and crossed himself. "And he asked your grandmother, his sister, for help."

"Help? Why in the world would my grandmother have helped him?" But Hellen's voice cracked. She didn't want to hear what the Seraphim of Glastonbury was about to tell her.

68

IN THE LIMOUSINE, DRIVING INTO ROME

"Your grandmother was having an affair with the man who ran the Society of Avalon."

The last sentence struck her like a sledgehammer. Tears came to her eyes. Her grip on the pistol loosened, and the weapon slipped from her fingers. Tom moved the gun away and gently took hold of her trembling hands. She was breathing heavily.

"In her defense," the Seraphim went on, "she only found out about the Society's dark machinations little by little. She was not in favor of their methods, either."

Hellen said nothing. Tom looked at her, not knowing what to say. Hellen's grandmother had had an affair with the psychopath who thought he was King Arthur? *That's rough. Really rough*, he thought

"But your grandmother *did* help her brother. Father Montgomery was given a new identity and disappeared into the priesthood. He told me that he was the only one to ever get out of the Society alive."

Hellen's head was spinning. Until today, she'd always believed that Father Montgomery had been murdered by AF, most likely by Ossana herself. But now it seemed that the Society of Avalon was involved, and to make matters worse, her grandmother had been mixed up in all of it as well. She'd always wanted to know more about her family's background, had always wanted to find out why her grandmother's amulet had opened doors for them in Valletta when they were looking for the sword, but she had never considered anything like this. Tom was still holding her hands, and it helped her focus on the true reason for their mission. Hellen shook herself and clamped down on her thoughts.

"We're actually here to find out something about an amulet that was in my grandmother's possession until the day she died." Suddenly, something occurred to her. "Father Montgomery even had a sketch of it in his notebook."

"We suspect that it's the amulet of the sorcerer Merlin," said Tom. He raised his hands apologetically. "Yes, I know it sounds absurd, but that's why we're here. We need more information about it, and we had hoped that you and Father Montgomery could help."

The Seraphim nodded, and his eyes grew sentimental. "She used to say that all the time."

Hellen and Tom looked at the man in amazement. "What? What did she say all the time?" said Hellen, who had managed to win back a little of her composure.

"That the amulet—which that terrible man gave her, by the way—was the amulet of Merlin. He always called your grandmother his Morgan le Fay."

His last words left Hellen cold. That was something she did not want to hear. "My grandmother never had . . . I mean, he and she never . . ." she said, her words stumbling.

"Oh, no. Your grandmother ended it soon enough. It was another time, thank God. It was a few years later that she met your grandfather."

Hellen sighed with relief. She wasn't actually related to those madmen, at least. "What else do you know about the amulet?"

"Nothing. Only what I've told you."

"At least now we know for certain which amulet we're looking for. And we've had quite a lot of experience in getting things back that we've already found," said Tom, an unmistakable trace of sarcasm in his voice.

Cloutard, silent until now, spoke up. "We're almost there."

Tom looked at the priest. "Sorry about the shock we gave you back there, but there's a lot at stake. If it's not too much trouble, please don't send the police after us," said Tom, and Hellen gave the Seraphim her most apologetic look.

The man nodded wearily, but there was a look of understanding in his eye. "I'm glad I've been able to get all that off my chest and to have the information benefit those who can use it."

He laid his hand on Hellen's shoulder consolingly. Then his expression darkened.

"What is it, Eminence? Is there something else you can tell us?"

The man closed his eyes and laid his head back. Hellen's muscles tensed again. There *was* something else.

"It's to do with your father," he said, almost inaudibly. "I don't know exactly what it's about. Your great-uncle told me that he disappeared from one day to the next. He was on an assignment, following some plan or other, something big. Your grandmother knew—"

The priest's voice cut off in mid-sentence as his head jerked to the side. Blood sprayed across the back of the car, and the Seraphim, a hole through his head, collapsed sideways. From the corner of his eye, Tom saw the motorcycle racing away.

69

IN THE LIMOUSINE, DRIVING INTO ROME

"WE HAVE TO GET AWAY FROM HERE," SAID CLOUTARD. "IF someone connects us with that shot, we are finished." He acted without waiting for a response, pushing the accelerator to the floor. The limousine raced away, tires screeching.

Hellen was staring into space. The Metropolitan's murder had shaken her, but so had his last words.

Father.

Assignment.

Plan.

Something big.

Those same words rattled through Tom's mind. What could the Seraphim have meant? Did Edward, Hellen's father, have something to do with AF? The idea was not that far-fetched. He and Count Pálffy, who had planned AF's Barcelona attack, had shared history. Pálffy had been Edward's mentor for years, they had worked together on excavations for Blue Shield and they had traveled half the world together—until the day Edward had vanished without a trace.

Tom decided to keep his thoughts to himself for now. He knew he might be on the wrong path entirely, the whole AF mess in recent years was too much, even for him. A few days earlier he'd been close to accusing van Rensburg of being AF's commander-in-chief, and now he was even looking at Hellen's father. Who next? He needed a vacation. Badly. But first they had to find the damned Fountain of Youth. And as for the amulet, they were still getting nowhere.

Hellen, silent for some time, now spoke up: "That my father could be involved . . . it has to be a misunderstanding," she said softly, more to herself.

"*La famiglia* has a safe house on the outskirts of Rome," said Cloutard, changing the subject. "We need somewhere to rest. We have been sleeping in cars and planes for days. We need to sleep in a normal bed and regain our energy, because we are not going to hold out much longer otherwise. We also have to decide what to do next."

Hellen was shocked at the suggestion. She had to process all this new information. "We can't just put our feet up!" she protested.

"Hellen, François is right. We need rest. A tired soldier is likely to become a dead soldier."

Cloutard drove out toward the Parco dell'Inviolatella Borghese, a large park on the northern edge of Rome. Close to the park they drove up to what looked at first glance to be a closed *trattoria*, set back a little from the road. Tom could well imagine what the restaurant was really a front for, but he didn't ask Cloutard any questions—his mafia contacts had helped them out several times already. They pulled up in front of the restaurant and Cloutard went straight to the entrance. He knocked on the door and it opened almost immediately. Cloutard was embraced, and Tom and Hellen were waved inside.

"There is a dead priest in the car. Please take care of it," said Cloutard, and the man hurried outside. Hellen was still sunk deep in her thoughts. "The guest rooms are on the next floor," Cloutard went on. "I am going to lie down for a few hours, *je suis épuisé*. Let us reconvene when we have had a little sleep."

"I couldn't possibly sleep now," said Hellen.

Tom could sense her inner turmoil and helplessness. "You need to rest, too, Hellen. Or you'll fall apart at some point, and that won't help your mother at all," he said.

Hellen knew he was right. "Let me just take care of one thing, please," she said. Tom frowned but nodded for her to go on. "I can't stop thinking of Father Montgomery's notebook, and his sketch of the amulet."

"Where's the notebook now?" Tom asked, sensing a spark of hope.

"At Blue Shield HQ in Vienna. When they transferred me from the hospital in London to Vienna, my things were sent to the office. But you found the Chronicle without the notebook, so I didn't give it any more thought."

"Then let's ask Vittoria to find it and check it out," Tom said.

Hellen was already on the phone. She quickly explained the situation to Vittoria. "Can you scan the sketch of the amulet, please, and run it through every image library you can find? We have to know where it comes from. And call Fábio, Cloutard's friend. He'll be able to help, I'm sure. He'll have access to databases Blue Shield can't reach."

Hellen ended the call and looked at Tom. "Maybe a few hours' sleep isn't such a bad idea," she said. Then she shook her head, took out her phone again and dialed a number. But the call went to voicemail, and she hung up.

"Papa isn't answering. I have to talk to him as soon as I can. I need to know what this is all about," Hellen said. She climbed the stairs wearily to one of the sparsely furnished rooms.

But is that such a good idea? Tom wondered.

70

MAFIA SAFE HOUSE, PARCO DELL'INVIOLATELLA BORGHESE, NORTH OF ROME

THE BRIGHT *PING* OF HELLEN'S CELLPHONE DRAGGED THEM both mercilessly from sleep. Suddenly wide awake, Hellen hastily reached for her phone.

"Vittoria's sent a message," Hellen said, and she kicked Tom in the side. He needed a little longer to wake up.

"And?" Tom murmured, yawning. "What did she find?"

Hellen scrolled through the message. "They found a logo in an image database. It's the same as my amulet."

"A logo? Like . . . of a company?"

"Yes. She found it on a website that's not online anymore."

"How do you find an offline website?" Tom scratched his head and tried to bring some order to his tousled hair— their brief sleep had turned it into a rat's nest.

Hellen had to smile. How could a tough guy like Tom, who could be utterly brutal and merciless to those who deserved it, be so sweet at the same time? In a different situation, she would have jumped him on the spot, but . . . she nipped the thought in the bud. "I'm no Internet expert, Tom, but even I've heard of the 'Wayback Machine.' It's a digital archive of the entire Internet. I read somewhere that they have more than six hundred billion websites already archived in it. It also means you can see what a website looked like years ago—which is particularly useful, of course, if a site goes offline."

"Wow, the things you learn. What website did she find it on?"

Hellen scrolled down, then let out a squeal and held the phone under Tom's nose.

"The Loge of Myrddin—International Grand Lodge of Druidism," he read from the display.

"A Druid order!" Hellen said excitedly.

"Druids? Like the one who mixed the magic potions in the Asterix books?" He thought for a second. "Getafix, with the golden sickle and the mistletoe?"

"Probably not quite like that, but close."

"Druids are still around today?"

"Well, the International Grand Lodge of Druidism apparently still exists, but they don't have anything to do with the old Celtic Druids these days. It's more of an association, like the Freemasons. They trace their lineage back to the 'Ancient Order of the Druids,' which has existed since the Enlightenment. They're all about humanity and human rights."

"But what's the connection to Merlin?"

There was a knock at the door. "*Vous allez bien?*" Cloutard asked through the door. Apparently, Hellen's squeal had woken him.

"All good, yes," Hellen said, and she got up to open the door for the Frenchman.

"Vittoria found something," said Tom. "Getafix is going to give us a hand."

Cloutard frowned. "Asterix is practically a religion in France. One does not joke about it."

"But Tom's right," Hellen said, and she explained what they knew so far.

"Vittoria dug up a membership list for the Grand Lodge of Druidism, and there's no mention of any 'Loge of Myrddin.'"

"Myrddin . . . that is the Celtic name of Merlin, *n'est-ce pas*?"

Hellen nodded. "Oh, Fábio found more on the Dark Web." She scanned further through the message. "Something on an urban-explorers' website."

Hellen grinned at Cloutard, who rolled his eyes. Searching for the Chronicle of the Round Table, he and Hellen had found themselves in a tight spot with some urban explorers in an abandoned hotel. "Not again. I have had more than enough of empty buildings."

"The Loge of Myrddin seems to be based in a castle in the Sainte-Baume region, in the south of France. That's the only clue they could find. According to the website, the castle is called Château du Maître-Mage."

"Castle of the Master Magician," Cloutard translated for the bewildered-looking Tom.

"Which would suit Sainte-Baume nicely," Hellen murmured.

"A little more info, please," said Tom curiously.

"The Sainte-Baume region is where Mary Magdalene was said to have spent her last days, in a hermit's cave. The region still draws pilgrims. And modern druids, too."

"But didn't you say the Druid lodge wasn't connected."

"There are druids and Druids. These ones are from esoteric circles and call themselves shamans or druids."

"Ah. The ones who do fire-walking and stuff like that?"

Hellen nodded, but she had already moved on.

"According to the Dark Web community, the castle isn't empty; it's still inhabited. The photos on various 'abandoned places' websites are apparently just a disguise. The Order still seems to be active, and they still practice Merlin's old magic and rituals."

Tom was on the verge of making another crack about magic potions but decided against it.

Cloutard frowned. "This is a very, very thin lead."

"But it's the only one we have. It's all they could find that connects to my amulet."

"Fábio is a real geek. If he did not find anything else, then nothing else exists."

"Then we see where this thin trail leads, for better or worse." Hellen said. In the meantime, she had opened Google Maps. "Sainte-Baume . . . it's a long drive from here."

"Then we'd better get going," said Tom.

71

SAINTE-BAUME FOREST, THIRTY MILES
EAST OF MARSEILLE, FRANCE

TOM, HELLEN AND CLOUTARD HAD DRIVEN IN SHIFTS during the long journey from Rome and had lost count of how many radar traps they had triggered. The family in Rome had given them a Toyota Land Cruiser to use for the journey. Tom had taken the third shift and was now guiding the car along a narrow forest road that wound its way up to the ridge of the Sainte-Baume massif. Hellen sat beside him. She had punched the GPS coordinates they'd received from Fábio for the Druids' castle into the Maps app and was navigating Tom through the last few miles. It was already after dark.

Dense fog filled the valleys, and clouds had closed over the moon. Their headlights were all the light they had, and they flooded the surroundings in ghostly light.

"*Alors*. From what I can find online, the castle has been empty and falling apart for years. I hope that it really is just camouflage and that we are not driving into a blind alley" said Cloutard.

Hellen nodded. If it really was a blind alley, her hopes were at an end. They had the shield and the sword, certainly, but they had no idea where the amulet could be. Pálffy had taken it from her in Malta, so logically it must now be in the hands of AF. Her only hope was that more than one such amulet existed. Maybe Merlin's followers had all worn one like it, like the rings worn by the Society of Avalon. If this Druid order really used the amulet as their logo, then the château would be the place to find out something about it.

They rounded the last curve slowly, and the path opened into a clearing about the size of a football field.

The castle, in the center of the clearing ahead of them, loomed in the headlights, and their hearts sank. The place was a ruin. Smashed windows, crumbling walls, bushes growing waist-high among the rubble. One of the watchtowers had collapsed, and all the walls and even the impressive main entrance were covered with creeping vines.

Hellen had to work to pull herself together. Tom could see her struggling against her tears. It looked as if they'd run straight into the blind alley Cloutard had just mentioned.

They parked the car at the edge of the clearing and got out. Tom wanted a closer look. He swung the bag containing the shield and sword onto his back and with a flashlight in his hand, he stomped through the tall grass toward the castle. But the closer he got, the worse it looked.

Compared to the reality, the images they had seen of the castle and its surroundings online had been flattering. Cloutard moved around one side of the building with a flashlight of his own. He found a tree that had grown up the wall, its branches digging into the stonework and roots heaving the entire side off the ground. One section of the roof looked as if it had been blown off in a storm; the shingles were broken and strewn across the clearing.

"I can't believe it. We've come so far. It can't be true, damn it." Hellen swore so loudly that a flock of birds in the treetops abruptly flew away. She kicked a rock on the ground in front of her against the large entrance door, mostly covered with ivy and wild grapevines.

Tom and Cloutard looked at her sadly. At that moment, the moon appeared from behind the clouds, and from the corner of his eye, Tom saw it reflect on something on the wall beside the front door. It glinted for a second, then disappeared as the moon was swallowed up again by the clouds.

"What's that?" he said half-aloud, and he swung his flashlight to the place where the moonlight had reflected. As he moved closer, he saw it again. "Hey!" he shouted to the others. "There's something here." Hellen and Cloutard hurried over. Tom had begun tearing the creepers away from the walls to get a closer look at whatever was causing the reflection.

"What have you found?" Hellen said excitedly, a glimmer of hope in her eye again.

"Call me crazy, but I'm pretty sure it's a security camera."

Cloutard came closer and nodded. "*Oui, mon ami. C'est une camera de surveillance.*"

"Hello? Is anyone here?" Hellen began hammering like a lunatic at the entrance, and Cloutard was worried that the rotten thing would fall off its hinges beneath her blows. Unsurprisingly, there was no response. But Hellen wasn't giving up.

"Hello? Is anyone here? Hey, Druids of Myrddin!"

She picked up a stone and used it to continue pounding tirelessly at the door.

"I think the camera just moved," Tom said, and he swung his flashlight onto the small glass panel, behind which the lens seemed to stare out at them.

Astutely, Hellen reached into her bag and took out Father Montgomery's ring. She held it in front of the lens.

"Society of Avalon. Father Montgomery. Seraphim of Glastonbury!"

If Hellen's voice had not been so desperate, rapping out the names like that would have sounded comical, but none of them were in a laughing mood.

"Tom, hold the sword and the shield in front of the camera," Hellen shouted. Tom did it. "Caliburnus and Pendragon's Shingle!" Hellen cried.

Suddenly, they heard a creaking sound. At first barely audible, it quickly grew louder. Hellen stopped banging and shouting. Tom had his flashlight trained on the door and they watched as, inch by inch, it began to open.

72

CHÂTEAU DU MAÎTRE-MAGE, SAINTE-BAUME FOREST

HELLEN DIDN'T HESITATE FOR AN INSTANT AND PUSHED through the gap in the door. Tom tried to hold her back, but quickly realized it made no sense and followed her through. Cloutard also pushed through the gap, and the heavy door creaked closed behind them.

"After driving up that mountain to get here, I did not think it could get any spookier," said Cloutard. "Why do we always have to do these things at night?"

"Oh, come on, you old crook," Tom said. "What could happen? All we're likely to find here is a few old geezers in robes. But here,"—Tom tossed him the sword—"now you can defend yourself properly."

Tom had packed the shield away in his backpack again and slung it over his shoulders. They looked around, the beams from their flashlights sweeping the crumbling masonry. They followed a passageway through to a small inner courtyard. There, too, the condition of the castle did not improve.

As if from nowhere, seven figures in long robes suddenly materialized from the shadows, their hoods pulled low over their eyes. Startled, acting on instinct, Tom reached for his gun, but Hellen shook her head and held him back. Cloutard reflexively raised the sword but immediately felt extremely silly and lowered it again.

The man in the center, presumably the high priest of the order, stepped forward and swept back his hood. A wizened face appeared. Tom had expected a bushy beard and long hair, as he and millions of others had come to expect from sorcerers—from Gandalf to Dumbledore to Getafix, they all looked alike—but this man was bald, and his face shaven perfectly smooth. He could have been sixty years old or ninety, or anything in between.

"Welcome, seekers," he said, spreading his hands wide. "As we have seen, you possess two of the three treasures of the great king," the old Druid said. His voice sounded strange, less like one man speaking and more like the sum of several voices speaking in absolute synchrony, like the chanting of a perfectly rehearsed choir. "Please follow us," he said, and the six others, heads bowed, turned and formed a corridor that led to the shadowy door from which they had probably emerged.

Hellen needed no more convincing, hurrying after the high priest.

"We've come because we're looking for the amulet of Merlin. It used to—" Hellen began, but the high priest interrupted her.

"Patience, my child." He opened the door and ushered their three visitors inside.

A small, circular hall opened in front of them. Torches flickering around the walls offered sparse but warm light.

"Please, sit," the dignified old man said, and pointed to three chairs. Together with the seven for the Druids, they formed a circle, in the center of which was a relief of the order's symbol— the same symbol that had adorned Hellen's grandmother's amulet. The priests closed the door and sat down. Tom, Hellen and Cloutard, looking around curiously, did the same.

"So, you seek the amulet of the Sorcerer," said the high priest, whose high-backed chair was a little more elaborate than the others.

"Yes. As I was about to say, the medallion used to be in my grandmother's possession. We need it to find the Fountain of Youth."

For a moment, a murmur ran through the room. The high priest raised his hand, and his guild brothers fell silent. He gestured to Hellen to go on.

In a torrent of words, Hellen overwhelmed the Druids with everything she felt she had to tell them—the Fountain of Youth, her mother's struggle for life, the shield and the sword and their desperate search for the amulet. She even mentioned the Chronicle of King Arthur. Cloutard, meanwhile, leaned over to Tom and stowed the sword away in his backpack.

The high priest listened in silence to Hellen's muddled explanations. She knew it must all sound completely absurd to him, but she didn't give a damn.

"Many come in search of the Fountain of Youth," the old man began, after Hellen had fallen silent.

"It isn't about youth for us. My mother . . . it's about my mother. She's close to death, and I can't stand to lose her" Hellen said, her voice steadier now.

"You seek the arcanum, then?"

"It really exists? The panacea described by Paracelsus?"

The old Druid nodded slowly. "As I said, many search . . . but few are worthy."

"Worthy?" Tom asked.

"The Sorcerer arranged it so that only a pure soul can collect the waters of the Fountain of Youth."

"So, you mean even if we find the Fountain of Youth and give its waters to my mother to drink, there is no guarantee it will make her healthy again?"

The Druid nodded again.

Hellen looked at Tom in despair.

"We're not just looking for the Fountain and the arcanum to save her mother," Tom said, "but to prevent them falling into the wrong hands. Evil people are also seeking the power of the fountain."

"That is very likely. Humans have searched for it for centuries. But Myrddin knew they would. Our wise master devised a test to determine whether a person is worthy of the power."

73

ROAD TO CHÂTEAU DU MAÎTRE-MAGE, SAINTE-BAUME FOREST

THREE ARMORED, 300-HORSEPOWER SUVs, APTLY NAMED "Scarabees" rolled the last hundred meters at a walking pace. Twenty heavily armed men with state-of-the-art battle gear ran through their final preparations. The weather was on their side. The wind had picked up, and the whistling and rushing all around them in the forest drowned out the crunch of their enormous tires on the forest road.

"Yes, sir. We've located them and we'll be in position in a few seconds. They can't escape . . . yes, the Seraphim is dead, but I don't know how much he revealed. I'll keep you informed," said Tristan. He ended the call and tucked the phone out of sight inside his tactical vest.

The three vehicles came to a stop in the clearing some distance apart. Tristan jumped out of the middle vehicle first, and ten of his men gathered around him.

"You four take the back, you four the flanks, and you two come with me," Tristan ordered. "And don't forget the C4."

Before heading to the front door, he gave a curt signal to the men who'd remained with the vehicles. A man appeared through the top hatch of each and removed the cover from the bank of floodlights mounted on the roof.

"Remember, the sword and the shield are all that matter. No prisoners."

The men nodded and ran to their positions.

A few minutes later, the castle was surrounded. There was no way out.

74

CHÂTEAU DU MAÎTRE-MAGE, SAINTE-BAUME FOREST

"A TEST?" HELLEN'S COURAGE SANK. *WHY WAS EVERYTHING always so damned complicated?* She thought. "What kind of test? What do we have to do?"

The high priest turned to his brothers, and they leaned closed and conferred in low voices.

"The suspense is killing me," Tom whispered.

"Suspense I could live without," Hellen replied softly. "This is all taking far too long. We don't even have the amulet, and now we have to pass some kind of test . . .?"

Hellen's despair was gradually starting to show. She choked back a sob, but quickly pulled herself together again.

After talking with the other Druids for a few minutes, the high priest turned back to Tom, Hellen and Cloutard. "We have decided that your search is just, but the way ahead is difficult," said the old man. He nodded to one of his brothers, who stood and left the room. The wind whistled through chinks in the ancient walls and the torches on the walls flickered wildly. Wood creaked.

"This place is getting spookier and spookier," said Cloutard, looking around nervously.

"What's the matter with you, François?" Tom asked.

"I do not know, but somehow I have a very bad feeling about this. It is as if something terrible is about to happen."

Cloutard's musings were interrupted by the Druid's return. He leaned close to the high priest and handed him a small cloth bag.

"Whether a pure soul resides in you, my child, we will soon discover," the high priest said. He stood up and crossed the circle to Hellen, who also stood up. "I will explain to you step by step how to find the Fountain of Youth. We know the way, but we do not know the starting point. You need to discover that for yourselves."

Hellen sighed again.

"Mark my words precisely. If you make the slightest mistake, you will not find the Fountain of Youth, nor will you ever find your way out of the forest again."

"The forest? Which forest? Fangorn?" Tom asked.

Suddenly, they heard three unexpected sounds in quick succession. With each one, the hall grew brighter. Blinding light poured through the gaps in the boarded-up windows. The Druids, startled, rose to their feet with a scraping of chairs.

"Wagner, I know you're in there. All we want is the shield and sword. Bring them to me and no one has to die," a voice suddenly growled through a megaphone.

"Did I not say, *mes amis*, that you should listen to the old Frenchman now and then? My gut is never wrong."

75

CHÂTEAU DU MAÎTRE-MAGE, SAINTE-BAUME FOREST

"What is that? What's going on?" the old man asked with fear in his voice.

"Those are the men we told you about," said Hellen. "Tell me what you wanted to tell me, quickly, please."

The Druids exchanged anxious looks, but then the high priest focused on Hellen again. He leaned forward and spoke softly into her ear.

Tom and Cloutard, meanwhile, had raced back to the courtyard to try to find out what they were up against. They dashed up the stairs to the watchtower, dilapidated but still standing, and took cover behind the decaying battlements.

"Wagner," the megaphone voice shouted into the night. "Bring me the artifacts and I'll let you all go unharmed."

"Three armored trucks and definitely more than ten men," Tom whispered, risking a quick look.

"You have no chance," the voice continued. "You can't

escape. As you can see, I've come prepared. The castle is surrounded."

"How do I know you'll keep your promise?" Tom called back. He took out his pistol and checked the magazine.

"You have my word of honor."

"Your word of honor isn't worth shit," Tom yelled back. He looked at Cloutard a little wistfully. "I've only got two clips. We won't get far with that," he said to Cloutard. "Our friends in hoods down there aren't likely to be some sort of supernatural ninja Druids, are they?"

Cloutard shook his head. "What now?"

"Honestly? I have no idea. Not yet, at least. Come on, let's get back to the others," Tom said, and they ran back downstairs.

"This is your last warning," Tristan growled through the megaphone.

As Tom and Cloutard reached the courtyard, a bone-shaking explosion rattled the castle. Their car, parked on the edge of the clearing, had exploded. The overcast sky flashed orange-red for a fraction of a second.

"We've got to get out of here somehow, fast. Brice's man is outside with a small army," Tom reported when they were back in the circular room. He stopped and observed Hellen and the Druids.

"Give me your hand, my child," said the high priest.

Hellen did as he asked. He placed his hand atop hers then closed her fingers, so that neither Hellen herself nor Tom or Cloutard could see what he had given her.

"Remember what I told you, every word, and you will find the fountain."

Hellen looked down at her hand. She was taken aback by what she saw, and Tom and Cloutard also saw it immediately: a pale, greenish shimmer emanating from her hand.

The Druid looked at his six brothers, and they nodded as one.

"Have no fear, my child. You are truly worthy," the high priest said, seeing her amazement. "Now come, we can help you escape," he added calmly, and he pointed to the door through which one of the Druids had disappeared earlier.

"But what will happen to you?" Hellen asked, glancing again quickly at her hand.

"Nothing can happen to us, but you have to protect the fountain."

"*Quoi?*" Cloutard suddenly said, staring in disbelief at his phone, where a message had just appeared.

"What is it?" Tom asked, going to him. The Frenchman held it out for him to see.

If you want to survive, central courtyard, now! the message read.

"Who . . . ?"

But that was as far as he got. A deafening and all-too-familiar noise roared over the top of the castle. Tom, Hellen and Cloutard looked at each other and ran. A raging storm blasted them with leaves and dust as they reached the courtyard. The Druids had followed them into the open, and everyone looked doubtfully toward the sky. Above them hovered a black helicopter, and a rope ladder tumbled to the ground beside them.

"Come on, hurry!" Cloutard shouted. He ran to the ladder and waved his friends over frantically.

"But who is it?" Tom shouted over the hellish roar of the chopper.

"I do not know, but it is our ticket out of here," Cloutard answered. He reached for the ladder, but more shots from below forced the helicopter to ascend, pulling the ladder out of his reach. Everyone ducked as more bullets flew at the helicopter from all around the castle.

Tom gazed up at the brightly illuminated chopper—a perfect target for the surrounding soldiers. He didn't hesitate but ran back up the watchtower stairs. From the top, he opened fire immediately, but not at the soldiers— he aimed at the Scarabees' floodlights. For a moment, the soldiers ceased fire, took cover, and refocused their attack on Tom, who dropped into cover behind the battlements. Shards of stone flew around his ears as bullets slammed into the masonry around him.

That gave the pilot, whoever it was, enough time to try again. When Tom saw that Hellen and Cloutard were hanging safely from the ladder, he signaled to the pilot to ascend. Again and again, Tom ducked from cover and shot at the floodlights until he'd taken out the last one. He reloaded. The helicopter gained altitude, dropped its nose, and flew directly toward Tom.

Now Tom targeted the soldiers, emptying his second magazine. When the helicopter was close, he broke cover, ran two steps, and leaped over the side of the tower. Bullets whistled around his ears as his hands wrapped around the last rung of the ladder. The helicopter disappeared into the night.

76

"I'M GOING TO DO THIS ALONE," SAID TOM AS HE CLIMBED out of the car.

"Like hell you will. This is about *my* family," Hellen said, climbing out after him.

"Hellen, it's far too dangerous."

"Dangerous?" Hellen snapped. "Have you forgotten everything we've been through in the last few months? We're going to do this together, as a team." She crossed her arms defiantly.

"I would do what she says, *mon ami*. This is a discussion you cannot win," said Cloutard, and he treated himself to a small sip from his flask.

"Thank you, and that's exactly what I'm talking about: I don't want to lose you." Tom looked Hellen in the eye. "We don't know what's waiting for us out there."

"Out there" was the AF yacht. Ever since the helicopter had materialized overhead at the castle, it had been one thing after another.

"Do you really believe Isaac Hagen's story?" Tom asked Cloutard, looking at him intently and changing the subject. He didn't want to talk about the mission ahead. "You seem to know him better than we do."

"I would not say I 'know' him," Cloutard said. "So far, I have not been able to figure him out. Which would suggest to me that he is telling the truth. He has tried to kill us multiple times, but then again, he has also helped us multiple times. He organized the Chronicle for us, after all, and we cannot forget that he saved our lives at the Druids' castle. But then again, when we swapped the Klimt for the Chronicle, he showed a very different face again . . . honestly, I do not know what to make of him. The fact that Hagen is MI6 is an advantage. It means one less person who wants to wring my neck because of the Klimt."

"If what he told us is true, then I can understand his behavior. It was all part of his assignment," said Tom.

"I don't believe a word he says," Hellen sneered.

"Why not? He wouldn't be the first undercover agent to work his way up inside an organization in order to take it down from the top."

"I just don't believe him. No way is he an MI6 agent. They're the good guys. Do you remember what Hagen's done since we first ran into him on Madeira?"

"Well, 'good guys' is a pretty flexible term," Tom said. "MI6 is about as good or evil as the CIA or Mossad. They do what benefits them, and they don't give much consideration to individual lives."

"My mother could get the truth out of him in five minutes," Cloutard threw in.

"We'll find out soon enough whose side he's on," said Hellen.

"The fact is, he got us the Chronicle," Tom said. "And he saved us from the castle and told us that the amulet is on the AF yacht, which is anchored here just off Monte Carlo. Without him, we'd have no idea where to look."

Hellen nodded. Tom was right.

"I just have a bad feeling about having you along. There's a lot less chance of me being spotted if I'm by myself. There are dozens of armed men on that yacht, and who knows what else," Tom said. He went around and opened the back of the car.

"One more reason for me to come. You'll need backup."

"I have backup. Hagen will be on the yacht," Tom said, although he knew that argument was chancy at best. He opened a small transport case, took out his SIG Sauer P226 and began to clean it.

"Are you two suddenly best friends? I do *not* trust this super-spy Hagen."

"Hellen," Tom began, but Cloutard, still sitting in the passenger seat, caught his eye. The Frenchman only shook his head. Tom turned away with a resigned sigh.

He was silent for a moment, then said, "Okay. But you do what I say, when I say it, understood?"

"Aye, aye, Captain!" Hellen saluted, smiling broadly.

"When was the last time you did any diving?" Tom asked, placing the pistol back in its case.

But before Hellen could reply, François spoke up. "He's here," he said, and he climbed out and joined his friends.

A pair of headlights turned from the street onto the industrial wasteland. Once the headquarters of a thriving freight company, half-ruined shipping containers and the rotting hulks of small boats now gave the place all the charm of a junkyard.

Tom was astonished to see an almost seventy-year-old truck chugging toward them. It was a Saurer M6, off-road capable and used in the past to haul anti-aircraft artillery —a blocky beast vaguely reminiscent of a fire engine, with side panels, hatches, and doors behind which anything could be stowed. The roof was a tarpaulin.

A diminutive Italian man about sixty years of age climbed out of the truck.

"Signore Pedersoli. It's good to see you again," said Tom, shaking his hand.

"Benvenuto, Tom Wagner," the gaunt man said. He removed his hat, which made him look more like an old fisherman than an international arms dealer. He counted several countries' secret services among his customers, but Tom, too, had occasionally made use of his services.

"From what I've heard, you were able to put my equipment to good use at Lake Como," Pedersoli said, smiling at Tom. He turned to Hellen. "And you must be the young woman Tom went to war for back then." He shook her hand. "I'm happy I was able to help."

Hellen smiled, reddening a little. On their search for the stolen holy relics, Guerra had abducted Hellen and held her captive in a villa on Lake Como. Noah had put Tom in touch with Pedersoli, who had fitted him out with all kinds of useful gear.

"A terrible thing, about Noah. I never thought he would change sides. I worked with him at Mossad for a long time. Just terrible," Pedersoli said. He went to the back of his antique truck, opened the rear hatch, and slid out a few drawers on the side.

"Wow!" said Hellen when she saw what he'd brought. The interior was lined with a vast array of military equipment, and dozens of pistols and knives were neatly bedded in foam in the drawers.

"Oh, *mon Dieu*," was all Cloutard managed to say.

"I have everything you ordered. I was even able to rustle up the Zodiac Milpro Futura Commando 470."

"Excuse me, the what?" asked Hellen.

"An FC470 Combat Rubber Reconnaissance Craft," said Tom. "How else did you think we'd get out to the yacht?"

"Again—the *what*?"

"It is an inflatable raft," Cloutard explained.

"Why didn't you just say that to start with?" Hellen said, and she boxed Tom on the shoulder.

"I've also organized some radio-equipped full-face masks." Pedersoli proudly opened another drawer, this one containing three complete scuba outfits in matte black.

"Perfect," said Tom. "Then let's get unpacked."

77

OF THE COAST OF MONACO, MEDITERRANEAN SEA

"I AM STARTING TO GET SICK OF WATER AND CONSTANTLY having to change," Cloutard complained. He was sitting at the back and steering the Zodiac. This time, the Frenchman had had to swap his beloved Brioni suit for a skin-tight neoprene wetsuit. "This thing does not even have enough space for my flask."

Tom and Hellen only grinned and continued checking and adjusting their equipment. They had set off in the dark, launching from the boat ramp at the abandoned company grounds. Pedersoli had given them a quick training session on the diving masks and had helped them load the gear into the boat before they left.

With a GPS unit in his hand, Cloutard guided the small craft across the choppy sea, unhappily wiping the cold seawater from his face at regular intervals.

"Are you sure you want to do this? You can still change your mind," Tom asked. Hellen's face had changed color a little since they left the coast.

"Of course I'm sure. I'm just a little queasy, that's all. The sea's much calmer beneath the surface. I'll be fine."

Tom took her hand and looked into her eyes. "You know I love you, don't you?" he said, and he saw a sudden gleam in her eyes. "I would never forgive myself if anything happened to you on this mission. Remember your promise. If I say 'duck,' you duck. If I say, 'jump overboard,' then you do it, whatever position I'm in."

Hellen tried to say something, but Tom didn't let her. He pressed a finger to her lips. "Promise me."

Hellen placed her hands on Tom's cheeks, pulled him close, and kissed him. "I promise."

"When you two are done making eyes at one another, we should focus on the job," said Cloutard, and pointed toward the horizon.

The massive AF yacht glowed white like an iceberg in the moonlight. They were still a long way from the six-hundred-foot ship when Cloutard stopped the motor and the Zodiac bobbed like a cork on the swell. Tom and Hellen slipped into their air tanks, positioned their masks, and pulled on their flippers. Tom checked the mesh bag a final time—it contained a few surprises for Noah that he'd found among Pedersoli's arsenal. His silenced SIG Sauer P226 and several magazines were stuffed inside his waterproof tactical vest. The SIG was the Navy Seals' weapon of choice, so it would no doubt prove its worth here, too.

Cloutard put on a headset and turned a dial on his radio. "Channel five, can you hear me?" he asked.

Hellen and Tom raised their hands and circled their thumb and finger, signaling "okay."

"Loud and clear," said Tom.

"Yes, sounds good," said Hellen.

"*Bonne chance*. And I want both of you back in one piece," Cloutard said.

"François, you know what you have to do?" said Tom, and the Frenchman gave them a thumbs-up.

Tom and Hellen looked at one another, nodded, and fell backwards over the side of the Zodiac and into the Mediterranean Sea.

78

OFF THE COAST OF MONACO

"Wʜᴀᴛ ɴᴏᴡ?" Hᴇʟʟᴇɴ ᴀsᴋᴇᴅ ᴡʜᴇɴ ᴛʜᴇʏ'ᴅ ᴀᴛᴛᴀᴄʜᴇᴅ and activated the last limpet mine—Tom's surprise for Noah.

"There's a sea-level hatch on the starboard side, near the stern. Behind it there's a small dock for the speedboat and the jet skis. That's where we get in." The last time Tom had been aboard the yacht, they'd brought through that same opening in the side of the ship. He had also been able to memorize some of the yacht's layout as Ossana had escorted him to the upper deck to meet Noah.

"*If* Hagen keeps his word and opens it." Tom could clearly hear the skepticism in Hellen's voice.

"He won't skip out on us. He brought us the Chronicle, remember?"

"Yes, and he got a damn good price for it. I'll only believe he's a good guy when I see it in black and white."

"François told us he's a man of his word."

"Yes, and we need to have a serious chat with him about that. He didn't tell us he was in contact with Hagen for almost a year."

"Yes, we do, but not now," said Tom, and he glanced at his dive watch. "It's almost time."

Hellen and Tom had reached the stern and drifted outside the hatch waiting for it to open.

"Uh, Hellen . . ." Tom asked hesitantly.

"Yes?" Hellen said, looking nervously at her dive watch.

"Before we go in there, I have to ask you something," he said.

"Is it important?" Hellen said. "Hagen's supposed to open the door any second."

"Will you . . ."

But Hellen didn't hear the rest of his words. All she heard through the radio was white noise. "What did you say? There was some kind of interference, I think. All I heard was noise. I didn't understand a word."

Tom clamped his teeth together and sighed. *High-tech equipment worth thousands and thousands of dollars, and it chooses this moment to die on us.*

"I said, will you—"

Just then, part of the hull moved inward, and a huge, double-winged door opened ponderously.

"Well, that's promising," Hellen said, and she was already swimming into the dock when Tom grasped her arm and held her back.

"Before we go in, you have to answer a question for me. We might not get another chance." He took a deep breath. "Will you marry me?"

Hellen stared wide-eyed at Tom through her mask, her face lit by Tom's small flashlight, the only light they had. Tom felt the blood rushing through his veins and thought his heart must be pumping at a hundred and eighty beats a minute, at least. All sense of time vanished. The moment between the question and Hellen's reaction felt like an eternity. Holding each other closely they floated almost motionlessly just below the surface, in the endless dark of the sea. The only sound was the rush of air as they breathed inside their masks.

In the background, ghost-white, the door continued to open, inch by inch.

"Thomas Maria Wagner," Hellen began. "I don't know anyone in the entire world with a worse sense of timing than you. No one else could think of a more inappropriate place to ask me that question."

She stopped speaking but went on staring at him. Their masks were almost touching.

"I love you, and I won't make the same mistakes again . . ." Tom stammered, unsettled.

Still, she said nothing.

"I never should have let you go. You're just—"

Then Tom suddenly saw it, and he stopped in mid-sentence. A single small tear broke from Hellen's left eye and trickled slowly down her cheek. Then her face came to life. Her expression softened, and her eyes became more radiant than Tom had ever seen.

"We're—"

"Oh, shut up, you idiot!" Hellen's answer came suddenly, and a shudder ran through Tom's body.

Without warning, she grabbed his arm and pulled him with her into the dock. They surfaced quickly, and Hellen pulled off her mask before helping Tom out of his. Then she looked deep into his eyes.

"Yes," she said. "Yes, yes, yes, yes, yes!"

For Tom and Hellen, the world stood still for a moment. This was their moment, and no one could take it from them.

79

ABANDONED INDUSTRIAL PARK ON THE BORDER OF MONACO

CLOUTARD SWITCHED OFF THE OUTBOARD AND DRIFTED the last few yards to the dock, then jumped out and began pulling the Zodiac up the ramp. He looked out and saw the small white point—the yacht—glittering on the horizon. Tom was a capable man, but Cloutard was still anxious. Would *they* be able to find the amulet and get out in time? Concerning the last part, Cloutard still had a few things to take care of. His hand moved toward his chest, instinctively looking for the flask containing his beloved cognac, before he remembered that there had been no room for it inside the wetsuit. He sighed. He could have really used a shot of Louis XIII just then. He grasped the handle on the boat and hauled it higher out of the water. Then he grabbed the radio and went around the building, back toward their car. As he turned the corner, he froze.

The back of the car was open. Cloutard stepped back and spied around the corner. Silence. Nothing moved. Where was Pedersoli? He was supposed to be watching the car and the artifacts. At least his truck was still there. Cautiously, Cloutard darted to the car, staying low.

"*Non, non, non,*" he said softly to himself, moving around the car. The back had been broken open and the sword and shield were gone. "*Putain de merde!*" he spat, slamming the rear hatch angrily. He hurried over to Pedersoli's truck, yanked open the driver's door—and the arms dealer's body fell out onto him. Cloutard recoiled in shock and dropped the two-way radio. Pedersoli lay lifeless before him, a bullet in his head. As soon as Cloutard gathered himself again, he picked up the radio. He pressed the "Talk" button. "Abort, abort! It is a—"

But that was as far as he got. A hard blow struck his head and he fell unconscious.

80

Tom and Hellen floated in the middle of the dimly
lit, deserted dock. The kiss lasted a long time, but finally
and with a heavy heart, they broke it off.

"We should get going," said Tom tentatively.

"Yes, we should."

They swam to the dock, peeled off their flippers,
unbuckled their oxygen bottles, and let it all sink to the
floor. Tom retrieved his pistol and they moved slowly up
the steps that led out of the water and onto the landing
stage.

"See? Hagen kept his word," Tom whispered. He was
having trouble staying focused.

"Yes, but where is he? I thought he was going to help us,"
Hellen countered softly, as distracted as Tom.

Tom abruptly stopped and raised his fist beside his head
to signal "stop." Then he pointed to the right to a niche

behind the parked jet skis. They dashed across and took cover.

The doors of the glass elevator slid open and two men with submachine guns stepped out. When they saw the open hatchway, one of them immediately reached for his radio.

Tom moved fast. He stepped out and took both down with targeted shots before either could say a word.

"Come on, help me," said Tom, putting the pistol away inside his vest. Hellen slowly emerged from the recess in the wall. She looked at the two dead men as if in a trance and gulped. She had seen Tom shoot someone dead more than once during their adventures, and yet it astounded her every time just how cold-blooded and precise he could be when necessary. Yes, the men were the foot soldiers of a terrorist organization, but taking someone's life was still anathema to her.

"Hellen!" Tom hissed. "Now!"

They grabbed the two men by their feet and pulled the bodies over the wooden landing stage to the niche where they had just been hiding. Tom pulled the cover off one of the jet skis and threw it over the bodies. Then he pulled out his gun again, moved quickly to the dock's control panel, and closed the outer hatch.

"What now?"

"We can't use the elevator, for obvious reasons," Tom said, pointing to the transparent cabin. "We have to get to the office where Noah met me last time. If the amulet is really on the ship, that's where it'll be."

"Do I hear a trace of doubt?" Hellen teased, but Tom ignored the jab.

"The office is on the top deck," he said, and he pointed to the marble stairway—complete with gold handrails, indirect lighting, and wood paneling—that led upward beside the elevator.

Tom led the way, pistol at the ready, as they ascended the stairs. Just before they reached the next level, Tom stopped and ducked back. The crackle of a radio had warned him. Hellen stopped just behind him. A sentry strolled past on the landing, from which countless doors and passages led in all directions. For a moment, the man paused and looked around. Tom had him in his sights, his pistol pointing at the back of the man's head as his other hand moved toward his knife, but Hellen held him back. She shook her head imploringly. The man moved on and disappeared into a corridor.

When they reached the next floor, they were through the lower decks and now found themselves on the main deck. Five levels to go. In front of them stretched a huge foyer, no less impressive than the lobby of a luxury hotel. Two curving stairways led up to the deck above. In the center of the lobby, a gigantic crystal chandelier hung over two decks, and there was marble, gold, glass, and crystal as far as the eye could see.

They took the last steps cautiously, Tom's eyes cutting left and right.

"All clear," he whispered, stepping into the foyer.

The sound of submachine slides being racked made Tom and Hellen jump. Around them, on the gallery of the floor above, four men appeared, aiming down at them.

81

ABOARD THE AVALON

"WELCOME ABOARD THE *AVALON*." NOAH POLLOCK'S VOICE resonated in the enormous foyer. For a half-second Tom thought about going on the attack, but it would have been suicide. Back-to-back, he and Hellen stood in the center of the room and looked up in dismay.

"Tom Wagner and Hellen de Mey," Noah began. "So happy you could make it. I've been expecting you." Noah opened his hands invitingly as he descended the broad stairway.

Four more guards emerged on the main deck and held them at gunpoint as Noah approached. Tom and Hellen raised their hands.

"No, no. Hands down, please. I'm hurt! You're my *guests*," said Noah. He held out his hand to Tom, who reluctantly handed over his pistol.

"SIG Sauer P226. Nice," Noah said. He unscrewed the silencer and, after a quick inspection, passed it to one of his men. "So you think you're a Navy Seal now? What happened to your Glock?" But Tom ignored him.

"Didn't I say it was a trap?" Hellen whispered, giving Tom an angry glare. "Hagen is a son-of-a-bitch. And you're too trusting."

"This way, please," Noah said, and he nodded toward the glass elevator. His men stepped back. Tom and Hellen entered the elevator, the same one Tom had ridden with Ossana to the top deck. Noah joined them.

The instant the door closed and the elevator began to rise, Tom grabbed Noah by the chin from behind, whipped out a knife, and pressed the blade to his throat. Hellen backed away, startled. But Noah only laughed.

"Tom, what are you doing? There are more than fifty armed men on this ship. You won't get out of here alive, not unless I want you to."

Tom looked around. The glass cabin slowed as it reached the top level, and the doors slid open. They were met by two men, who instantly leveled their weapons at Tom and Hellen.

"Back it up!" Tom snarled. He increased his pressure on the knife. A few drops of blood appeared beneath the blade on Noah's throat.

"Tom, don't," said Hellen. She placed a hand on his shoulder and shook her head, and Tom, reluctantly, let his hand drop.

Noah took the knife from him. At the same time, he signaled to his men to lower their weapons. "We're all civilized people here. We don't have to solve everything with violence," he said as he stepped out of the elevator.

Tom was surprised at this sudden burst of sanity in his former partner, but bit back any commentary. They followed Noah through the double doors into the large penthouse suite.

"Please, take a seat."

"I'd prefer to stand," said Tom. He crossed his arms.

"Put your fucking ass on the sofa!" Noah snapped without warning. He had his back to them and was gazing out into the night. One of the guards grabbed Tom by the shoulders and pushed him down onto the sofa. Hellen sat down, too.

"Leave us alone," Noah said without turning around. He underscored his order with a dismissing wave. When the guards had left, Noah turned around. "I've got to say, I'm impressed. One of these days, you'll have to tell me how you got out of the Wewelsburg. A drink? Whiskey sour, right?"

"Noah, what's going on?" Tom began. "What happened to you? We were friends. We wanted to make the world a better place. But look at yourself."

Tom was angry and full of loathing, wanting to take Noah down . . . but more than anything, he was sad. He pitied his old friend. They had been through thick and thin together, but Noah had betrayed him and switched sides.

"Tom, you still see everything in black and white. The world isn't that simple."

"You can keep that 'fifty-shades-of-gray' bullshit to yourself. You screwed me over. You betrayed everything we stood for, and now you've killed the Pope and hundreds of other people and you're working for the asshole who had my parents killed."

"If you want to change the world, you have to be willing to make a sacrifice or two. But apart from that, I'd ask you to be a little patient before passing judgement on me."

"Oh, sure, but you know what's strange? Somehow, it's always someone else who makes the sacrifice, while you wallow in luxury. I made up my mind about you a while ago now. I was wrong about you."

"People skills were never your forte. Your best friend's a crook, your girlfriend's mother can't stand you, and back when we were with the Cobras, no one took you seriously, no one really saw you as part of the team. You've always been an outsider, and you always will be. Look at yourself. Aside from your talent at blowing things up and causing headaches for everyone around you, you aren't much use to anyone."

Tom looked at Hellen and her smile warmed his heart. He knew Noah was wrong, and Hellen's "yes" to his question was the proof of it. Nothing and nobody could spoil what they had. Tom smiled calmly back at Noah. He felt an inner peace, as if were exactly where he needed to be. No uncontrollable emotions were taking over, driving him to recklessness. He was no longer alone. He had a responsibility—a responsibility to Hellen, his future wife.

A knock interrupted Tom's thoughts. A moment later a

door opened and a guard came in with a box in his hands. "Sir, our divers found these," the man said, and he set the box—containing the limpet mines Tom and Hellen had attached to the hull—on the table.

They shared a look of horror, and any thoughts they had about getting out of there alive vanished.

"Ah," said Noah. "I see you haven't just come for the amulet."

Hellen's eyes widened. "Where is it?" she hissed. "It's mine. It was my grandmother's."

"Hellen, don't be so melodramatic. We're not in a soap opera. Can we act like grown-ups? The amulet never belonged to your grandmother, and certainly never to you. It belongs in the hands of a powerful man, a man who will change the world and who's prepared to make countless sacrifices to guarantee his success—a man who is not only the leader of AF, but someone who has far more power than you can possibly imagine."

Noah's diabolical grin reminded Tom of Jack Nicholson's Joker in "Batman."

"I'm sorry, but it seems you've been misinformed," Noah continued. "It isn't here, or at least, not yet. The leader has it." He checked the time. "You'll have to excuse me, but he will be arriving soon. You haven't earned it, but you're going to get to meet this great man face to face. After that, what becomes of you will be entirely up to him."

Hellen looked at Tom in alarm. She could only guess at how he felt. Very soon, he would meet the man who'd ordered the killing of his parents. And *she* would see the man who ordered the hit on her mother.

Tom's eyes narrowed. His gut told him that tonight, there on the yacht, would be the final showdown. The conflict between them and AF, which had started with the Habsburg diamond affair, would end. What he didn't know was who would be standing afterward.

"Take them below and lock them up. I'll deal with them later," Noah said to the guard.

82

BLUE SHIELD HEADQUARTERS, UNO CITY, VIENNA

VITTORIA RUBBED THE WEARINESS FROM HER EYES. SHE yawned. She'd been sitting and staring at her computer for hours, watching as maps were compared with the pattern Hellen had found on the inside of the shield. She sat up and reached for her coffee cup. It was empty, so she stood up and climbed over Fábio's legs. He had fallen asleep beside her and lay in his armchair with his legs outstretched. Her cup in her hand, she left the office to make herself a fresh brew. She put the cup in the coffee machine and pressed the "triple espresso" button. The machine ground to life. She took the sugar and poured three large teaspoons into the hot drink, hoping it would be enough to revive her. She trudged slowly back into her office, sipping at the cup, when a sudden beeping roused her from her drowsiness. She stopped in her tracks and stared at the monitor from the center of the office for a moment. A large red banner had appeared. "Match Found," it said in large white letters. She scrambled back to her desk, shook Fábio awake, and sat down again.

"Hey, Fábio, we've found something," she said.

"Wh-a-a-a-a-a-t?" Fábio sat up straight, stretched, and let out a long yawn. Then he rubbed his eyes and turned to the monitor.

"The computer actually found a match," Vittoria said. "Look."

She called up the map section and zoomed out a little. They looked at the screen and then at each other.

"So, our magic forest is in France, between Carcassonne and Montségur?"

"Looks like it."

Vittoria reached for the phone and tapped in Hellen's contact. It rang. "*You have reached the voice mailbox of Hellen de Mey*," she heard. A little surprised, Vittoria hung up and checked the time. Then she called Tom's number and waited, which also went to voicemail. She got the same result with François.

"No one there," Vittoria said, and she put the phone aside thoughtfully.

"Sorry to hear you're out of luck," they suddenly heard a female voice say behind them. Startled, Vittoria and Fábio spun around—and stared down the barrels of three pistols. "But your friends have their hands full with other things. They couldn't possibly take a call now. It's doubtful they'll ever be able to again when my boss is finished with them."

"And who would you be?" Vittoria asked acidly.

"Aren't we temperamental? I like that. But who I am doesn't matter," the brunette said in a Hungarian accent. "We are only here to take back what is ours." She looked toward the desk, where the three parts of the Chronicle of the Round Table lay beside the scanner. A nod was enough: one of the men with her took the old leather scrolls and placed them carefully in a flat flight case he'd brought along. "And what do we have here?" Slowly, the woman approached Vittoria and Fábio, keeping her eyes on the monitor.

"Nothing. That's just—"

"Don't insult my intelligence, Ms. Arcano," said the brunette, cool. "It looks to me as if you're one step closer to finding the Fountain of Youth."

Vittoria looked at the woman without flinching. *Who is she? How does she know all this?* she wondered, and she glanced questioningly at Fábio. Fábio, who'd been sitting silently the whole time, spoke up.

"Take what you want and get out of here," he said frostily.

"Easy, big fella," the woman said. After a verifying glance at her men, she put her gun away. She took out her phone and gestured meaningfully at Vittoria and Fábio. Reluctantly, they moved aside and let her reach the desk.

She plugged her phone into the computer, pressed a few buttons, and copied all the data connected to the Chronicle. When she was done, she put her phone away inside her jacket, took out her silenced pistol once again, and fired several shots into the computer before sidling back to her men.

"Tie them up," the woman said, and she left the office.

83

STOREROOM ABOARD THE AVALON, OFF THE COAST OF MONACO

"WE'VE GOT TO FIND A WAY OUT OF HERE," SAID TOM, AND he began searching through the crates and cupboards in the storeroom they'd been locked inside.

"What difference does it make? It's over. We walked into a damned trap, and we've blown any chance we had of getting the amulet," Hellen said angrily. She was sitting on a beer crate, resigned. "We're trapped here, and my mother is running out of time. The doctors only gave her a few more days to live, and those are already up."

"Hellen, trust me. We can do this. We've always worked it out. Besides, we're a real team now." He went to her and took her hands in his. "You and me," he said.

"Team is short for 'Trapped? Expect A Miracle,' which means all we can do is put our trust in François, now," Hellen said.

It made Tom proud to hear something that silly come from her. Unable to find anything useful in the crates, he sat down beside her. "Cloutard would have called out the cavalry by now to come and save our butts," he said.

"If he's in time. And if AF's leader really shows up here, then it's game over for us. Now that we're in his hands, he won't hesitate to kill us."

"You have to look on the bright side. Maybe it really is your father, if what the Seraphim told us was true. Then there's at least a chance *you* will survive."

Hellen looked at Tom and had to laugh. "You know, I keep thinking you've said the dumbest thing that can possibly be said, and you keep outdoing yourself. If we were already married, what you just said would be grounds for divorce. But yes, you're right, that would really be the cherry on top of everything else, wouldn't it?" Her words laden with sarcasm, she said, "Mother's on her deathbed after being poisoned with God-knows-what on the orders of my father, the international terrorist kingpin." She looked at Tom and hesitated for a second. "And you can't forget: if that's true, then my father also ordered that your parents be killed."

They looked at each other for a moment, then both shook their heads.

"No way. Neither of us really thinks Edward is behind all this."

"Of course not," said Hellen, and she leaned against Tom, who put his arm around her.

They sat in silence, but separated like teenagers caught making out moments later when the door was unlocked. But they could only watch in disbelief as two guards dragged in Cloutard's unconscious body and dumped him at their feet. The door closed again.

"So much for teamwork," Hellen sighed.

They set to work trying to wake their friend. Finally, a sharp slap in the face from Hellen got him to open his eyes.

"*Où suis-je, que s'est-il passé?* Where am I? What happened?" he murmured.

"You're alive. That's the main thing," said Hellen.

"What happened to you?" Tom asked.

"I returned to the ramp . . . there was . . . Pedersoli is dead," Cloutard stammered brokenly. He probed gingerly at the back of his head, where he'd been struck. Then he was suddenly wide awake. "The artifacts! They have the artifacts!"

Hellen looked from Cloutard to Tom. Panic rose inside her and she turned chalk-white. She sank awkwardly to the floor. It was really over now. They'd lost everything. Even Tom, subdued, leaned against the wall.

84

BELOW DECKS ABOARD THE AVALON, OFF
THE COAST OF MONTE CARLO

"WHERE'S 007 WHEN YOU NEED HIM?" HELLEN ASKED
after the three had sat in silence for a while and digested
their defeat. They'd been locked in their makeshift cell
for more than an hour now.

Tom paced back and forth like a panther in the small
room. "If Hagen is really what he claims to be, and if
Noah found out, then we have to assume he's dead," he
said.

"That doesn't sound particularly inspiring," Hellen said.

"*Merde*," Cloutard swore. He'd tried yet again to pick the
lock but failed. "If Sister Lucrezia saw me now, she would
be very disappointed," he said, and he sat beside Hellen
on the floor.

"Now we're the ones who will need a miracle if we're
going to get out of here alive," Hellen murmured. "But
I'm afraid we used them all up in our last few
adventures."

"At least we will not die of thirst," Cloutard added, taking a bottle of beer from the crate.

A commotion in the corridor made them sit up. Once again, a key rattled in the lock.

"Quick, pass me a bottle," Tom whispered, positioning himself behind the door. It swung open and one of the guards tumbled inside, unconscious. Hellen, Tom, Cloutard turned to see the battered face of Isaac Hagen.

"What are you waiting for, an engraved invitation?" Hagen said, taking the guard's submachine gun.

"Thanks. I was starting to fear the worst," said Tom, taking the pistol from the unconscious man's holster. "What happened to you?" he asked, taking a closer look at Hagen's injured face.

"They caught me when I was opening the hatch and interrogated me. When they finally left me alone, I managed to get free."

"See? He didn't abandon us," said Tom, looking directly at Hellen. "You're always so distrusting," he needled.

"This way," said Hagen.

"No, we have to go up," Hellen protested. "We need the artifacts and the amulet."

"Maybe. But for now, this is the way. We have to do a little scouting first."

A little later and one deck higher, they reached a corridor with a door at the far end. Hagen produced a keycard and placed it on the card reader on the wall beside the door.

"You think that'll work?" Tom asked, watching back down the corridor, guarding their rear.

"I don't think they've erased me from the system yet. They were far too busy dancing a tango on my face." Hagen placed his hand on the scanner, and the subsequent buzz made them all breathe easier. Hagen pulled open the door and moved through swiftly.

"Hallelujah," said Tom, entering the control room last. "Just like at Wewelsburg."

Computers as far as the eye could see. Hagen was already sitting at one of the terminals and tapping furiously at a keyboard. "We have to hurry. The tech guys could show up for their shift any minute."

"What are you doing?" Hellen asked.

"First, I want to put as much evidence as I can onto a hard drive. And second, from here we can see the entire yacht." He pointed to the huge monitor on the wall. A grid showing dozens of surveillance cameras appeared. Tom, Hellen and Cloutard gazed up at it.

"Camera thirty-seven," Tom said, and he pointed to one of the top rows. Hagen zoomed in on the feed from camera thirty-seven until it filled the screen. It was the camera monitoring the helideck. In the pale light of dawn, they could see a helicopter approaching from the distance.

"That has to be the leader," said Tom, studying the image. Suddenly, Noah appeared at the edge of the screen and waited. When the black helicopter landed, Noah, ducking slightly, ran to it and opened the side door. Two men descended the extending steps to the deck. With a deep, submissive bow, Noah greeted the man exiting the helicopter.

Tom, Hellen and Cloutard looked at each other in dismay.

"It can't be," said Tom.

85

CONTROL ROOM, ABOARD THE AVALON

"Where did they go? We need another angle," Tom said, clawing impatiently at the back of an empty chair when Noah and the leader vanished from camera thirty-seven.

"Just a sec." Hagen switched back to the overview screen.

"There," Cloutard said. "Number thirty-three."

"Is that really . . .?" Hellen whispered. Her voice was weak.

"It certainly is," Tom gritted out. "Who else would Noah be sucking up to? The commander-in-chief of AF is—"

"Berlin 'the Welshman' Brice," Cloutard said, finishing Tom's sentence and inhaling deeply.

Tom looked steadily at the monitor. So he'd been face-to-face with the man responsible for his parents' deaths countless times in the last few months. He'd even worked with him. "Are you seriously telling me we spent weeks jetting halfway around the world with that asshole, and that I even went to him directly for help? He shot Ossana dead, his own foster daughter, just to avoid blowing his cover."

"Let's not forget that he tried to detonate a nuclear bomb in Europe," Cloutard threw in.

Hellen laid a hand on Tom's shoulder, but he drew away convulsively. He racked the slide on his pistol and stormed back to the control room door.

"Tom, don't!" Hellen called after him. He stopped.

"She's right," Hagen said. "There's not much you can do by yourself. We have to do this together."

"Wait, look at this," said Cloutard.

Tom turned back. "Can we get sound on this?"

An image from another camera now filled the monitor. The image showed the leader's office. Tristan stood beside the door to the outside deck while Noah mixed a drink. He handed it to Brice, who was staring out the window into the distance. He took a swig from the glass, then set it on the desk. From inside his shirt, he lifted out the amulet, which he was wearing on a chain around his neck.

"My grandmother's pendant," Hellen whispered.

Hagen looked up from his terminal for a moment and watched the scene.

Brice placed the amulet on the desk in front of him, where Excalibur—the Holy Weapon—and King Arthur's shield already lay. He sat down and took another swig from the glass.

"Where's the sound?" said Tom impatiently. "We need to hear what they're saying."

"Sorry. The camera doesn't have sound," said Hagen. "But I'm done here. We can go."

"Then let's finish this," said Tom, striding swiftly back to the door.

"Wait. Let me go ahead. I know my way around here," Hagen said. He slipped the hard drive inside his jacket and grabbed the submachine gun.

In single file, they crept down the corridor to the stairway in the foyer, Tom again bringing up the rear. At the end of the corridor, just before they reached the foyer, they stopped.

"How are we going to do this?" Tom asked.

"Just before they snatched me, I was able to call for reinforcements," Hagen said. He checked his watch. "They should be here any minute."

"Sounds good. Then we should wait," Tom said. "We might just have a chance."

Hagen nodded.

They didn't have to wait long. In the distance, they heard the roar of approaching helicopters. Suddenly, a shot rang out from one of the decks above.

86

LEADER'S OFFICE, ABOARD THE AVALON, OFF THE COAST OF MONACO

From one second to the next, all hell broke loose aboard the yacht. The rattle of machine gun fire. Screams. Chaos. Dozens of guards ran up to the outer deck, ignoring Tom and the others completely.

"It's now or never!" Tom yelled, and he sprinted up the curving stairs.

"Damn, Wagner's really insane," said Hagen, and he went after him. Hellen and Cloutard did their best to keep up. They ran up the stairs to the top deck, ducking flying bullets and ricochets. When they reached the office, Tom kicked in the double doors and charged inside.

The scene that he found inside was confounding. Brice sat at his desk, staring into space. He didn't move a muscle. Tristan was lying dead on the floor, the contents of his cranium decorating the panorama window. Noah was standing in the middle of the room with Tom's SIG Sauer in his hand.

"*Putain de merde*," Cloutard gasped when he stepped into the room.

"Drop it," Hagen snarled at Noah, who immediately let the pistol fall to the floor.

"Tom. You're right on time. I've got a present for you."

Tom, who still hadn't worked out what was happening, swung his gun toward him. "What's going on here?"

"Allow me to introduce the leader of Absolute Freedom. This is the man who was pulling the strings in Barcelona, the man behind the plans for the El Dorado gold, the man to blame for murdering the Pope—and for murdering your parents, too," said Noah, and he pointed at Berlin Brice, who sat in his opulent executive chair with wide, staring eyes.

"What's wrong with him?" asked Hellen, who had noticed that something about Brice was off.

"How observant of you, Hellen. I mixed a little something very special into the poor man's drink. He's paralyzed from head to foot. He can't speak, either, but he can hear every word we say. Also—and this is far more important —he can feel everything. His senses are a hundred times more acute than normal."

Tom looked Noah in the eye and was suddenly completely at a loss. But he kept his gun on him. "Why are you doing this, Noah?" he asked softly, more to himself than anyone else.

87

LEADER'S OFFICE, ABOARD THE AVALON

Tom looked intently at Noah, whose smile was bitter. Hellen had moved up beside Tom, now. She could easily imagine the emotional turmoil he must be going through. His arms sank and then he suddenly raised them again, over and over. His fingers clenched the pistol tightly. Cloutard face was also worried. No one knew what was going on. In the background, the sounds of battle between the MI6 agents and the AF guards faded into the background.

"Why am I doing this?" Noah began, and he paced back and forth slowly and deliberately. "That's a good question. Why do people do the things they do? Pick one of the seven deadly sins and you have your answer. In my case, though, the question isn't quite so easy to categorize. Why, for example, did I betray you and switch sides? Well, if you recall, you were mostly to blame for that. It was your naïve recklessness that sentenced me to life in a wheelchair, after all. And when I got the chance to walk again, I took it, simple as that."

"That's it?! I was your partner . . . your friend!" Tom cried. He took a step toward Noah, jabbing the pistol forward as if it were a sword.

"We were all your friends," Hellen said, and for a moment laid a hand on Tom's shoulder. Tom struggled to regain control of himself, and Noah went on.

"Were we friends? Really?" He turned away and stalked through the room, gesticulating as he went. "I used to be like you. And then, all I could do was sit and watch while you ran around having all the fun while I sat behind my desk, decaying slowly. But suddenly, when I started working for AF, I felt good again. For a little while, at least. I felt like I was in the right place. People were finally taking me seriously, I had responsibilities, I was accepted . . ." Noah slapped both his thighs and gripped them tightly, ". . . and I will be eternally grateful to this man for getting me out of that fucking wheelchair."

He took several long strides back and forth, as if to show how well his legs worked.

Tom looked at his former friend. Slowly, unstoppably, a deep pain rose inside him. His grip on the pistol slackened. He'd had no idea how Noah felt after he'd been confined to a wheelchair because of Tom's mistake. He could hardly imagine the bitterness of a man suddenly relegated from being one of Mossad's top agents to life as a desk-bound IT specialist.

"Finally, I was myself again. I was stronger than ever before." Noah balled both fists until his knuckles cracked. "And I had power I'd never had. I could really make things happen. The leader gave me a mission, and at the same time he gave my life new meaning. It was worth something again."

Hellen shook her head slightly, and Tom raised his eyebrows incredulously.

"I'm not asking you to understand. No one ripped the ground out from under your feet." Noah dismissed his own last words with a wave and was silent for a moment. He went on: "But what matters far more is that you were never able to find out AF's true master plan. The organization chose to call itself Absolute Freedom for a reason. We're not some terrorist organization out to spread fear and chaos, carrying out random attacks around the world for money or more power, and you can forget any religious goals. We have a far more noble calling. But as with everything in life, you have to—"

Tom interrupted him. "Don't say a single word about making sacrifices. My uncle? Did he have to give his life so you could walk again? Or my parents? Did they need to be sacrificed to ensure peace in the Middle East? And what about all the rest who've died because of you and this idiot's desire to be an arch-villain?" he said, pointing at Brice. "Were they all just sacrifices to this psychopath's Great Plan? The fact is, he, you, and thousands of other megalomaniacs all through history still haven't understood the concept of 'making sacrifices.' We owe the gods nothing. The only debt we owe is to ourselves and our fellow human beings." Tom's voice was cutting. Everyone in the room could feel the flint in his words, his icy glare, his emotional coldness.

"How's the air up there on your high horse?" Noah said. "But I know you're not interested in global politics, social injustice, or any of the other things that are going to hell on our planet, to say nothing of actually understanding them. Then again . . ." Noah let out a laugh, somewhere between malice and despair. "Then again, it must be clear even to you that things can't go on as they have been. Humanity is spreading like a cancer. The only thing it strives for is growth. More. Higher. Faster. Further."

The twisted look on Noah's face made Hellen shudder. She pressed close to Tom. Even Hagen, who'd seen a lot in his career, was looking at Noah in horror, even a little fear. Noah's emotions were spilling over.

"We're working overtime to destroy ourselves. Plundering the earth's resources, wasting energy, overpopulation, over-aging, economic growth at any price. And politicians everywhere look on and don't lift a finger. And why? Because they want to be re-elected. Because they don't want to lose anything. They think of themselves, nothing else."

"Noah, you can't be serious. You can't tell me that AF did all it's done to save the world."

Noah's posture and expression suddenly changed. Tom's words seemed to have flattened him, like a steamroller. He suddenly grew meek. His insane, rapturous expression vanished instantaneously, and he looked withered, defeated. For a moment, he buried his face in his hands, and a bottomless desperation seemed to take hold of him.

"I believed it. I actually thought we could do it."

"That you could do what? Save the world?" Hellen said now, practically spitting the words.

Noah rubbed his face with his hands and nodded silently. "Yes. I really believed it."

Though Cloutard, Hellen and Tom deplored what Noah had done in the last two years and the atrocities he'd committed in AF's name, they couldn't help feeling a little pity for him now.

"I'm tired. I'm tired of all the violence, tired of all the intrigues. Tom, you were right. I realized too late what I'd gotten myself into. AF is bigger and more powerful than we ever thought. And I saw too late that *he* . . ." he pointed with an outstretched arm at Brice ". . . is a megalomaniac. He, the commander-in-chief of Absolute Freedom. He, the Welshman. And King Arthur."

Tom spluttered and burst out in a fit of coughing. He looked at Hellen and Cloutard—on them, too, Noah's last words had had a similar effect.

"Excuse me, what did you just say?" said Tom, shaking his head suspiciously. "He thinks he's who?"

Noah looked at Tom. "What do you mean?"

"I thought I just heard you say that Brice here was King Arthur."

"He is. The Society of Avalon is an AF cell, and my wonderful boss here has a weakness for anything Arthurian, which is why he presided over it personally," Noah said. "Why do you think this ship is called the *Avalon*?"

"*Vous aussi, mon Dieu,*" said Cloutard.

"This just keeps getting better," Hellen added.

"It's true. And who knows who else he thinks he is . . . God, maybe?" Noah joked. He was standing behind Brice now and patted him on the shoulders. Brice's eyes stared intently at Tom. Noah moved around to the side of the desk, leaned on the desktop, and lowered his head. He shook himself and laughed bitterly. "But you know what the real irony is? All I did was put myself in another, metaphorical, wheelchair. Except that this time I couldn't steer it myself. And now it's not about my legs anymore, but about my life."

Hellen took a step toward Noah and wanted to say something, but Tom held her back.

"Let him talk, Hellen," he whispered.

Noah straightened up again and turned away. "My life's a mess. I've murdered for Mossad. I've spread terror around the world for AF. I doubt there's a place for me in Paradise, and I wonder whether they'll even take me in hell."

His voice broke as he spoke the last words, and he turned away from them and gazed out over the sea. He was completely drained. Slowly, as if it demanded super-human strength from him, he turned around and looked at Tom.

"And then I was tasked with planning your murder. I was supposed to kill Tom Wagner. And something in me fought back."

He moved toward Tom, who stiffened. He was ready for

Noah to fly at him any second. He distrusted him as deeply as he could distrust anyone. But nothing like that happened.

"I'm a lost soul. I've done everything wrong with my life. And for once I want to do something right. I want to set the world free." He turned away again and went back behind the desk, where Brice still sat motionless, panic in his eyes.

"Noah, it's over. You can't free anyone anymore, least of all yourself," Hagen said. "Your men are dying or being arrested as we speak, whichever they choose. The only question is, which path will you choose?" Hagen still had his gun on him and took a step forward.

"The path of survival, of course," Noah said, and he stopped behind Brice's chair. "Before you take me in, there's one small thing I have to do. Let's call it the first step toward restitution." He patted Brice's shoulders again. The leader's eyes twitched back and forth in panic. "I admit, it isn't completely selfless. The depths to which this man would go taught even me to be fearful and cost me countless hours of sleep."

"What is it you want?" Tom asked.

"I want to give you the chance to take revenge on the man who ordered your parents' murder. At the same time, you'll be freeing the world of evil incarnate."

Tom stared at Noah incredulously. Seconds passed. Tom realized that he was no longer aiming his pistol at Noah, but at Brice. For a brief moment, he toyed with the idea of simply pulling the trigger. His finger curled repeatedly around the trigger.

"Tom," Hellen said gently. "He isn't worth it."

"No. He really isn't." Tom lowered his gun and turned away. "You're out of your mind."

"Oh, Tom. This is what you've always wanted. Just look at the state you were in when you sent Guerra to meet his maker back in Barcelona."

"If you think I'm going to shoot a defenseless man in cold blood, then you're really on another planet."

"You don't have to shoot him in cold blood. His senses are so wired by the drugs than any pinprick will feel like he's been run through with a sword." Noah dug his fingers into Brice's shoulders, and Brice's eyes conveyed only too well what he was feeling.

Tom was stunned, speechless.

"He isn't going to torture him, and he certainly isn't going to kill him," Hellen said, looking at Tom. "Brice is going to help us bring down the rest of his organization."

"Ah, we're taking the high road, are we? Tom, this is a refreshing twist. I wouldn't have expected it from you. But you know what? Then I guess . . ." Noah leaned down to Brice and pinched his cheek, then looked up at Tom, Hellen and Cloutard with a diabolical grin and said, ". . . I'll just have to free the world myself."

The crack as Brice's neck broke shook all of them to the bone. With a swift, skilled twist, Noah had snapped the helpless man's neck.

Tom reacted first, but he was too late. He leaped across the desk and dragged Noah to the floor. Noah didn't even try to defend himself. He only laughed. Tom turned him onto his back and his hands closed around Noah's throat. All he had to do was squeeze. But he knew he wouldn't do it.

"Come on, Tom," Noah gurgled, urging him to do it. "End it!"

"Sorry to disappoint you, but we're taking the high road, remember? Besides, we still have a lot of questions for you about AF—first of all, who's in the next level down. Now that you've killed Berlin Brice, you're going to have to do the talking."

Noah closed his eyes and Tom could see tears tracking down the sides of his face. "I'll tell you everything," he said, his voice faltering. "Everything I know."

88

EASTERN PYRENEES, FRANCE

Tom stared ahead like a zombie as he steered the Jeep Renegade along the narrow forest road. So much had happened in the last few days. It was a lot to process. And, of course, they still had a goal: the Fountain of Youth had to be found. But as tough as Tom was, what he'd learned on the yacht was not easy to digest. Berlin Brice, the man responsible for the death of Tom's parents, was dead, and for a long time he'd been practically under Tom's nose. Noah, who'd gone from being a friend to an enemy, and now back to a friend—of sorts—had been taken into custody by Hagen's MI6 colleagues. His fate was uncertain. Tom had a pretty good idea what MI6 would do to him in order to extract everything they needed about AF and its followers. He caught himself sympathizing with Noah, at least a little. He looked across to Hellen, slumped in the passenger seat beside him. She, too, was staring off into emptiness. Her mother was at death's door, and she had still had no opportunity to talk to her father. The affair the Seraphim mentioned was hanging over her head like the Sword of Damocles and was obviously eating at her.

But they had no time to brood. They had flown out with the Avalon's helicopter as soon as the ship was under MI6 control. Now that they had all three artifacts—the sword, the shield, and the amulet—they could enter the magic forest that the Chronicle and the Druids spoke of. Aided by Vittoria's research, at least now they knew where to start. They had transferred from the chopper to the Jeep at Carcassonne Airport for the drive to the heavily forested region in the foothills of the eastern Pyrenees, to the place Vittoria had marked on the map.

"The area fits perfectly," said Hellen. "It's exactly what I'd expect. Carcassonne and Château de Montségur have always been mystical places: the Catharist heretics, the Albigensian Crusade, and all the conspiracy theories about the Templars and the Priory of Sion have their roots here. I didn't know Merlin had made it this far, but with all the Arthurian stuff we've experienced so far, I don't think anything can surprise me now."

"Are you sure?" Cloutard murmured from behind. "I mean, we are driving to a *magic* forest, are we not?"

Cloutard had made himself comfortable on the back seat. He had his hat pulled low over his face and was in the middle of a nap—well-deserved, after the exertions of recent days.

"I'm awfully glad we scanned the entire Chronicle and stored it in the cloud before that Katalin woman showed up at headquarters. The damage she did was effectively zero."

"Yeah, that could have been a real disaster . . . but you should try to get a little rest yourself," Tom said quietly. "We've got at least two hours to go."

"I'm all right," said Hellen, but her voice betrayed her. She was at her limit, just as Tom and Cloutard were. But at least there a little fresh hope now—they were closer to finding the Fountain of Youth, closer to a miracle for her mother.

"What about you?" Hellen said. "How are you handling it, knowing that the man who killed your parents has finally paid for it?"

"Honestly, I can't really say. It doesn't bring Mom and Dad back. Don't get me wrong. I'm glad AF has been destroyed. I'm glad Noah's in custody and that the world is a little bit safer. But I'd made my peace with all of that when Guerra died. It was only in the last few days that everything came to the surface again when I found those papers in the Wewelsburg. I feel different, I guess, but I can't say yet if it's really an improvement." He looked at her. "But I'm looking forward to our future together."

Hellen returned his smile, although there was some pain in it, too. "It's the same for me. Once we're over this last hurdle and have saved my mother's life, we can finally breathe easily again. We can stop constantly looking over our shoulders."

Her eyes returned to the amulet and the stone given to her by the high priest, which she held in her hands. Absently, she let the pendant her grandmother had given her slide through the fingers of her left hand. The bulbous amulet, one side of which was emblazoned with a Maltese cross, had countless small holes in its surface. She recalled how she had shone Tom's flashlight on it at the grave of Grand Master Jean de la Cassière in Valletta, how it had shown them the way they had to go and led them to the Sword of Peter, also known as Excalibur.

She hefted the polished green stone from the Druids in her right hand. A faint, mysterious green light pulsed from it, or seemed to. As she observed the faint shimmer, her eyes lost their focus.

"The light of God

Is the beginning

And the end."

The voice of the Druid, like many voices speaking at once, reverberated in her head. And then it came to her. She finally understood his first clue.

89

EASTERN PYRENEES, FRANCE

"THE PENDANT SHOWED US THE WAY!" HELLEN SUDDENLY cried. "Remember in Valletta, when we shone your flashlight through the amulet and the Grand Master's coat of arms appeared? It actually showed us which way to go."

"Yes, but . . .?" said Tom. "You think it'll do it again?"

"Yes. Because the Druid gave me clues about how we can find the Fountain of Youth."

"Why do these old guys always speak in riddles? Imagine if your car's GPS explained the route like that? Why didn't he just tell you straight out?"

"*Mon ami*, you are acting as if this is your first search for a lost artifact," Cloutard murmured from the back seat, woken by Hellen's outburst. "People used to tick a little differently than we do today. And sometimes, that was a good thing."

Hellen placed the stone in her lap and focused all her attention on the amulet.

"I've tried for years to open this amulet, you know. I've failed every time. But it *must* open, I'm sure of it," Hellen said. She turned the pendant in every direction, examining every detail. "I just don't get it," she said, and dropped her hands into her lap. When the amulet touched the stone already there, the stone flared brightly for a moment.

They heard a click, and Hellen looked up at Tom.

"What is it?"

"It's opened. The stone . . ." Hellen said, and she opened out the two halves of the amulet to reveal a recess carved out inside it: the negative of a very specific shape.

"The light of God

Is the beginning

And the end."

"That was the first clue the Druid gave me," Hellen said, her voice trembling. "'The light of God.' Do you see it? It was the stone from the meteorite, the skystone, the one that helped us on our search for the Grail. Light played a part in that, too."

Tom raised his eyebrows as Hellen picked up the stone and placed it in the hollow inside the amulet. The glow intensified, and they exchanged excited looks. The green light from the stone poured through tiny openings in the amulet. Hellen held her hand in front of it and looked at the pattern it cast on her palm. From one side, it projected the Grand Master's coat of arms, on the other just a collection of green dots.

"Stop the car!" Hellen yelled.

Cloutard almost fell off the back seat when Tom hit the brakes. "*Que s'est-il passé?*" he said, sleep-drunk.

Even before the car had come to a complete stop, Hellen opened the door and jumped out, ran around, and opened the back of the Jeep. Tom followed her.

"What are you doing?" he asked.

She took out the oversized backpack in which they were carrying the shield, pulled it out and laid it on top of the pack with its back upward. "You'll see in a minute," she said, and she held the glowing amulet over the shield. Countless green dots were projected onto the pattern of lines on the shield. "Now I understand why the Druids couldn't tell me the exact starting point. You need the amulet to find it," Hellen said, elated.

Adjusting the angle and distance with her arm, she aimed the green points of light at the ends and intersections of the numerous lines until they matched perfectly.

"*Fantastique*," said Cloutard, who had joined them in the meantime and stood yawning and rubbing his eyes.

"Wow!" was all Tom managed to say.

"There! That's where we start," Hellen said, and she pointed to one green dot that glowed larger and brighter than the others. She hung the pendant around her neck, then took her iPad out of her backpack and called up the maps of the area that Vittoria had sent. "Here! Here is the 'beginning and the end,'" she said breathlessly, and she placed her finger on the map.

90

FOREST, EASTERN PYRENEES, FRANCE

HELLEN WAS TOO EXCITED TO EVEN THINK ABOUT SLEEP during the rest of the drive. The map showed a remote point at the end of the barely passable forest track.

Tom stopped the car. "This is as far as we can go," he said. "François, time to wake up." He shook Cloutard, who'd fallen asleep again as soon as they had moved on, until he woke up, then went to the rear of the Jeep and grabbed the backpack containing the shield and sword and slung it onto his back. He checked his pistol, pushed it into its holster, and snapped the holster to his belt. Then he took a large bag out of the back and tossed it to Cloutard, who was stretching his weary bones. "Here. Don't expect me to carry everything. From here out, we have to go on foot."

Cloutard looked at Tom in horror as he shouldered the bag. "My God, Tom, what is in here? Gold bars? Lead? Bricks?"

"Just a little while ago, you said I was acting as if I'd never searched for ancient artifacts before. We've been through a lot just in the last few days, and I want to be ready for anything. The clock's ticking and we're probably only going to get one chance. So you get the honor of carrying the gear."

Cloutard snorted, but he knew Tom was right.

"Got everything?" Tom asked. Hellen nodded and patted her own backpack.

"It does not look very welcoming," Cloutard said as they looked ahead down the narrow path that vanished into the dark, tangled undergrowth.

"Belize, when we found El Dorado, was inviting and civilized by comparison. I didn't know an ancient forest like this still existed in Europe," Hellen agreed. "Certainly not anything as dense and grim-looking as this. It's like night in there."

Hardly a ray of sunlight managed to penetrate the greenery overhead. Centuries-old trees loomed two hundred feet high and fallen branches created an obstacle course between the densely packed trunks. The path was hard to make out beneath the foliage, bushes, and fallen trees, and even harder to follow.

"Which way?" Tom asked.

"The starting point only marked one of the lines on the map, so I'd say we just follow the path and see where it leads. There's nothing else we can do right now."

"Okay. Then let's go," said Tom, and he climbed over the first fallen tree trunk and stomped off down the trail. Hellen and Cloutard followed close behind.

About an hour later, they came to a fork in the path. They stopped. The forest around them had hardly changed. If anything, it had gotten even denser, more impassable, and spookier.

"If it wasn't for this fork, I'd have sworn we'd already passed this way. Somehow, everything here looks the same," said Tom. He pointed to a fallen tree and a moss-covered boulder beside it. "We passed something exactly like that twenty minutes ago. The only difference is, now there's a fork that wasn't here before." He scratched his head.

Hellen nodded.

"Very true," Cloutard agreed. "Everything does look the same. But we cannot have walked in a circle, with the fairies building a fork in the path in the meantime, could we?" He did not sound as if he completely believed what he was saying.

"Probably not," Tom agreed.

Dust and pollen danced in the golden rays of the afternoon sun that, here and there, managed to pierce the canopy.

"When this is all over, we are going to discuss my role here," Cloutard puffed, putting down the heavy bag.

"Do you still miss your Brioni? Those overalls you got from Hagen really suit you."

"Yes, in fact, I do. At least I have a hat, but that is not what I mean. I am more the brains than the brawn. Besides, I think I am getting a little too old for this." Cloutard took off his hat and wiped the sweat from his brow. "Well, Hellen, what now? What was the Druids' next clue?"

91

FOREST, EASTERN PYRENEES

"Avoid the bears,

For only from the dragon's mouth

Flows the blood of the fallen knight

To guide you to your goal."

TOM AND CLOUTARD LOOKED AT HELLEN DUBIOUSLY.

"Have you been sneaking Cloutard's cognac?" Tom asked.

"What can I tell you? Those were the Druid's exact words," Hellen said. She was as much at a loss as her friends.

"'Avoid the bears'? Does that mean there are bears here?" Cloutard heard a cracking sound behind him and spun around.

"There must be all kinds of animals here. Probably even werewolves," Tom said with a smile. He leaned toward Cloutard and made claws with his hands. "*Loups-garou*, François!"

"That is not funny at all," said Cloutard, looking around.

"What does the GPS say? Are we still on course?" Tom asked.

Hellen took out her handheld GPS, where she had uploaded the rudimentary map engraved on the shield and overlaid it with the actual area and turned it on.

"What the hell?" she muttered, and she knocked impatiently at the display. "Look at this," she said, passing the handheld to Tom.

The map was spinning wildly in a circle, and their position marker jumped back and forth on the display and sometimes disappeared completely.

"Hmm. Modern tech isn't always much use. We'll have to go old-school." Tom passed the device back to Hellen, then rummaged in a side pocket of Cloutard's bag until he found a compass. "Uh-oh," he said.

Cloutard and Hellen were beside Tom instantly, peering over his shoulder. The compass needle was also going crazy.

"What now?" Cloutard asked. He sat down on a small rock to rest, but a gust of wind suddenly whirled up a flurry of fallen leaves, and the Frenchman jumped up again. Tom and Hellen were also startled.

"This is a very strange forest. It was spooky enough at the Druids' castle, but that was a walk in the park compared to this." Cloutard reached into his jacket with a trembling hand and took out his flask of cognac.

"How did people used to find their way if they didn't have a compass?" Tom said. The question was rhetorical, and all three, without saying a word, looked up.

"Apart from the fact that it is broad daylight, we cannot even see the sky through the treetops, so steering by the stars is out of the question," said Cloutard.

"That's it," Hellen squealed. "The stars."

She took out her iPad and opened an app.

"*Ma chère*, how are we supposed to . . .?" Cloutard said, pointing to the sky again.

"Well, not the stars, exactly, but the constellations. The bear and the dragon are constellations." She tapped through the app until she found what she was looking for. "The Draco constellation winds around Ursa Minor. Look." She tapped on the constellations listed on the app. "So '*avoid the bears*' means something like, we should follow the dragon constellation around Ursa Minor until we get to the dragon's head."

"All well and good," Cloutard said. "But we still cannot see the stars."

"We don't need the stars in the sky. It's much simpler." Hellen pulled up the photograph of the shield. "Constellations are basically just points connected by lines."

She peered closely at the confusion of lines engraved on the shield, tracing a finger over several of them. "Here it is, look. If you isolate these lines, they match the constellation Draco perfectly. We have to go this way." Hellen pointed down the right-hand branch of the fork and was already marching away.

92

FOREST, EASTERN PYRENEES

ANOTHER HOUR PASSED, AND THEY KEPT GETTING THE feeling that they were walking in circles. Again and again, they saw trees, rocks, and roots jutting from the ground that they were sure they'd seen before, and yet the path itself seemed a little different each time.

The idea that they might never find their way out of the forest again had already occurred to each of them, but none dared to say it out loud.

Hellen, who had been looking at the ground in front of her, looked up for a moment. A short distance ahead, a bright clearing had suddenly appeared.

"We should have seen something that bright much sooner," Hellen murmured. Tom was also dubious. It was as if someone had snapped a light on from one second to the next and the clearing had only come into existence a moment earlier. But he kept his fanciful magic-forest ideas to himself—they were drained enough as it was.

But what they saw next just made it worse: the path came

to an end. Without warning, a chasm about twenty feet across, and at least as deep, opened in front of them, with no end in sight to the left or right. And from where they stood, they could not see whether the path continued on the far side.

"Going around doesn't look like an option," said Tom, noting the sweat streaming down Cloutard's face.

"How do we get to the other side?" the Frenchman asked.

"We don't even know if we *have* to get across," Hellen answered. "First we have to figure out where to go from here. At least we've deciphered the first half of the clue."

"Well, for my money, this more than qualifies as 'the dragon's mouth,'" said Tom, looking down into the small gorge. "And we've got 'the blood of the fallen knight,' too." He pointed down to the creek splashing along the bottom of the ravine. The water was a bright crimson. "Where the heck *are* we? And where did this gully suddenly come from?"

Hellen took out the iPad, opened her offline maps app, and checked their surroundings.

"We are here," Cloutard said, tapping on the display. "And none of this is shown. No ravine, no creek— certainly not a red one. According to this, there is only forest, and apart from trees only more trees. How is that possible?" He was clearly upset. The strain of the last few hours—the last few days, in fact—were starting to wear on the usually urbane Frenchman.

"What were you expecting, François? This is a *magic* forest," Tom said with a grin, unable to restrain himself.

"The creek is easily explained," said Hellen. "In Peru, there's the Pukamayu, the red river. It gets its color from copper and other metals and minerals in the rocks. So red water isn't exactly extraordinary. Finding a stream like that *here*, though, is a little odd . . ."

"I'm telling you, this is Fangorn," said Tom.

"The forest with the talking trees from 'Lord of the Rings'? No, this is more like Mirkwood, the creepy forest from 'The Hobbit,'" Cloutard said in reply.

"Boys, can we stay focused?" Hellen snapped. Cloutard and Tom looked like two kids whose mother had just read them the riot act. "Fact: the app is clearly wrong. No ravine, no creek."

"We've dodged the bears, and 'the dragon's mouth' probably means the ravine. That just leaves the last two lines. What are they trying to tell us?" Tom said hurriedly.

93

FOREST, EASTERN PYRENEES, FRANCE

HELLEN REPEATED THE ENTIRE CLUE:

"Avoid the bears,

For only from the dragon's mouth

Flows the blood of the fallen knight

To lead you to your goal."

"One way to read it would be that we're supposed to follow the stream. But that seems too simplistic to me, somehow." She studied the map again. "No, no, no, not now, please!" she suddenly cried.

Tom saw her eyes suddenly fill with tears. The iPad display had turned black and wasn't reacting at all. Hellen tried the start button again, but the tablet was dead.

"But it was fully charged two hours ago. It was full when we left the car," Hellen said, looking imploringly at Tom, who wrapped her in his arms.

"The GPS and compass went haywire, too. I'm not surprised to see the iPad's given up the ghost, too. But we've made it this far—we can do this. Besides, we still have the shield, and that can show us the way."

"You're right," she said. "Get it out."

He lifted the shield from the backpack and Hellen, exhausted, crouched over it on the ground. Tom sat down opposite her, and they peered at the engravings on the curved inner surface.

"We should be here," Hellen said, pointing at the spot that represented the dragon's head in the constellation. "Which means this line has to be the ravine. But that doesn't help us."

Despair threatened to drown the little strength she had left. Tears trickled down her face and dripped from her chin onto the shield. She hung her head and wept bitterly.

Tom leaned across and held her hands in his. "You're the strongest, smartest, bravest woman I've ever met, and those are only some of the reasons I love you and want to marry you. I know you'll find a way. You can do it," he said gently.

Hellen suddenly fell silent. No sobbing, no crying, nothing. She grabbed the sides of the shield and jumped to her feet—she was back. "I've got it. I know what we have to do. Look at this."

Tom and Cloutard looked at her in amazement and leaned over the shield.

"What do I see there?" A tear had fallen into a notch on the shield and now ran along one of the lines. "The blood of the fallen knight," she cried. "We don't have to follow the creek. We need its *water*, the 'blood of the knight.' When we pour it onto the shield, we'll see which line we need to follow next."

94

FOREST, EASTERN PYRENEES, FRANCE

WHILE TOM AND HELLEN ARGUED ABOUT WHICH OF THEM would climb down to get the water, Cloutard had already found a way. He'd taken a rope out of the bag, uncoiled it, and tossed one end down into the stream. When he pulled it up again, he dripped a little of the water onto the shield.

"*Excusez*," he interrupted the ongoing quarrel between the two turtle doves. "Stop squabbling, come here, and look at this."

Taken aback, Tom and Hellen looked at Cloutard and suddenly felt very silly. They joined Cloutard and watched as the red liquid flowed along one of the engraved lines—but not the others, from which it simply pearled away, as if from a waterproof coat.

"This is how you solve a problem with brains before action," Cloutard said proudly, coiling the rope again.

"François, you're a genius," Hellen said.

Once Tom had oriented the red line to the environment around them, he chuckled. "We'll see how our favorite philosopher handles action—he won't like what we have to do next."

Cloutard paused his coiling. "*Non.*"

"Oh, *oui*," Tom replied. "Our path is over there," he said, and he pointed across the ravine.

"Even a thinker has to act sometimes, François," said Hellen, her motivation returned.

From his backpack, Tom took out a folded Glock shovel. He unfolded it and tied it to one end of the rope. Then he stood at the edge of the gulch, dangled the end attached to the shovel a couple of feet below his hand, and swung it in a circle several times. When he let go, the shovel flew in an arc over the gully, landing among rocks on the other side. Tom pulled at the shovel until it was firmly wedged in a cleft.

"You first, Hellen," Tom said as he wrapped the other end around a tree a few yards back from the edge. He tied the rope at knee level and pulled it tight.

"My friends, I am really too old for this. I will just wait here for you," Cloutard said. It was no longer just the heat and strain that were making him sweat. It was pure fear, too.

"It's child's play, old man. Even you can do this," Tom said. "Just watch Hellen."

95

FOREST, EASTERN PYRENEES

Hellen clipped her backpack on securely, lay down beneath the rope, and swung her legs up over it. Hand over hand, she pulled herself across the ravine.

"I do not know if I ever told you this, but I am not especially fond of heights," said Cloutard tentatively.

"You can do it. Just don't look down," Tom said, and he clapped Cloutard encouragingly on the shoulder. Hellen, already on the other side, waved back at them.

"Easy-peasy!" she called.

"Your turn," said Tom.

Trembling nervously, Cloutard stepped over to the rope, took off his hat, folded it as well as he could, and stuffed it inside his overalls. Then he did what he'd seen Hellen do. Slowly, and looking rather helpless, Cloutard squeezed his eyes closed and pulled himself across bit by bit.

"Don't stop. You're doing great. Keep going," Tom called.

Suddenly, a jolt went through the rope, and it came free from the tree trunk. Cloutard fell and Hellen screamed in panic and Tom leaped forward, just managing to grab the rope and keep his feet as it dragged him forward. Just inches from the edge, he dug in his heels and stopped Cloutard's fall.

"I've got you, don't let go!" Tom yelled, and he pulled the rope up again with all his strength. It still sagged a little in the middle, but at least he'd been able to stop Cloutard from hitting the rocks on the other side. "Hurry up! I can't hold it forever!" he shouted, his face red with exertion, and sweating now with fear himself.

Finally, Cloutard made it to the other side. Tom breathed easily again and looked across. Hellen helped Cloutard over the edge, and the Frenchman immediately collapsed, exhausted. He pulled out his hip flask and took a big mouthful.

He earned that one, Tom thought with a smile.

Once Tom was also safely across, the rest of the path was relatively uneventful, though the steady incline made them work hard. After half an hour, the trees gradually thinned out to reveal a high rock face. The barely recognizable path led directly to a crack in the rocks. Barely a meter wide, the fissure curved out of sight after only a few yards, and they could not see what lay beyond.

Tom, Hellen and Cloutard looked at one another doubtfully, all thinking: *should we really go in there?*

"We've come this far," Hellen said.

"As long as we do not have to climb across any more canyons," said Cloutard.

"Let's go. We're almost there," said Tom, and then cut himself off before saying what he was thinking. So close to their goal, he didn't want to remind Cloutard that they still had to go back, which would naturally involve crossing the gully again.

One by one, they squeezed through the fissure until they reached the entrance to a cave.

96

CAVE IN THE FOREST, EASTERN PYRENEES

<small>INSIDE THE CAVE, THEY AT FIRST BELIEVED THAT THEY HAD</small> reached a dead end, but then Tom discovered a collapsed passage.

Working together, they were able to push aside some of the boulders that blocked its mouth, and in a few minutes the opening was big enough for them to slip through. This time Tom led the way. He took off the backpack containing the artifacts and climbed through the hole. When he reached the other side, Hellen passed him the backpack, then Cloutard's and her own, before climbing through herself. Cloutard came last.

"Hurry up, let's go!" Tom called back, waving his flashlight. He'd already gone ahead down the long passageway. As fast as they could, Hellen and Cloutard followed him along the low tunnel, roughly hewn from the rock, until they reached a chamber about ten feet across.

The light from Tom's flashlight swung across the wall in front of them. Four overlapping stone disks, each about three feet in diameter, were mounted on it, arranged like the petals of a flower. Hellen wiped away the dust and cobwebs and discovered reliefs of crosses, lions, and dragons beneath the centuries-old grime. Together, one quarter of each of the disks formed a picture in the center of the "flower"—a picture of a shield.

"It is a combination lock," said Cloutard.

"But how do we find out which combination to use? There must be hundreds of possibilities. And some of the symbols are so worn they're not even recognizable anymore," said Tom. Time had clearly left its mark on the disks.

"Two hundred and fifty-six, to be precise," said Hellen drily.

"I assume it would be too easy to just turn them so they match the image on our shield?" said Tom.

"Yes, that would definitely be too easy," Hellen agreed, studying the symbols and their possible combinations.

"We can always use a skeleton key," Tom joked, holding up a block of C4. Cloutard smiled, but Hellen took no notice at all. Mentally, she was back in the circular room at the Druids' castle. She could still feel the high priest's breath as he whispered the second-to-last clue in her ear.

"Triumph over the father,

And the secret will reveal itself.

But remember,

You only have one chance."

Hellen repeated the Druid's words as her fingers glided across the edges of the weathered, exfoliated panels.

"What's that supposed to mean?" said Tom with a trace of exasperation, going off to examine the rest of the chamber.

After a few minutes, the scraping of stone on stone made Tom turn around.

"What are you doing?" he asked, startled.

Hellen was turning the stone disks. She took a step back when she was finished.

"*Incroyable*," Cloutard whispered when he recognized the picture that the sections they'd thought were worn away now formed. Together, they created the outline of a dragon—primitive, but perfectly recognizable. They stared expectantly at the wall, but nothing happened.

"At least the earth isn't shaking, and the walls aren't caving in. I'd call that a plus," Tom said.

"I don't understand. King Arthur's father's familial coat of arms was a dragon. Even his name, Pendragon, contains 'dragon,'" Hellen said, and she slid despairingly down the wall until she was sitting on the cave floor. "We've come so far, and now—"

"I've got it!" Tom suddenly cried. "We have to *kill* the dragon. According to the legend, didn't St. George kill the dragon with our sword?" He reached over his shoulder and slid the sword out of his pack.

Hellen looked up. "Of course! 'Triumph over the father, and the secret will reveal itself.' Which is roughly the same as: kill the dragon and the door will open." She jumped to her feet and ran to the wall with the stone disks. In the center, the disks formed a curving, diamond-shaped opening. Hellen pushed her hand inside carefully.

"Are you sure that's a good idea?" said Tom as Hellen's arm disappeared to her elbow in the wall.

"I can feel something," she said.

Suddenly, she shrieked and was pulled hard against the wall. She writhed and pulled, her face screwed up in pain. Tom and Cloutard turned white as ghosts and jumped toward her—and then there was silence. Hellen pulled her arm out, grinning from ear to ear. "See? I can make dumb jokes, too. Give me the sword."

"Never do that again," Tom said with relief.

"Never, please," said Cloutard, grasping demonstratively at his chest. "My heart won't take it."

Tom handed her the sword.

"I felt a small slot inside," she said, and she pushed the sword into the opening. They heard a click. She grasped the sword by the end of the hilt and turned it clockwise. Another click. Quickly, she pulled the sword out again. The ground began to vibrate underfoot. Dust trickled from the chamber roof and the four disks moved apart. The vibrations grew stronger as a gap appeared in the middle of the wall and the two sections ground slowly apart.

97

CAVE IN THE FOREST, EASTERN PYRENEES

HELLEN'S EYES GREW MISTY AS SHE GAZED INTO THE SPACE that had opened before them. She just stood there. Cloutard and Tom had run in immediately and were looking at everything around them like children at Christmas.

"How about that?" Tom shouted. "We made it. We're here!"

Hellen didn't move. All the stress and sleeplessness lately were too much for her. Finally, she had discovered the Fountain of Youth. Saving her mother was within her grasp.

"Come in, Hellen. We've done it!" Tom cried.

The chamber was circular, about thirty-five feet across. In the center, a small stone pillar narrowed to a tip about three feet above the ground. Around it stood thirteen life-size stone statues. One was unmistakably Merlin, and the rest represented different knights. Each had their left arm stretched forward, directly over the central stone obelisk.

"Do not keep us in suspense, *ma chère*. What is the final clue?"

Hellen finally entered the room, moving directly toward the stone in the center. Around the center of the pillar ran a smoothly polished circular basin, reminiscent of a basin for holy water. Around the rim, thirteen channels were arranged, like the rays of the sun. Hellen leaned over the basin and her breath suddenly caught in her throat—the pendant around her neck, which had slipped free of her overalls and was now dangling over the basin, suddenly blazed more brightly than ever before.

"Hey, you boys need to see this. I think we're right where we're supposed to be," she said. She slipped the chain over her head. Cloutard and Tom stopped looking around and turned to her. Almost in a whisper, she spoke the Druid's final words:

"Through the power of God,

And the shelter of the father,

The sorcerer's spell will

Give you eternal youth."

Hellen crouched and ran her fingers over the gleaming inner surface of the basin, tracing the grooves in the stone. She raised her eyes. The statues' thirteen outstretched arms reminded her of the sun's rays as well. Looking closer, she noticed small holes in each of the palms.

"As cryptic as usual," Tom said.

"You never were much of an abstract thinker," said Hellen. She moved around the basin, looking at the figures more closely. "If I'm reading things right, we have to insert the sword into one of the channels to trigger some kind of mechanism. Then, I hope, water will flow from one of the arms into the basin."

"That seems to make sense," said Cloutard. "But which channel? What mechanism?"

"I haven't thought that far yet," Hellen replied. She moved from one figure to the next. "These are all knights of the Round Table. One of them must be King Arthur, and this one is obviously Merlin." She had stopped in front of one of the heavily weathered statues, carved with a long, flowing robe.

"Merlin certainly lives up to the cliché," said Tom. "He looks like Ian McKellen as Gandalf."

"One channel aligns with each statue," said Cloutard, now standing at the basin himself and examining the radiating grooves. "So it makes sense that, by inserting the sword, you would choose which 'faucet' to use, for want of a better word."

"I agree," Hellen said. "And this," she held up the amulet, "has to return to the hilt of the sword, to allow the water to flow over it and acquire its curative powers."

"God's espresso machine," said Tom.

"Yes. In a sense, that's exactly what it is," Hellen agreed.

"So, all we need to figure out is which statue to choose and how to turn the damned thing on," Tom said.

98

CAVE IN THE FOREST, EASTERN PYRENEES, FRANCE

"Through the power of God,

And the shelter of the father,

The sorcerer's spell will

Give you eternal youth,"

Hellen repeated. "'Through the power of God' means you can give God's power to the water by using the stone."

"So far, so good."

"The '*sorcerer's spell*' can only refer to Merlin, which means the sword has to pushed into the slot that points to Merlin. He was an alchemist, after all."

"Makes sense."

"But the second line isn't clear to me at all," said Hellen, and she moved farther around the circle. "'The shelter of the father,'" she muttered over and over.

"Which one is Arthur's father?" asked Cloutard.

"That's the problem. Pendragon isn't obviously any of them. I'm not even sure which one represents Arthur. Apart from Merlin, they all look about the same."

"I'd always pictured men in shining armor," said Tom. "These look more like Roman legionnaires."

"That's because the plate armor you're thinking of was only developed in the late Middle Ages. The Arthur legend goes back much further, to the fifth century A.D. —about eight hundred years before that kind of armor was invented. Some historians believe that Arthur actually fought the Anglo-Saxons as a high-ranking leader of the Roman Empire in Britain."

"Well, this one here looks like he's asking a lady to dance. Or like he's a waiter, except someone stole the towel draped over his arm."

"Tom, can you be serious for once in—" But Hellen's stopped speaking as she looked at the statue Tom was talking about. She went over to him and kissed him passionately. "Tom, you're a genius. That's it! Don't you see?"

"*Quoi?*" said Cloutard in surprise.

"The arm is held like that because it should be holding a shield—Pendragon's shield! The purpose of a shield is protection, the shelter of the father!" Hellen was grinning from ear to ear.

She removed the amulet from its chain, opened the pommel of the sword, and placed the amulet inside. The pommel closed with a satisfying click. Tom took off his pack and Cloutard lifted out the shield and hurried to the statue with the outstretched arm.

"Ready?" Hellen asked, setting the tip of the sword into the slot aligned with Merlin.

Cloutard nodded.

"What do I do?" asked Tom, who'd been feeling a bit useless the whole time.

"You have to catch the water," said Hellen.

"With what?"

Hellen frowned. "Damn. Don't tell me we forgot to bring a bottle?"

Tom's eyes lit up and Hellen read his mind. Both of them turned to Cloutard.

"Oh, *non, non*. I just refilled it in the bar on the yacht."

"Out with it," said Tom, holding out his hand to the Frenchman.

Cloutard reluctantly leaned the shield against the statue and took out his flask. "*Un moment*, please. One last sip," he said. He lifted the flask to his lips and guzzled until Tom jerked the flask out of his hand.

"Seriously? I don't want to have to carry a drunken Frenchman all the way back to the car," Tom said, pouring the rest out on the floor.

"*Quel sacrilege*," said Cloutard, and his face described the five phases of grief: denial, anger, bargaining, depression and, finally, acceptance.

"Ready now?" Hellen asked, and both nodded.

But Tom wasn't sure. He was prepared to catch the water in the hip flask, but his gut was telling him they'd missed something. His eyes moved from knight to knight, taking a final close look at all of them.

Hellen pushed the sword into the slot and heard the first encouraging click. Then Cloutard lifted the shield and placed it onto the knight's arm.

"Stop! Don't!" Tom cried. But it was too late. Cloutard had already released the shield. The knight's arm sank slowly. Another click sounded through the room, but no water appeared. Instead, the earth trembled beneath their feet. All they could do was watch helplessly as the entrance to the chamber closed.

99

VIENNA GENERAL HOSPITAL, AUSTRIA, TWENTY-FOUR HOURS LATER

"AND WHAT HAPPENED THEN?" THERESIA DE MEY ASKED. She was sitting upright in bed and was listening in fascination to the stories that Tom, Hellen and Cloutard were telling her. Edward, Vittoria, Fábio, and Adalgisa were also listening.

"As you can imagine, we all panicked a little when the heavy stone door closed," Cloutard said.

"I didn't panic," said Tom. "I still had the C4." He and Hellen looked at Cloutard and laughed.

"Sorry. After finishing half the flask, I admit I was a little tipsy," said Cloutard in justification.

Hellen continued: "We calmed down again pretty quickly. Tom had noticed that one of the knight statues was wearing a medallion around its neck, a pendant just like grandma's," she reported. "It was hardly visible at all. All you could see were thin lines that represented a pendant on a chain, and the weathering had made them almost invisible."

"And as we all know, sorcerers are particularly good at camouflage and misdirection," said Tom. "So I thought, maybe Merlin pulled a trick like that and had hidden himself among the knights. Long story short, we started over, but this time with the right statue. The water flowed over the stone into the basin. We caught it in Cloutard's flask and Skinner picked us up in the Hercules from the airport in Toulouse."

"Thank you. From the bottom of my heart," said Theresia, and she hugged her daughter close. "And you, Tom, come here. You'll be family soon."

"Okay, okay, you're welcome," Tom murmured into the pillow when Theresia hugged him so tight that he could hardly breathe.

"Come on," said Edward. "Let's not overdo it. She still needs to rest. We should go."

"All right," said Hellen, standing up. "We'll come and visit again tomorrow."

Just then, the doctor entered the room. "Oh, pardon me," he said. "I thought you'd already left. I just wanted to check in on our patient. As you can imagine, we're all beside ourselves. It's truly a miracle. We'd done all we could."

"It is," said Hellen, with a knowing wink at her mother. She was the one, after all, who had secretly given her mother the water from the Fountain of Youth just a few hours before, without the doctors' knowledge.

"Thank you, doctor, for everything you've done for my wife," said Edward. He shook the doctor's hand and went out of the room. One by one, Adalgisa, Vittoria, Cloutard and Fábio said their goodbyes and followed Edward out.

Hellen went to her mother's bedside and gave her a heartfelt kiss on the forehead.

"And Tom, thank you for looking after my daughter so well," Theresia said.

"I always will," was all Tom replied. With his arm around Hellen's waist, they went out to join the others.

100

FRANÇOIS CLOUTARD'S VILLA, FORT TABARKA, TUNISIA, A FEW WEEKS LATER

"Can you explain to me why I let myself get talked into wearing a bowtie that I have to tie myself?" Tom looked in annoyance into the floor-length mirror and tugged cloddishly at the ends of the tie. "Why can't I just get one of those pre-tied ones with an elastic neckband?"

He was standing in a room more reminiscent of the Palace of Versailles than the medieval fortress they were really in.

After helping to put Ossana and AF out of commission during their search for the sword, Cloutard had finally regained his beloved fortress on the peninsula close to the city of Tabarka in Tunisia. Ever since the shootout, when he and Tom had fled in his helicopter more than a year earlier, no one had really looked after the place, so he'd spent many hours in recent weeks getting everything back in order. The renovations had been enormously expensive, and with Fábio's and Adalgisa's agreement he had decided to cash in his nest egg at the private bank in Luxembourg.

"Elastic? *Mon Dieu*, Tom, you are a complete Philistine. A man marries once in his life, and he should at least be decently dressed for the occasion."

Tom had lost count of how many times he'd already tried, but he untied it and started over.

"As your best man, I am responsible for ensuring that you look your best," Cloutard said. He went to Tom, pushed his hands away, and took matters into his own hands. Seconds later, Tom had a perfectly tied bowtie around his neck. "That is simply part of the basics of being a gentleman," Cloutard said. He looked out Tom's bedroom window. In the courtyard below, a lavish banquet was being set up. "No, damn it! We are putting the flowers out just before it starts! They won't last ten minutes in this heat. Do I have to do everything here myself, *pour le diable*?" Cloutard bellowed down, and the three waiters busy setting everything up ducked in fright.

Tom grinned. "Now, now, François. Don't get so upset. A gentleman doesn't go yelling his head off like that."

Just then, the door opened, and Sister Lucrezia rushed in. "Signor Cloutard, we have an emergency!"

101

FRANÇOIS CLOUTARD'S VILLA, FORT TABARKA, TUNISIA

THERESIA CIRCLED HER DAUGHTER, INSPECTING HER wedding dress one last time. She could not remember the last time she had seen her daughter wearing a dress —it had probably been before all the insanity with AF began, when she and Tom first met and attended the Opera Ball together. But this dress was considerably more sumptuous than anything she had worn before.

Hellen's father leaned on the balustrade and looked proudly at his daughter. "I never thought I'd live to see this. When the Taliban were holding me in Afghanistan, there wasn't much that gave me strength." He went to his daughter, embraced her for a moment, and kissed her forehead. "But the hope that I might hold you in my arms again one day and see you as happy as you are today helped me endure a lot of the pain and torture."

Hellen didn't like to imagine what her father had suffered in the years after he had disappeared. "I'm so glad that's over, and that you're back with us now," she said. She opened her arms wide and the three embraced for a few moments. Hellen could not recall the last time she had been so happy. And soon she would marry the man she loved, and all the people that mattered most to her and Tom would share the day with them.

"You could have just told us you were working for the CIA, or at least given us a tiny hint after you came back," Hellen said to her father, unable to keep a hint of reproach out of her voice.

"That's right. We had no idea what you were doing," Theresia added. "We wouldn't have asked for details, but maybe just to know you were working for the CIA in Afghanistan, that you spent years as a prisoner there before the CIA got you out again . . . you could at least have told us that much." Her tone of voice made it clear that both women shared the same deep concern.

"I was taken completely by surprise when the Seraphim told me that grandma had been involved with Brice, the Society of Avalon, even with AF," said Hellen. "And even though she had turned her back on all of that, I was afraid you might be mixed up with it as well. But that's all been put to rest now. I'm so glad the Agency gave you permission to at least tell us who you were working for there."

Hellen's mother had decided to resign as head of Blue Shield. She wanted to catch up on at least a little of the time she and her husband had lost when he went missing. They were planning to retire to the island of Santorini in Greece.

Theresia looked at her watch. "It's almost time to go down," she said. Hellen saw her mother's eyes grow misty, but she had never looked more radiant than she did then, leaning against Edward. Hellen was not the only one to feel that she had never experienced a lovelier moment in her life. And the day was just beginning!

102

TOM'S BEDROOM, FORT TABARKA, TUNISIA

CLOUTARD HAD LEFT THE ROOM LIKE A STARTLED CHICKEN, running off with Sister Lucrezia to deal with some emergency in the kitchen, and Tom stood alone in front of the mirror and thought back on everything they had been through. Though the outlook had often been bleak, in the end everything had turned out for the best.

Only one thing dampened his mood: Tom would have given anything to have his parents with him on this special day. That would have made his and Hellen's wedding perfect, but no one could change that now. Even if AF was finally defeated, and those guilty had been brought to justice, his parents' fate could not be undone. Berlin Brice, the Welshman, the commander-in-chief of AF, had tasked Jacinto Guerra with the bombing in which Tom's parents—along with many, many others—had perished.

The work of various police forces and secret services around the world had revealed that Tom's parents had probably just been in the wrong place at the wrong time.

As it turned out, Brice had initially known nothing of Tom's connection with the bombing in Syria. He only found out when the confrontations between Tom and AF became more frequent.

But all of that was little consolation. Tom's parents had fallen victim to a cruel attack by an even crueler organization. The only bright spot was that its leader was now dead, and that Noah, his right-hand man, was sitting in a maximum-security prison cell. Captain Maierhofer had told Tom that the information retrieved from the situation room on the yacht, and the hard drive rescued from the Wewelsburg, had led to numerous arrests worldwide. The Welshman had done his job very well indeed, putting AF people into important positions in business and politics. Many had been shown to have collaborated with the terrorist organization and were now behind bars as a result. AF would never be able to hurt anyone again.

Tom and Hellen had been shocked to discover that AF's bloody history had actually begun with the King Arthur cult. It seemed that as a young archeologist, the Welshman had discovered the first clue to the artifacts in the mountains around Snowdon—that was the genesis of the dreadful story that had claimed so many lives.

There was a knock at the door and Tom was jolted from his thoughts as Captain Maierhofer entered the room. They had never had a particularly good relationship, ever since Tom's early days with the Cobra antiterror unit. But now they could finally put their differences aside. Maierhofer had even been surprisingly happy when Tom invited him to the wedding in Tabarka.

"It's time, Wagner."

Maierhofer, as always, had deliberately mispronounced Tom's surname, saying the "a" in his typically drawn-out, Viennese fashion: "V-a-a-a-a-hgner". Tom grinned and took a final look in the mirror, straightened everything one last time, happy to shortly be marrying the most beautiful woman in the world.

"By the way, Tom, I just saw on the news that they've announced 'habemus papam' after one of the longest conclaves in history. Seems there were some discrepancies and dissent among the cardinals, but the ex-camerlengo, Cardinal Monteleone, is the new Pope."

Tom made a face. Monteleone was not exactly a worthy successor, but right now he didn't give a damn. And the Sword of Peter, with UNESCO's help, had fortunately been returned to its rightful place before the Vatican had taken any legal action. The intervention of the Austrian Chancellor, whose life Tom had once saved, had helped convince the Vatican to decide against pursuing the thief. For Tom, the new Pope was just one more reason not to have anything to do with any of that stuff ever again.

The moment he stepped into the courtyard and saw the fruit of Cloutard's efforts, the ill-tempered Monteleone was forgotten. The Frenchman had redecorated the old fortress completely, turning it into a fairy-tale castle. *Why couldn't Cloutard have been a wedding planner instead of a crook?* Tom wondered, as he stepped out and surveyed the small crowd of guests. They had managed to gather everyone who mattered to Hellen and himself: Tom's grandfather, Arthur Julius Prey, and Vittoria Arcano were there. Father Lazarev, whom they had not seen since the affair in Nizhny Novgorod, was officiating; the FBI agent

Jennifer Baker was sitting next to the four nuns, Lucrezia, Bartolomea, Renata, and Alfonsina; Eon and Kiara van Rensburg were there with their ever-present butler, Wikus de Waal. Fábio and Adalgisa. Even Cloutard's mother had made the strenuous journey from Tuscany. Even Isaac Hagen, Tom's former arch-enemy, who had turned out to be an undercover agent for MI6 and had played a major role in destroying AF, was celebrating the day with them. A few of Tom's former Cobra colleagues had made it as well, as had several of Hellen's friends from her time at the Museum of Fine Arts. Tom took a few deep breaths, then strode down the aisle between the rows of seats to the altar at the front. Seconds later, a door opened and Hellen stepped into the courtyard at her father's side. Accompanied by the "Wedding March" from Felix Mendelssohn-Bartholdy's "A Midsummer Night's Dream," she walked slowly toward Tom. Nothing could make the moment more perfect.

103

COURTYARD AT FORT TABARKA, TUNISIA

"THE DAY YOU WALKED INTO MY LIFE SHOWED ME something that I wasn't ready to admit for a very long time," Tom began his vows. "It wasn't the thrill of jumping off a cliff. It wasn't the adrenalin rush of a motorcycle chase, or the rush you get looking death in the eye—none of that was missing from my life. It was you. You are what finally made my life exciting and made my heart happy. You showed me a path that I don't want to walk alone anymore. Your smile when you wake beside me in the morning, your courage, and your passion remind me every day what a lucky man I am, and what's truly important in life. We have been through everything together, we've had good times and bad times, but you are my best friend and the love of my life. And I know that, together, we can make it through anything. As long as my heart beats, you will be the reason it does. Hellen de Mey, I love you with all my heart."

A smile and a sob of happiness escaped Hellen when Tom finished. Her tear-filled eyes gazed deep into his as he slipped the wedding ring onto her finger. A silence followed. Theresia dabbed a few tears from her face and looked blissfully at Edward. A trumpeting sound suddenly broke the momentary silence as Cloutard loudly blew his nose. Tom and Hellen laughed, and Father Lazarev took over.

"If anyone here can show just cause why this couple should not lawfully be joined in holy matrimony, let them speak now or forever hold their peace."

Another silence. The only sounds were the crash of the sea and the cries of seagulls. Tom and Hellen looked out smiling at the small gathering, then turned back to Father Lazarev, who went on contentedly with his address.

"Then by the power vested in me, and with God's blessing, I now pronounce you man and—"

A gunshot reverberated between the old walls.

"I have an objection," Katalin Farkas shrieked, appearing suddenly in the courtyard. Tom and Hellen stared at her in disbelief. There were muffled screams and the scraping of chairs as the guests turned around in shock. Maierhofer and three of his Cobra colleagues were already on their feet, but Tom signaled to them to remain calm as he moved in front of Hellen, pushing her behind him.

"You've taken everything from me! You've destroyed everything that Berlin Brice and Count Pálffy spent their entire lives working for," Katalin spat. "They wanted to change the world." Flailing her arms wildly and with a maniacal look in her eyes, she waved the pistol in all directions as she moved through the crowd toward the wedding couple. "I loved them, and now they're both dead. Why should you get to have my happy ending?" Katalin screamed. Her seemingly out-of-control flailing stopped, and she leveled the pistol directly at Tom.

Two shots and a high-pitched scream rang through the courtyard. Tom flinched and looked down at himself, but he hadn't been hit. He spun around to check on Hellen and froze. From beneath his jacket, she had taken the pistol that he'd pushed into his belt and fired at Katalin. He smiled with relief.

"Now if she'd been waving a Saracen sword instead of a pistol, that would have been an excellent movie reference," Cloutard whispered to Tom.

"Can you please explain to me why you felt the need to bring a pistol to our wedding?" Hellen said, looking furiously at Tom. He gulped.

"Uh, well, you never know, right? Ever since I've known you, I've had to watch my back 24/7. I'm sorry, I . . ." he said. He felt like a kid caught with his hand in the cookie jar and was trying to talk his way out of it as elegantly as he could.

Finally, a mischievous smile appeared on Hellen's face.

"I love you," Tom said with relief.

"I know," Hellen replied with a smile. "We have a very crazy life." And they stood and watched as Maierhofer and his men tackled the still-raging Katalin and dragged her away.

"We have a very nice medieval dungeon here at Tabarka,"

Cloutard called as he rushed off to show Maierhofer the way down.

"That was a great shot, by the way," said Tom. Hellen had shot the pistol out of Katalin's hand, which had caused Katalin's gun to fire as well, giving Tom's Cobra friends time to reach her.

"Honestly? I was aiming at her head," Hellen said with a shrug.

104

TERRACE OF FORT TABARKA, TUNISIA

"I now pronounce you man and wife."

Not waiting for permission, Tom drew Hellen close and sealed the ceremony with a kiss. Katalin's brief interruption was forgotten. Cheers, applause, and a storm of confetti filled the courtyard. The beaming couple strolled between the guests, who had lined up in two rows, and on to the terrace overlooking the sea, where the wedding dinner was to take place. The guests followed them out. Everyone was looking forward to what Cloutard had conjured up in his kitchen with the help of the four nuns. Tom had to smile. The first time he had dined here with Cloutard, he had thought the eccentric, affected Frenchman to be a true madman—and his opinion in that regard had not changed much at all.

The newlyweds took their place at the head of the main table and the rest of the tables quickly filled. Then Cloutard rose to his feet and clinked his champagne glass with a fork, and everyone fell silent.

"Making a speech now, François?" said Tom.

"*Mes amis*, I speak now not only in my function as best man, but more importantly, as the chef."

"Hear, hear," came from the other end of the main table, where Edward and Theresia were sitting.

"I wish to beg your undivided attention for sixty minutes, no more. I would like to take the opportunity to explain in a little more detail the five-course meal, and to relate one or two rather important anecdotes about the dishes I have selected. I hope none of you are too hungry just yet."

Complete silence fell. No one could believe their ears. Cloutard was going to talk about the meal for an hour before it even began?

"*Bande de fous*, I am only messing with you. The first course is already on its way."

Three waiters appeared to cheers and laughter from the guests and began to serve the food. Cloutard smiled at Tom, raised his hip flask, toasted Tom and Hellen, and took an invigorating swig of Louis XIII.

The party was in full swing, and Cloutard stood and headed for the kitchen to supervise the next course. Only with the untiring assistance of the nuns had he been able to make all the preparations for the exquisite dishes he had concocted for the guests. And as long as he kept himself busy, he did not have to think about the problems he still had to face—he had not delivered the Klimt to the person who had commissioned it, after all. Today was for celebrating, but the grim reality would catch up with him tomorrow.

"Monsieur Cloutard, do you have a moment?"

Cloutard turned to see Eon van Rensburg, who had followed him into the kitchen.

"Monsieur van Rensburg, can it wait? I still have four courses to prepare," Cloutard said, furrowing his brow.

"Of course, monsieur. But come to me after the meal."

Three hours and four more courses later, the guests were all exhausted. The food Cloutard had served was among the best anyone there had ever eaten. The guests had separated into smaller groups and were all having a splendid time. Maierhofer and Fábio were talking shop about the latest automatic weapons and other modern gadgets used in counterterrorism, while Adalgisa kept bringing up how those technologies might also be put to "other uses," which got Maierhofer quite unsettled. The nuns and Father Lazarev were heatedly discussing the incoming Pope, while Jennifer Baker and Vittoria sat together and compared the training standards of Interpol and the FBI. Isaac Hagen was once again being taken to task by Cloutard's mama, and Tom's grandfather, who had once traveled the world as a photojournalist, took a few photographs with the wedding couple and Hellen's parents to remember the day.

Cloutard spotted the van Rensburgs and went to find out what was on the multibillionaire's mind.

"You wanted to talk to me?" Cloutard began.

"Of course, my friend." Eon had stood up and gone to meet Cloutard halfway. "I only wanted to say that I have taken care of the matter with the Klimt."

Cloutard looked at van Rensburg in surprise. "But how did you even . . .? What do you mean, monsieur?"

"Your employer wanted Klimt's 'The Kiss,' but I was able to interest him instead in another piece from my collection. He allowed himself to be appeased with that, and you are no longer in his debt."

Cloutard's jaw dropped. "But . . . but monsieur, I have no idea how to thank you."

Eon van Rensburg looked back at his wife and smiled mildly. "You will find out very soon how you can thank me. Shall we have a word with our newlyweds?"

"Mr. and Mrs. Wagner?" Kiara van Rensburg called, waving to them. "Could we borrow you for a moment?"

Tom, Hellen joined them, and all three looked at the van Rensburgs curiously.

"I'm sure you remember, when we lent you the shield, that I mentioned owing me a favor?" Eon began.

Tom, Hellen, and Cloutard shared an uncertain glance. Kiara reached into her handbag and took out an envelope, which she handed to Hellen. Hellen quickly scanned the document inside and let out a sharp squeal of excitement.

Eon van Rensburg smiled and gazed intently at all three. "Have you ever been on a *real* treasure hunt?"

EPILOGUE

In his career with Mossad, Noah Pollock had been a prisoner many times. In fact, the prisons had often been far worse than his cell at Dartmoor. It wasn't the Ritz but compared to the filthy holes in which he'd been held and tortured in Syria and Iraq, his cell here was rather cozy. The food was decent, and he had access to the prison library. He hadn't had time to read for years.

He had just stretched out on his cot with Friedrich Nietzsche's *Thus Spake Zarathustra* when the small peephole in his cell door slid open.

"On your feet, hands against the wall," the guard snapped. Noah's wrists and ankles were cuffed, while a second guard watched the process closely with his gun drawn. Then Noah was led from one end of the prison to the other, to a small room containing a chair and table with a telephone on it.

The guards pushed Noah onto the chair and chained him to the center of the table, then left the room. When the door was locked, the telephone rang. Noah picked up the receiver.

"Congratulations, Mr. Pollock. An outstanding performance on the yacht. You should be nominated for an Oscar."

Noah immediately recognized the voice on the other end of the line. He would have known the cold voice of his commander-in-chief anywhere.

"Thank you, sir," he said.

"Everyone swallowed it. For Tom Wagner, his team, and the entire world, the leader of AF is dead, and the organization has been smashed. At the same time, we've gotten rid of the Welshman, those idiot Knights of the Round Table, and the Society of Avalon. You've done brilliant work. And now we can take our time and start again, in the background, a little less brazenly and publicly than before. Unfortunately, things with Pálffy and Ossana got a little out of control. AF should be orchestrating things in the background, not making headlines in the world press every other day."

"You're absolutely right, sir."

"That should suit you, shouldn't it? 'By way of deception, thou shalt wage war'—that was Mossad's motto, after all?"

"That's right, sir," Noah replied, keeping his responses curt. "How long do I have to stay here in Dartmoor, sir?"

"Noah, I have to get off the phone. We'll sort this out as soon as we can and get you out of there."

· · ·

Two thousand miles away, a man replaced a receiver on its cradle and looked back over his shoulder.

"Who was that, darling?" asked Theresia de Mey. She had just walked into the room and was smiling at her husband.

"No one important, sweetheart. Just a few details about our move. I'll be out in a moment," Edward said.

Theresia de Mey smiled, kissed her husband on the forehead, and went back out to the terrace.

Edward de Mey watched her go out. He felt nothing for this woman, no more than he felt for his daughter, Hellen. It was all feigned. Everything was secondary to his true goal.

In college, he'd been recruited by Berlin Brice for the newly-formed successor organization to the Nazi's "Ahnenforschung" project. He still recalled exactly when the revelation had first come to him: the knowledge that he was special, that he had a purpose, that he saw interrelationships between things differently than others did. And also, the revelation that he had to act if he wanted to guide the destiny of the world. It had happened when he and Brice discovered the cave of the old Round Table in Wales. It was there that he had felt the energy of the old myths for the first time. He knew he'd found Camelot. There, in the cave in Snowdonia, he had felt the power slumbering in those ancient treasures. It had struck him like a lightning bolt, and there and then he decided to take all of that secret, ancient knowledge for himself. He would not share it with anyone.

He had tried to get rid of the Welshman, leaving him behind in the cave and blowing up the entrance. But like the insect he was, Brice had managed to crawl out again and had sworn eternal revenge. For a moment in Egypt, he thought Brice had recognized him, but his imprisonment by the Taliban, from which Pálffy had ransomed him with diamonds, had left its mark—that, and the fact that more than thirty years had passed since their last encounter in the cave.

He could not explain it, but after the incident in the cave, he had felt an indescribable power inside him. He had felt invincible. And ever since that day, he had been.

His mind had devised complex plans with ease, and in no time at all he had worked his way to the very top of the organization and had built up a network of his own. He had deceived and exploited secret services and criminal organizations alike for years. And everything had gone perfectly, until the day he allowed his old mentor Count Pálffy to make a decision, and he had failed in his attempt to assassinate the Pope and to detonate a nuclear bomb beneath Barcelona. Until that moment, AF had always operated in the shadows. No one had noticed them, and his power had grown step by step, artifact by artifact, myth by myth. Taking advantage of the resources of the CIA, for whom he had acted as a double agent, had been child's play. And it had been just as easy to connect Katalin first with Pálffy, and then with Brice, and in the end, she had been able to steal the amulet from him. Ossana had gotten her hands on it after killing Pálffy but never handed it over, so he had sent Katalin to take it from her. Katalin had had Pálffy and Brice wrapped around her finger every step of the way, but her appearance at the wedding had been her tour de force. Edward had loved every second of it.

Men like Brice and Pálffy were vulnerable because they were governed by their loins. But for him, sex had never held much interest. The power that emanated from the old myths had always been much more fascinating.

The Florentine diamond affair had been a good test. Momentum had picked up in Barcelona, and for a while he had given his soldiers, like Ossana and Noah, free rein. But they had suffered one defeat after another. True, Wagner had been very lucky. But he had always come out on top. That was the reason Edward had reappeared personally, orchestrating their little de Mey family reunion just to get closer to his greatest enemy and call the shots directly. From that moment on, everything had once again gone perfectly to plan. Every trail he laid—the abandoned AF site in Egypt, the Wewelsburg, even the last great set piece on the yacht—he had planned himself, and all of it had worked. Noah had done his job well, but he had still failed too often against Wagner. He had no intention of ever getting Noah out of prison and was even considering having him eliminated before long.

Because Edward de Mey did not make mistakes. Now there would be time to forge new plans—plans that, this time, would be perfect. The list of artifacts Count Pálffy and he had assembled many years ago was far from finished. There were so many secrets, treasures, and powerful relics out there, just waiting for him to find them, and then to guide the world in the direction he knew was right. There were too many people on Earth as it was. One could easily cull the herd.

Of course, he would have to put up with Theresia—and presumably, now and then, Hellen and Tom, too, but all that was just a small bump on the road to true glory. Here, on Santorini, he would find the peace and quiet he needed. He would let the dust settle for a while and then rise again like a phoenix from the ashes, greater and more powerful than ever before. And the first thing he would do would be to eliminate that infuriating Tom Wagner once and for all. He could not allow any more interference of that kind. But there would be time enough for that.

He stood up and went out to join his wife on the terrace. It was time to play the good husband for a while.

At the opposite end of the bay in northern Santorini, just over half a mile from the de Meys' terrace, a man was holding his breath. He was out of practice, to be sure, but in his youth, he'd been very good. In the beginning, there was hardly anything that he'd enjoyed more or that had spurred his ambition as much.

Isaac Hagen had joined the British Army at eighteen and become a member of the Special Air Service, the SAS, nine years later. The training had been tough, and the six weeks he'd spent in the jungle had nearly killed him, but he had graduated among the top three in his unit and afterward could choose for himself which direction he wanted to go. He decided to train as a marksman, and to this day he still held the SAS record.

He was a little rusty these days, of course. After leaving the SAS and joining MI6, he had filled a series of other roles. But it was like riding a bicycle: once you mastered the skill, you never forgot how to do it.

Hagen could see the target through his telescopic sight and held the trigger at the pressure point. He was still holding his breath, waiting for his target to shift slightly to the right. Neither he nor his rifle moved a millimeter.

Three seconds passed. As a marksman, Hagen had learned to stay calm and wait for the perfect moment. His pulse beat evenly.

Patience is a virtue, he thought, as the seconds passed.

Then his moment came. With the crosshairs centered on his target's head, he squeezed the trigger. And it really was like the old days.

A bullet entered the head of Edward de Mey, the true leader of the terrorist organization Absolute Freedom, and he fell to the terrace, dead.

———

THE END OF
of
"THE SWORD OF REVELATION"

Tom, Hellen and Cloutard
will return in their next adventure.

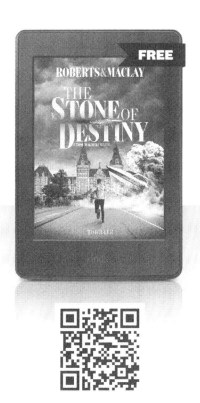

THRILLED READER REVIEWS

"Suspense and entertainment! I've read a lot of books like this one; some better, some worse. This is one of the best books in this genre I've ever read. I'm really looking forward to a good sequel. "

———

"I just couldn't put this book down. Full of surprising plot twists, humor, and action! "

———

"An explosive combination of Robert Langdon, James Bond & Indiana Jones"

———

"Good build-up of tension; I was always wondering what happens next. Toward the end, where the story gets more and more complex and constantly changes scenes, I was on the edge of my seat"

———

"Great! I read all three books in one sitting. Dan Brown better watch his back."

———

"The best thing about it is the basic premise, a story with historical background knowledge scattered throughout the book–never too much at one time and always supporting the plot"

———

"Entertaining and action-packed! The carefully thought-out story has a clear plotline, but there are a couple of unexpected twists as well. I really enjoyed it. The sections of the book are tailored to maximize the suspense, they don't waste any time with unimportant details. The chapters are short and compact–perfect for a half-hour commute or at night before turning out the lights. Recommended to all lovers of the genre and anyone interested in getting to know it better. I'll definitely read the sequel."

———

"Anyone who likes reading Dan Brown, James Rollins and Preston & Child needs to get this book."

———

"An exciting build-up, interesting and historically significant settings, surprising plot twists in the right places."

THE TOM WAGNER SERIES

THE STONE OF DESTINY

(Tom Wagner Prequel)

A dark secret of the Habsburg Empire. A treasure believed to be lost long time ago. A breathless hunt into the past.

The thriller "The Stone of Destiny" leads Tom Wagner and Hellen de Mey into the dark past of the Habsburgs and to a treasure that seems to have been lost for a long time.

The breathless hunt goes through half of Europe and the surprise at the end is not missing: A conspiracy that began in the last days of the First World War reaches up to the present day!

Free Download!
Click here or open link:
https://robertsmaclay.com/start-free

THE SACRED WEAPON

(A Tom Wagner Adventure 1)

A demonic plan. A mysterious power. An extraordinary team.

The Notre Dame fire, the theft of the Shroud of Turin and a terrorist attack on the legendary Meteora monasteries are just the beginning. Fear has gripped Europe.

Stolen relics, a mysterious power with a demonic plan and allies with questionable allegiances: Tom Wagner is in a race against time, trying to prevent a disaster that could tear Europe down to its foundations. And there's no one he can trust...

Click here or open link:
https://robertsmaclay.com/1-tw

THE LIBRARY OF THE KINGS

(A Tom Wagner Adventure 2)

Hidden wisdom. A relic of unbelievable power. A race against time.

Ancient legends, devilish plans, startling plot twists, breathtaking action and a dash of humor: *Library of the Kings* is gripping entertainment – a Hollywood blockbuster in book form.

When clues to the long-lost Library of Alexandria surface, ex-Cobra officer Tom Wagner and archaeologist Hellen de Mey aren't the only ones on the hunt for its vanished secrets. A sinister power is plotting in the background, and nothing is as it seems. And the dark secret hidden in the Library threatens all of humanity.

Click here or open link:
https://robertsmaclay.com/2-tw

————

THE INVISIBLE CITY

(A Tom Wagner Adventure 3)

A vanished civilization. A diabolical trap. A mystical treasure.

Tom Wagner, archaeologist Hellen de Mey and gentleman crook Francois Cloutard are about to embark on their first official assignment from Blue Shield – but when Tom receives an urgent call from the Vatican, things start to move quickly:

With the help of the Patriarch of the Russian Orthodox Church, they discover clues to an age-old myth: the Russian Atlantis. And a murderous race to find an ancient, long-lost relic leads them from Cuba to the Russian hinterlands.

What mystical treasure lies buried beneath Nizhny Novgorod? Who laid the evil trap? And what does it all have to do with Tom's grandfather?

Click here or open link:

––––––

THE GOLDEN PATH

(A Tom Wagner Adventure 4)

The greatest treasure of mankind. An international intrigue. A cruel revelation.

Now a special unit for Blue Shield, Tom and his team are on a search for the legendary El Dorado. But, as usual, things don't go as planned.

The team gets separated and is – literally – forced to fight a battle on multiple fronts: Hellen and Cloutard make discoveries that overturn the familiar story of El Dorado's gold.

Meanwhile, the President of the United States has tasked Tom with keeping a dangerous substance out of the hands of terrorists.

Click here or open link:
https://robertsmaclay.com/4-tw

––––––

THE CHRONICLE OF THE ROUND TABLE

(A Tom Wagner Adventure 5)

The first secret society of mankind. Artifacts of inestimable power. A race you cannot win.

The events turn upside down: Tom Wagner is missing. Hellen's father has turned up and a hot lead is waiting for the Blue Shield team: The legendary Chronicle of the Round Table.

What does the Chronicles of the Round Table of King Arthur say? Must the history around Avalon and Camelot be rewritten? Where is Tom and who is pulling the strings?

Click here or open link:

https://robertsmaclay.com/5-tw

———

THE CHALICE OF ETERNITY

(A Tom Wagner Adventure 6)

The greatest mystery in the world. False friends. All-powerful adversaries.

The Chronicle of the Round Table has been found and Tom Wagner, Hellen de Mey and François Cloutard face their greatest challenge yet: The search for the Holy Grail.

But their adventure does not lead them to the time of the Templars and the Crusades, but much further back into mankind's history. And the hunt into the past is a journey of no return. From Egypt to Vienna, from Abu Dhabi to Valencia, from Monaco to Macao, the hunt is on for the greatest myth of mankind. And in the end, there's a phenomenal surprise for everyone.

Click here or open link:
https://robertsmaclay.com/6-tw

———

THE SWORD OF REVELATION

(A Tom Wagner Adventure 7)

A false lead. A bitter truth. This time, it's all or nothing.

Hellen's mother is dying and only a miracle can save her...but for that, the team needs to locate mysterious and long-lost artifacts.

At the same time, their struggle with the terrorist organization Absolute Freedom reaches its climax: what is the group's true, diabolical plan? Who is pulling the strings behind this worldwide conspiracy?

The Sword of Revelation completes the circle: all questions are answered, all the loose ends woven into a revelation for our heroes — and for all the fans of the Tom Wagner adventures!

Click here or open link:
https://robertsmaclay.com/tw-7

ABOUT THE AUTHORS
ROBERTS & MACLAY

Roberts & Maclay have known each other for over 25 years, are good friends and have worked together on various projects.

The fact that they are now also writing thrillers together is less coincidence than fate. Talking shop about films, TV series and suspense novels has always been one of their favorite pastimes.

———

M.C. Roberts is the pen name of an successful entrepreneur and blogger. Adventure stories have always been his passion: after recording a number of superhero audiobooks on his father's old tape recorder as a six-year-old, he postponed his dream of writing novels for almost 40 years, and worked as a marketing director, editor-in-chief, DJ, opera critic, communication coach, blogger, online marketer and author of trade books...but in the end, the call of adventure was too strong to ignore.

———

R.F. Maclay is the pen name of an outstanding graphic designer and advertising filmmaker. His international career began as an electrician's apprentice, but he quickly realized that he was destined to work creatively. His family and friends were skeptical at first...but now, 20 years later, the passionate, self-taught graphic designer and filmmaker has delighted record labels, brand-name products and tech companies with his work, as well as making a name for himself as a commercial filmmaker and illustrator. He's also a walking encyclopedia of film and television series.

www.RobertsMaclay.com

Printed in Great Britain
by Amazon

16680281R00233